THREE SHALL BE ONE

THREE SHALL BE ONE

FRANCENA H. ARNOLD

MOODY PRESS
CHICAGO

Printed in the United States of America

*To those who have discovered
that the "Eternal Triangle"
becomes blessed reality when
Christ is made a living partner
in marriage*

Chapter One

Linda stood at the window and watched as her husband turned onto the sidewalk and broke into a run. At the corner of the vacant lot he glanced back to wave at her, then cut through the lot to shorten the distance to the depot. As usual he was late. Already she could see the smoke of the train as it came out of the woods beyond the station. She hoped Tony would catch it, but she must remember to ask him tonight. If he missed it, he had to wash the dishes alone that night. It was a game they had played ever since he had been rebuked by his office manager for too frequent tardiness. Tony most decidedly did not like to do dishes, and the game had been a more effective discipline than the manager's displeasure could be.

She waited until the chug-chug of the engine, borne on the autumn air, told her that the train had left the station again, then she pivoted around on her heel, put her hands on her hips, and stared in belligerent fashion at the room. She spoke vehemently, after a few moments of significant silence.

"Right now I am going to do something to this house. I'm not sure what, but it will be drastic, whatever it is. It will probably be a mess when I get through with it, but I don't care. I'm going to make it *my* house instead of my mother-in-law's!"

She looked first at one side of the room and then the other. With its new furniture, its expensive rugs and hangings, its bric-a-brac that a collector would have envied, it was a room to delight the heart of any lover of beautiful interiors. Every article in it was in harmony with its surroundings. The colorings were deep and rich with just the right amount of contrast. The pictures were few, but each one was exactly the picture needed at that particular spot. The lighting was, even at this bright morning hour, subdued. In all the room there was not one discordant note.

Linda, however, looked at it with acute disfavor. Then she crossed the hall and gazed at the dining room and its furnishings with the same expression of distaste. The kitchen appeared to arouse still more the spirit of rebellion that was building up in her.

She made a tour of the other rooms, tiptoeing past the nursery lest she waken the sleepers within. Returning to the living room she stood in the middle of the floor.

"I *am* going to do something! I hate this place. I *hate* this place! I hate *all* of it! The draperies make me seasick, the rug makes me nervous, and that grand piano gives me 'the willies.' I don't like bedrooms done in early American. I think all these 'just right' things are a pain in the neck."

She was speaking aloud with the abandon that came from a realization that she was alone in the house after weeks of constant surveillance.

"I know what I'd like to do. I'd like to get rid of the whole mess. I'd give the piano to that little church on the corner. They probably don't have one half as good. I'd like to stick the rugs and draperies into the furnace. Then I'd take that imported china in the dining room and practice throwing it at the big tree by the creek. That's what I'd *like* to do. Being half-civilized, I can't, but I'm going to do *something*. I'm going to go right now and throw those overfed flowers as far as I can send them. Then I'll go out in the lot and pick some weeds, some common little hobo weeds that are more suited to my style."

She seized the tall vase with its long-stemmed flowers,

turned with an angry shake of her shoulders, then stood transfixed with amazement and confusion.

"Tony! How did you get here?"

"Walked."

"You're supposed to be at work."

"I'm supposed to be on my way to work. But I forgot my brief case and came back. So glad I did. I wouldn't have missed this dramatic little scene for anything. Is it a habit of yours to go crazy as soon as I get out of the house?"

"I-I-I- was just—"

"You were just having a hate-fest against my mother, weren't you?"

"No. I-I—"

"Don't make it worse by lying! You do hate my mother and you can't deny it. You don't appreciate a thing she's done for us."

"I do so! That's what's the matter. I appreciate fully that she came into our apartment that was all our own, took us away from it, and fixed this monkey house up for us, then expects us to like it."

"Well, who wouldn't like it? It's much nicer than the apartment—nicer than anything *I* could expect to get for you for many years, if ever. I'd think you'd be grateful."

"Grateful? My eye! The apartment was *mine*. And there isn't one thing here that's mine except the babies, and if she had *her* way, she'd find something to do with them so that they'd get training more suitable for the grandchildren of the exclusive Mrs. Bannister!"

"Oh, be reasonable, Pat! Nobody wants to take the babies away from you. If you'd only try to—"

"Try? Haven't I tried? I let her sell all our stuff we had so much fun getting together. I let her drag us out here where—"

"Where it's lots nicer for us. There's fresh air for the kids, and a garden for you—"

"Excuse me! That garden is *not* for me. That's *your* bailiwick. I'd rather have one little cactus plant in my old kitchen window than that 'colonial' monstrosity."

"Oh, shut up!"

"I won't. I've been shut up for four months, and I'm—"

The door slammed, and she stood in amazement. Tony had walked out on her! She ran to the window and again watched him go down the street. The hot, angry tears blurred her vision, but she gazed after him until he had disappeared behind the clump of evergreens on the corner.

What in the world could have possessed her to say all those things to Tony? She would never have voiced her unhappiness had she dreamed of the possibility of his return. In her heart she had intended to get her outburst over and be composed by the time he came from work in the evening. Having kept still under all of the irritations of the past weeks, why should she have to lose control of herself just now when her mother-in-law had gone and she could enjoy life alone with Tony and the babies once more?

"I don't care," she whispered. "He's just too much of a mama's boy for his own good—or for my pleasure. Why doesn't he stand up to her? I wouldn't have let either of my parents interfere in our lives like she has been doing. They wouldn't have tried it though, bless their hearts. If there was any one thing I always had plenty of, it was freedom from parental interference. I guess I could have used a lot more. There ought to be a happy medium between my independence and Tony's—servility, that's what it is! I can't do a thing with him always siding with her."

An imperative call from the nursery put an end to her musing, but all morning as she worked the resentment within her would not be downed.

She and Tony had been happy until his mother came. He hadn't seemed like a mama's boy then. They hadn't had much money, but they had not missed it. They could always find something to do that didn't cost anything. It had been more fun fixing up the apartment with secondhand furniture than it would have been to go to all sorts of expensive places where folks thought they had fun. Both of them had had too much of that other in their lives already. An evening spent painting an old table was lots more enjoyable. She never would forget the hooked rug they made that first winter, working together over the frame through long evenings and getting a thrill as each detail of the pattern became clear. Where *was* that rug now? Had *that* been sold to a secondhand dealer? Or was it stuck away in a box in the attic with the dishes and cutlery and red enameled pans Tony's mother hadn't considered good enough for the new house? When she had time, she would look for it.

"If it's gone, I'm telling the world somebody had better look out! That was *my* rug. Tony gave me the materials the day we had been married three months, and I said I'd rather have them than an orchid. I wonder how *she'd* like it if I took some of *her* things and junked them."

As she hung the baby-wash in the sunshine of the back yard, she glowered at the neat paths and clipped boxwood borders of the garden that had been carefully planned and was given tender care even yet by a landscape gardener. The trees and bushes on the terrace likewise aroused her dislike.

"I don't like *any* of it. It's like a toy house in a Christmas village. I'd rather live in a grass hut in the jungle or in a sod house on the 'lone prairee!' Oh, *why* didn't she leave us alone?"

Going back to the kitchen to prepare lunch, she remembered that she had burned the eggs for breakfast and that Tony had refused to eat them.

"Before *she* came he ate everything I cooked, even when things were just messes. And when he was so sweet, I tried

11

harder and harder to learn. But now I feel like burning eggs every morning!"

The open door down the hall revealed the offending bedroom with its quaint wall paper and colonial furnishings. It also reminded her again of the hooked rug. That would have been the logical spot for it, right in front of the little rocker she loved to sit in when she rocked the babies. But Mrs. Bannister had banished that rug and bought one not half as pretty.

"It could have been nothing but spite that made her do that. And Tony just gave in like the mama's boy he is. When she's around, he has no more character than a hunk of jello."

She crossed the hall and stood in the middle of the room that Tony's mother had vacated the evening before. Everything was exactly as it should be, the bedspread draped evenly, the shade drawn to just the right point, the exquisitely dainty closet accessories in faultless order.

"How odiously neat! I wonder if anything will ever make me feel as if this room were a part of my house. Even you," she pointed accusingly at the photograph on the dresser. "You look slick and smooth and like a nice, fat, stuffed shirt. Now whyever did she leave you for? Does she think I like that picture? Well, I don't, Madame Mother-in-law! That's *your* Tony. Or rather, it's your *Chetwolde*. My *Tony* is a different guy altogether."

She rushed into the other bedroom and rummaged in a dresser to return triumphantly with a dilapidated billfold.

"Now, just look at the difference! *My* Tony is a *regular* fellow, a husband and dad in a million. Your Chetwolde is just your puppet, jumping around when you pull the strings."

She gazed contemptuously for a few minutes at the photograph in the silver frame, then let her eyes rest on the snapshot in the billfold. The laughing face that looked back at her brought sharp memory of a dear voice saying, "Oh, Pat, I didn't know love would be like this!"

In that instant her mood of rebellion was gone. Whirling on her heel she rushed into her own room and flung herself across the bed.

"Oh, Tony, Tony," she sobbed, "I can't stay mad at you. You're all I have, and I'll die if anything goes wrong between us. If you come home tonight and want to sp-spank me, it will be all right with me!"

Chapter Two

AFTER THE STORM OF TEARS had passed away, she lay quietly thinking over the life she and Tony had had together. She went back even farther than that and realized she had never known what real happiness was until Tony brought it to her. As far back as she could remember, there was the unhappiness that came because of the sharp quarrels between her parents. She could see them now over the breakfast table set up in some hotel room, her mother, lovely and sweet and utterly unreasonable, and her father heavy-eyed, unshaven, and exasperated at her mother's calm uncomprehension of whatever happened to be the point of difference that day. All the reconciliation scenes that came afterward, and the passion of their devotion at other times, never served to blot the memory of the quarrels from the mind of the little girl who often crept away to cry out her hurt in the arms of the wardrobe woman, Aunt Lucy. She used to wonder if husbands and wives always quarreled that way. And she wondered now why such a brilliant man as her father had married a woman who couldn't understand his language even when she used the dictionary. Linda had often helped her mother look up some of her dad's big words after he had slammed the door and left them. Or why had a woman of her mother's charm and beauty fallen in love with a clown? For that was what her dad was. He never denied it. The act that made his name known to theater-goers all over the country was nothing more or less than a piece of delightful clowning. Mother's act was all grace and beauty, while her dad just made laughs for folks.

They seemed as utterly unfitted for each other as a clumsy, lumbering moose and a graceful gazelle. Yet they had loved each other; with a love, however, that did not keep them from quarreling. Did her mother secretly admire and envy her dad his quick wit, and did he adore her for her beauty which was in contrast to his ungainliness? Linda wondered why she, their only child, had not inherited either the wit or the charm.

"I must have been a terrible disappointment to both of them," she mused sadly. "If I had been sweet and lovely like Mother or smart like Dad, maybe I could have held them together. If I had been the kind of child they could exhibit with pride, perhaps Dad wouldn't have fallen for Eloise. I know Mom wouldn't have married Tom if she could have got Dad back. Oh, what a mess it all is, and no wonder I'm the worst part of it. I never had a real family, and now Eloise is all that's left and she hates me. I *can't* let anything happen to Tony and me. It would kill me."

For four years Tony had been the center of her being. It all began the summer after she was a Junior in college. The vacation had started out badly. She had wanted to go with Mother and Tom to California, but Tom said no. Then the day after school closed, while she was waiting to find out what Dad had planned for her, came word of the plane crash in the mountains. She realized that, had she gone, she too, would have been killed. She had wanted Dad terribly then, and he had come to her at the dormitory. They had cried together, she for the mother who had never had time for her child, and he for the beautiful girl whom he had married and lost.

Oh, how she had begged to go with him when he left! But his eyes were sad and his manner nervous as he answered her, "I wish you could, but I don't think it would work out, little girl. Eloise isn't well and has to have quiet. We're going to Canada for two months. I'll arrange for you to go to a good camp this summer, and I'll meet you here late in August to get

15

ready for school. And, oh yes, there's something else. Listen, Lindy Lou, if anything ever happens to me, there's insurance enough to take care of you. It's all I've ever done for you, but it'll show you your Daddy did love you." Then he was gone. She had been sad and rebellious and very lonely when she had reached the camp in the White Mountains. She was *so* sick of spending her vacations in camps. How she had wished she knew where Aunt Lucy was! It would have been fun to spend another summer with her like the one she had had when the folks were in Europe. But this camp was—just another camp, and she loathed them all.

It was one night when she had been almost ill from moping all by herself, while the other girls played, that they had had guests from across the lake. A half-dozen young men came and gravely presented to the counselors a great stack of identifications, credentials, and references gathered from their billfolds and such letters as they could produce. With the counselors' consent they had been allowed to stay for an evening of fun.

One of the boys, the big bashful one whom the others called Chetwolde, had sought her out as she stood alone.

"I feel that way, too," he stammered. "May I stay here with you?"

He not only stayed then, but came back the next day, and the next, and the next. Lying now across her bed with lashes wet with tears of loneliness and shame, Linda forgot her grievance at Tony, forgot even the babies asleep in the next room, and remembered only the magic of the days and evenings that followed—the canoe trip up the river, the picnic on the island, the tableaux they put on one rainy night when she and Tony won the prize for the cleverest one. She could still imagine she heard one of the fellows announcing the winners "of this stupendous, colossal, unbelievably magnificent presentation from Shakespeare's immortal drammer An*tony* and Cleo*patr*y."

Later as they lingered behind the others in the walk through the dripping woods, the bashful Chetwolde had confessed to her the inferiority complex that made his life miserable.

"I think it started the first day I went to school. The teacher wouldn't believe that I knew my name. And when she tried to pronounce it, all the kids laughed. And everybody's been laughing ever since. Who else ever was named Chetwolde?"

"No one that I ever knew," she confessed. "If you were like my dad you'd laugh with them and make an asset out of a handicap. But you're just not that type. Couldn't you make them call you Chet?"

"I tried it several times, but it didn't go over. I had a second cousin who always managed to keep them reminded of Chetwolde. Whenever kids find out that another kid can be teased, they tease him. And I never had what it takes to bluff it through. Most of the fellows don't laugh anymore, and I'm trying to forget it. But if I ever have a son, I'm going to name him Mike or Pete. And I'm not going to keep reminding him that his mother was a Brewster and his grandfather a Chetwolde!"

He said that so fiercely that she had laughed. "Are the Brewsters and the Chetwoldes so bad?" she questioned.

He laughed with her, then answered soberly, "They aren't bad at all, as ancestors go. All of them had a lot to their credit. And it isn't old John Chetwolde himself that I don't like. It is just his name. If I had to be named after him why couldn't he have been named something that wasn't quite so funny?"

"I won't call you Chetwolde," she had promised soothingly. "I'll call you Antony—no, just Tony. May I?"

"I wish you would. I believe if I were called Tony I could be a different chap, one with some backbone. I think I might even—"

17

"Might even what?"

"Oh, nothing much. If you call me Tony, may I call you Pat? After all, what is An-*tony* without his Cleo-*pat*-ry?"

"O.K. I like that better than Linda."

"Don't let the other guys call you that, please. I want it to be my name for you."

She had remembered that unfinished sentence and wondered many times what he had intended to say. He might even have —what? Was the old complex still bothering him? Since those days he had married, had done well at his work, and had seemed to be happy. But did the presence of his mother and her constant use of the name "Chetwolde" still have an unfortunate reaction for him?

Shortly after college had opened that fall, he had called to tell her that he had a position with a company in the city near her.

"Oh, how grand!" she cried. "Isn't that luck?"

"Not on your life. There's no luck about it. You see Tony wanted to be near you so he chucked Chetwolde in a corner and came out here and got a job. That's all there is to it."

She hadn't understood then. She had been too happy to think about it. But now she realized he had had to break away from his possessive and domineering mother and had to start in a new position in a strange place. It couldn't have been easy, but out of love for her, Tony had done it. There probably had been quite a scene for, when they were married the next summer, Tony hadn't told his mother until it was over. He had urged that they wait until Christmas before going to see her. A bit more of her anger and rebellion crumbled as she thought of it. Tony had realized how his mother would resent her son's wife, and he knew from a lifetime of experience that he could not stand before her anger.

It had been a wonderful year, that first one. They had only

18

three rooms, and at first they had hardly any furniture. If they had been wise they would have bought furniture instead of taking that idyllic trip into the north woods. But they weren't wise. They were in love.

Oh, it had been such fun—the building of their nest. Tony had called it the "eyrie" because it was up so high. For a month they had slept with their mattress and springs laid on the floor, before they had money for the rest of the bed. And they had bought their kitchen equipment from the ten-cent store. They had eaten what seemed like a ton of one kind of breakfast food so that they could get some "real silverware." A wave of hot anger swept over her again as she remembered how that had been replaced by sterling flatware in a colonial pattern. Where was that precious "breakfast-food" silver now? She hadn't even known what had been done with it. Oh, why couldn't *she* have left them alone?

The answer to that was that the stately Mrs. Bannister never left *anything* alone—not if she saw any chance of changing it to suit her specifications of perfection. That first Christmas when they had visited her, she had begun on Linda before they had spent a day with her. She was not sharp nor scolding. Linda could have met open opposition. She was just gentle, sadly patient, and very determined. Linda could not yet look back on that visit, now two years gone, without a shudder of distaste. Had not Mr. Bannister been there to act as buffer, she would have deserted and run long before the week was over. That calm, quiet, stolid-appearing man knew, it appeared, just when to take over a situation and avert "civil war." Linda thought privately that had Mr. Bannister married Tony's mother ten years earlier when the boy was struggling with adolescent frustrations and psychoses, he might have been able to do victorious battle with even the Chetwolde complex.

"But he did get into the family in time to save that Christmas visit," Linda mused. "If it hadn't been for him, I probably would have gone crazy or compounded a felony, whatever that is."

The shadow of the visit could not survive in the happiness of their own home, however, and they soon forgot it. Linda, when she looked back, would always see the months that followed through a golden haze. And in May when the baby was born, both she and Tony were so happy that they thought nothing could ever trouble them again. She could close her eyes now and see the room in the hospital where she lay while Tony knelt beside her and tried to tell her what she meant to him. She could see the blue and white of the bit of sky visible through the window, and smell the scent of the roses on the table. And she could feel the tight gripping of Tony's hands on hers as he gulped and said huskily,

"If life gets any better, Pat, I can't stand it."

What had happened to dim that happiness and take away the shine from the love that had been so precious to them? Was it the hard work of caring for a baby in a tiny apartment where there was no place for quiet or privacy? Was it the fact that there never was enough money to do anything but provide the absolute essentials? It could not have been that, for they had laughed over the forced economies together, and the baby had been just fun even when she was cross. Linda had been afraid Mrs. Bannister would come and insist on instructing her in the arts and mysteries of baby care. But Mr. Bannister fell ill just then, and for months his wife was held at his bedside.

"Bless his heart!" she whispered now. "He saved me from her once again. It was almost as if he had that stroke on purpose."

No, that year had been happy in spite of the scarcity of money, in spite of the hard work, the inconvenient apartment, in spite of everything. Mr. Bannister had died in the spring, but although Tony had really loved his stepfather, it had cast only a slight shadow over their lives.

Could the fact that the babies were only a year apart be blamed for the rift between them. It *couldn't* be that. For Tony had said when he brought her and the new baby home, "Now we're a prefect foursome. Two guys and two gals! I wouldn't trade places with the—the—the chap that gets his weight in gold every year. He's a poor poverty-stricken mortal compared with me!" He had been a dear during those first weeks when she had been frantic with one baby teething and the other crying all the time because no food seemed to agree with it. He had even said one morning after an especially hard night,

"Aren't they sweet and cunning? Fighting through things like this with them just makes you love them till you ache."

No, it wasn't the hard times they had had last summer with the babies. With a cold certainty, Linda knew just exactly when the trouble began. In June Mrs. Bannister had unexpectedly appeared to visit them. Tony had looked from the window one Sunday afternoon and exclaimed, "Oh, no!" in tones of such disbelief that she had rushed to the window just in time to see the driver unloading a vast amount of luggage from a taxi while Mrs. Bannister stood by in her sweet, helpless way. Tony had gone down to help bring the bags and suitcases up the long flights of stairs, and Linda had stood dumbly in the middle of the floor wishing she could take the babies and run some place—any place—to get away from the woman who was even now climbing toward her and surely planning how she could rearrange their lives.

Of course, there hadn't been room for her. Where *could* one put a guest in a three-room apartment that already had four people squeezed into it? She had slept for two nights on the folding cot Tony had borrowed from a neighbor, then on the third morning had sallied forth from the house with the announcement that she had an idea which would be wonderful for all of them. Linda had hoped it meant she was looking for a small apartment for herself, or better yet, a hotel room that would be only a temporary shelter until she could return to her own home. But at late afternoon she returned with the announcement that she had bought a lovely bungalow in a nearby suburb, and they were all to move in two weeks.

"Just like that!" muttered Linda. "She *would* go out and find a place when other folks have to wait months to get one. I still have my doubts as to what she did to get rid of the former owners. I'll bet they had never thought of selling until she saw the house and decided she wanted it. I wouldn't be a bit surprised to meet their ghosts in the basement some dark day. And she never even asked us if we wanted to move. I most decidedly *didn't*, but we moved anyway. And from that day until ten o'clock last night this has been her house, Tony has been her Chetwolde, the babies have been *hers*. That's why I blew the lid off this morning. I have been boiling for four months, and something just had to blow up."

For another half-hour she lay there turning the problem of these unhappy weeks over in her mind. Tony seemed to have become a different person. Instead of his lighthearted boyishness that had taken all the sting out of hardship and poverty, there had come a moroseness that made her feel all the time as if he were displeased with her. In any difference of opinion between the two women he consistently, with an air of apology to Linda, accepted his mother's plans and ideas. Then in what Linda called his role of "The great appeaser" he would try to persuade Linda that it was for the good of all. In somber parade the events of those weeks passed her in review; the bickerings between herself and Tony in their room at night; the constant supercilious supervision that Mrs. Bannister gave to

22

every detail of their lives; the great amount of money that she spent on them, making Tony's salary seem not only insufficient for his family's needs, but completely unworthy of notice; the irritation that had become so much a part of her own life that she often feared to speak lest she betray it. But one other picture stood out above them all, the memory of Tony's face as he had gone from her this morning, his eyes sick and shocked, so different from the face that looked out at her from the picture in the wallet.

"You *are* weak, Tony," she whispered. "If you weren't you'd have taken over this situation and beat up both of us women until we learned to live together. But weak or not, you're my Tony, and I'm not going to let things get spoiled for us. I feel like I did when the staff at a hotel once gave me a doll house for Christmas, and then we moved during the next week and left it. Nobody, not even Tony's mother, is going to take my doll house this time. Tony is mine, and the babies are mine, and I'm going to *keep* them. What's the difference whether it's here, or in the little apartment, or in the middle of the Sahara desert? If the foursome is together, nothing else matters."

Chapter Three

Tony LOOKED AT THE PAPERS on the desk before him, then at his watch, at the papers again. He frowned in an effort to concentrate, and for a full fifteen minutes he worked doggedly. Then he uttered an exclamation of impatient disgust. Every form he had filled out since noon was wrong! He looked at his watch again, turned back to his work, started to write, then gathered up the papers and thrust them into a drawer. He closed the drawer with complete disregard of the disorder inside. Pushing back his chair he arose and stalked to the manager's office.

"I'm going home, Mr. Clint," he said shortly. "I don't feel well."

"Sure. Oh, sure. I'm sorry. Hope it's not serious."

"I'll be O.K. tomorrow. Thanks."

He'd better be O.K. tomorrow. Another day like this would put him into the nut house. The fifty-minute ride seemed interminable, yet he was glad for this time of quiet where he could relax and think a bit before he got home. What had ailed him this morning to make him speak to Pat as he had? He had not misrepresented things to Mr. Clint when he said he was not well. He *wasn't* well. He was sick all over with remorse and sorrow. How *could* he have yelled at her that way? And what was the matter with Pat that she should suddenly have become so furious about the house? He thought she had gotten over the hurt about having to leave the apartment. She hadn't said anything about it for several weeks, and he had been relieved to have it settled so nicely. He had thought that Pat had decided to take Mother's suggestions rather than to stand against them, and he was glad for that decision. It never did any good to oppose Mother. One might as well give in at once and avoid the unpleasantness that would otherwise bring an eventual consent.

He thought wearily of the many times he'd tried to oppose her and had always lost. Again and again he had tried to take a stand, but he could not remember a single victory. Well, one might call it a victory when he had given up the position Mother had obtained for him with Follingsted and Bradford, and had come here on his own. It hadn't been a real struggle. He'd done it while Mother was in California. Ever since, he had had a fear that in some way she would get him back with her old friends where she could have a part in his progress. He hadn't dared tell her he was going to be married lest she manage to prevent it. It had been over six months after the wedding before he had had the courage to take Linda to her. He loathed himself for not being able to stand against her, but he knew that to do so would be to precipitate a battle that might last for months. He remembered once when Aunt Anna had asked that he might spend a month with her. He had wanted so desperately to go that he had urged Aunt Anna and Uncle Ed to intercede for him. That attempt to break the cords that bound him had lasted for one whole winter, for Aunt Anna, also, was a Brewster and quite determined. But Mother had resented the pleasure he had shown over a previous visit and had been adamant in her decision. He had never seen his aunt again. Someday when the babies were older and could be transported about with a bit less than a truck load of paraphernalia, he'd like to take his family and show them to Aunt Anna. He'd heard that she sold the farm after Uncle Ed died, but her Christmas card had carried no address. He must write to some other relative for it. He would not ask Mother, he knew. She had never forgiven Aunt Anna, and it was best not to mention her.

One could not win out with Mother, and he wished Pat wouldn't try. If she would just accept things without struggling against the stronger force everything would be O.K. One had to admit that Mother's way usually was right even though it might not be one's own first choice. He hadn't wanted to move from the apartment any more than Pat had, but it *was* too crowded, and the babies needed the fresher air of the suburbs. It was nice for all of them out there. Mother loved beautiful things and had given them a home of which they could always be proud. Of course he himself would rather have earned it for Pat, but that would have meant years of waiting, and Pat deserved the best there was, right *now*.

What a girl she was! He remembered the first time he had seen her up at that camp on the lake. She was sad that night and his heart ached at the desolation in her eyes. When he knew her better, he learned the cause of the sadness and yearned to bring joy into the life of the girl that nobody wanted. He had found that she could be gay and lighthearted in the right environment. And he had discovered in her a warm sympathy that made him show to her the things in his own nature that he had carefully hidden from everyone else. He had loved her at once, but hadn't dared tell her so, for he could not believe she could ever love him in return. He thrilled now as he remembered his joy when she admitted her love.

As the train wheels clicked over the rails, he did not hear them. He was hearing again Pat's exclamation over the yellow roses that awaited them in their apartment after the honeymoon. There was little else in the way of furnishings in that apartment, but there was love and joy in abundance so they didn't miss the furniture.

It hadn't been easy for Pat those first months. A girl who has never had a home in all her life doesn't know much about the operation of a kitchen. But they had learned together, and at times their hilarity had brought the neighbors to the door in inquiry. Pat had been a good sport and hadn't let anything get her down. There had been the day they were planning to meet her dad downtown and had arrived at the stage door just in time to learn that he had collapsed in the middle of his act. She had been brave that night and all through the days that followed, even when she found that the stepmother who didn't like her had managed to get hold of such small bits of property as were left. The insurance policies that were in Pat's name had been allowed to lapse.

"I don't care, Tony," Pat had said. "Let's forget Eloise. Daddy loved me and meant to take care of me. But he couldn't, and I have you instead. That's all I need."

They didn't quarrel in those days. Why should they quarrel now when life was so much easier? Some place in the situation lay the key to the puzzle. *Why* were they so unhappy now? They had everything to make them happy, two lovely babies, a nice home, and each other.

But did they have each other when they could get so angry? He grew sick again at the thought that something had come between them. It couldn't be. It *shouldn't* be. Whatever it was, he would get rid of it.

Was it the lack of money? Pat's parents had always managed somehow to give her every material thing she might desire. It must have been hard for her to learn to live on a strict budget and do her own work, work for which she was totally untrained. But Pat hadn't seemed to mind. They hadn't quarreled last year when she had to wear resoled shoes and learn to darn his socks. They hadn't quarreled last spring when they gave up even the daily paper to save for another baby crib. No, it couldn't have been the lack of money. Even if it *had* been, that cause was gone. Mother had given them the bungalow, and they were released from the monthly bugaboo of rent. And for months, ever since she came last June, she had carried much of the expense of the household. They would be able to get along beautifully now, even without her help.

When had things begun to go wrong between him and Linda? It hadn't been just this morning. There had been irritation and querulous words at other times. It had been a long time since they had joked and played together as they used to. Pat had inherited a great deal of her father's quick wit, and when they were alone, she was a delightful companion. But of late there had been no laughter at the table. There had been instead quick irritation and tense nerves. When had it started? He pretended to try to decide, but deep down beneath his questioning lay the knowledge, and he knew he might as well drag it out and face it squarely. It had all started when his mother came. All his life Mother had directed and controlled him. By the time he had finished college, she had a position ready for him. She chose his friends. She managed his social life. He had wanted to go into business with a friend in another city, but she had overruled him. He had often considered a breakaway, but until he met Pat, he had never had sufficient incentive. Even after it was accomplished, he was afraid she'd find some way to circumvent him. And she had. When she came to them last summer, she had taken the reins as if they belonged to her, and he had not been able to prevent it. Pat probably thought him cowardly, but he knew, as she could not, how hopeless rebellion would have been. It seemed futile to start a battle that was lost before it began.

He had to admit that Pat had tried to keep up the old fellowship and fun under the new environment. But his mother's presence, her air of reserved disapproval at Pat's jokes, her hurt feelings if her opinion was disregarded, her jealousy if they enjoyed themselves without her—all these had dampened their spirits and caused nervousness that easily became irritation. He could see all this now, but he did not see how he could have avoided it with his mother in the home. He had met that sweetly stubborn gentleness too often not to be aware of the steel beneath it. He hated himself for not being able to assert his manhood and let his mother know that Pat was his wife, his very dear wife, and as such was entitled to his first love and consideration.

Yes, even greater than his anger with his mother was his disgust with himself. Why couldn't he speak out and assert himself as a man should? Why couldn't he sit down with Mother and talk it all out plainly? He knew the answer to *that*, all right. Mother wouldn't talk. She had a dozen ways of evading him, all of them more effective than his efforts. At first she would laugh indulgently and tell him he was "cute," as if he were an adolescent schoolboy trying to assume manhood. Then she would pretend to listen, but when he had finished she would kiss him, rumple his hair, and call him a "funny sweetheart." Then she would consider the issue closed. If he persisted, she would use other wiles and evasions. Eventually, unless he had wearied before then, it would end with tears, a headache, and perhaps a fainting spell. He'd never withstood the fainting acts. Try as he would, he could not take them. After one or two such experiences in his school days, he had learned the signs and always waved the white flag when the tears came. If only he could laugh at her as Dad Bannister used to! But he couldn't. Dad had been a middle-aged man whom she could not intimidate. But she had held the reins over her son ever since he could remember, and he did not know how to change the situation.

Even if he could survive the fainting spell the battle wouldn't be won. She would have some other hitherto unknown means of defeating him. He would lose in the end, and the longer the battle was the more severe would be the penalty exacted. It had been bad enough when he alone bore the brunt of her displeasure, but now with Pat and the babies to consider, he couldn't let her get angry at them.

Once when he was a small boy, he had been left at home under the care of a maid. The day was rainy, and after lunch he had been told to take a nap while the maid did likewise. As soon as he was sure she was asleep, he had stolen out of the house and sallied forth to investigate the delights of a neighborhood which hitherto had been seen only through the windows. Down one street and then another he had wandered, splashing happily through puddles and caring not at all for his wet shoes. He had come upon three other boys playing in the stream of water that flowed down the gutter, and had been invited to join them. Off came the shoes and socks, and with them all class barriers. He had found a tin lid that made a wonderful boat, and had entered it in an exciting race that led on for many blocks. It had been the happiest day of his life. But as the afternoon waned and the boys were wearily trudging home, judgment had descended. Mother and a policeman had found him, and the bright happiness of the day had been blotted out by a heavy cloud of parental disapproval. The next three or four hours had been so intolerable that even in memory he evaded them. For months he dreaded to ride through the streets for fear he would be seen by those luckier boys who could play in undisturbed freedom, and who had witnessed his shame. Of late the whole incident had come back over the space of the years to torment him. It had brought with it a fear, a cold, paralyzing dread. It was foolish perhaps, but very real; the fear that Mother would again, as in that long ago day, manage to shatter his happiness.

Oh, why couldn't he be a man and take the stand he should? If Dad Bannister were alive, he could manage the situation. Dear old Dad! He must have loved Mother in his queer, quiet way, but he had no illusions about her, and he knew how to deal with her. But now Dad was gone, and Mother had turned her thoughts and talent for management back to him and his family. He must have known on that June day four months ago what her coming might mean, for he could remember feeling sick and weak as he went down the stairs to meet her. He had not seen all the unhappy details, however, and they had been more trying than he could have dreamed. All he could do was to try to keep peace between the women, while all the time he had a consciousness of Pat's disappointment in him. Release had come at last, and Mother had gone for a winter in the South with an old friend. Perhaps by spring she would be reconciled to living in her own home with the two servants who had been with her many years. After he had taken her to the train last night, he had felt a sense of relief so great that he was ashamed of it. If he, the son, felt that way, how must it have been with Pat who had borne most of the unpleasantness? He had thought as he was drifting off to sleep last night that he must think of some especially nice thing to do for Pat to show his appreciation for the fine way she had kept sweet under the trying presence of a disapproving mother-in-law.

But even though he thought he understood how she must feel, he had been totally unprepared for the scene into which he had inadvertently stepped that morning. He had not dreamed that the resentment had been piling up in her mind and heart, ready to break the barriers at the first opportunity. How she must have fretted during all the weeks of apparent acquiescence! He had known she was hurt over the move from the apartment, and she had sulked for a few days when her furnishings had been thrown aside for Mother's choice. But he thought she had forgotten it by now. She had accepted Mother's domination quietly, and except for an unusual quietness, had shown no trace of those feelings which had burst with explosive force this morning. At the memory of that anger and his sharp, unsympathetic rebuke, a wave of terror swept over him. Why had he answered her so sharply when she was just saying and doing the things he had often wished to do himself? What would he do if he got home today and found that she wouldn't forgive him? Was this the way real trouble between husbands and wives started? He'd always thought that for some reason they quit loving each other and then began to quarrel. Now he was troubled by the realization that ugly quarrels could come even when they loved. Was that what was happening to him and Pat? He knew that her parents' divorce had been a blight on her childhood. Were his and Pat's babies to be endangered the same way? How could he live if anything came between him and Pat?

"It can't be," he thought desperately. "I was a heel to speak to her that way. I don't know what ails us. But we can't let anything break us up. We're going back to the happiness we had last year. I'm for Pat—first, last, and always. And the world, including my mother, had just better understand *that!*"

Chapter Four

Linda sat by the kitchen table folding the baby clothes she had taken down from the line. All the rebellion was gone from her heart, and in its place were shame and fear, shame that she had given way to the angry outburst of the morning, and fear of what would be Tony's attitude when he returned. It had been a long, lonely day, and she had had much time for reflection. Her thoughts had not been happy ones, and her sober face betrayed the state of her mind.

A step on the porch caused her to turn. Tony stood in the door, his face flushed and a self-conscious smile on his lips. In her surprise at seeing him at this early hour, she stared dumbly. He stooped to lift the toddler who had run with upstretched arms, then continued to look in Linda's direction as if waiting for consent to enter. At last she spoke.

"Oh, it's you."

"Yep. Sure is."

"You're home."

"Sure am."

"You came early."

"Sure did." Then he laughed, and Linda's heart and face lifted at the sound. "Now having settled all that weighty matter, would you discuss an item of *real* importance? How'd you like to grab an egg and a pickle or two and go for supper out by the dam?"

"A picnic? Oh, I'd love it! There's a great big tomato in the refrigerator, and a fresh bag of potato chips in the cupboard. We can stop at the store and get some hot dogs. You fix some bread and butter sandwiches while I make the baby's formula. Get two of those jars of Susie-Q's food off the shelf."

She pushed aside the unfolded portion of the clothes as if, with them, she was brushing away her discouragement and fears. In ten minutes the basket was packed and the wraps and blankets gathered.

"All O.K.," came Tony's voice from the nursery. "You take Susie-Q and the lunch, and I'll bring this young hippo and his blankets. Just don't let's get things mixed up. I'd hate to roast this fat pig and then try to put the hot dogs to sleep."

It was restful and quiet out by the dam. Indian summer, with all its glory of golden leaves and hazy distances, lay warm about them. The baby from his basket watched the rustling leaves overhead and laughed at the changing shadows. Susie toddled about gathering pebbles and acorns. Tony built a fire and whittled sticks for roasting forks. As Pat spread a cloth on the ground under a big tree whose branches leaned over the water as it rushed to tumble over the dam, she breathed deeply of the fragrant air. The tight nerves loosened, the tense muscles relaxed. Life was *good*—so *very* good. Her world was back in its proper orbit again, and it was good just to be alive. She looked up and saw Tony smiling at her. With one quick step he was at her side and his arms held her close.

"O.K., sweetheart?"

"O.K.," she answered happily.

But late that night when the babies were tucked into their cribs and Tony lay quietly beside her, the fear returned. What did lie ahead of them if they could get as angry with each other as they had been that morning? Try as she would she could not banish her feeling of oppression. When her restless tossing would not be stilled, she slipped from her bed and stole into the living room where she could be alone with her troubled musings. The evening in the woods had been beautiful, and it was dear of Tony to plan it. But the pleasure of it could not blot out that picture—that of herself standing in the middle of this same room ranting shrilly against his mother while Tony stood, white and angry facing her. His furiously spoken, "Oh, shut up!" rang in her ears. Would she ever forget it? And would the same scene recur at some unexpected moment? Would it become a habit? Would the quarrels grow more frequent until they seemed constant, as in her dad's and mother's case? She hoped she'd never try to wheedle her husband with tears as her mother had done. But if anything happened to cause a rift between her and Tony, she couldn't stand it. She shivered as if the room suddenly had turned cold.

Tony's voice spoke softly as he knelt down beside her. "Any room at this mourner's bench for another penitent, honey?"

She moved so that he could share the window seat against which she was leaning.

"What is it, Pat?" he questioned.

She bowed her head on the seat and her voice came, muffled and low. "What happened to us, Tony? What happened?"

"I don't know," he said soberly. "I thought of it all day long and couldn't find the answer. Even tonight when we were at the dam, I couldn't forget it. I don't want to quarrel with you *ever*, Pat."

"I don't *want* to either. But we *did*."

"I'm as ashamed as you could ever want me to be."

"But I don't want you to *have* to be ashamed. And I don't want myself to have to be. But we both are. And if we quarreled like that once, we could do so again."

"What caused it all, honey?"

"I don't know and I'm sure you don't. I just felt like raving. So I raved. And when you came in you felt like slapping me—"

35

"Pat! I didn't do that, did I?"

"Only figuratively. But you did feel that way, I'm sure. Oh, Tony, I'm frightened. It could happen again!"

They sat holding on to each other like children who were afraid of the dark. Tony's voice was sober when he spoke.

"If we know what we're afraid of we ought to be able to avert it."

"How? It just sneaked up on us."

"We're well educated. We've both studied psychology. We ought to be able to analyze ourselves—to find out, as it were, why we tick as we do. If we understand that, we should be able to steer away from disaster. That's what psychology is for, to help us to understand and appraise human conduct."

"Horrors! I don't want to be psychoanalyzed or appraised. But if it will help in any way to prevent such a scene as I put on this morning, I'm willing to try. But don't ask me to dissect myself. I know too much about me already, and most of it isn't nice."

"I'll report on you right now. You're the sweetest and best thing that ever came into my life. And I love you so much that I'd die if anything ever took you from me."

"That's how I feel about you."

"Then if it's mutual there's no point of disagreement. So we'd better go back to bed."

They had been lying quietly for so long that Tony was sure she was asleep when Linda's voice came again.

"Tony, what is a mourner's bench?"

Tony's voice was full of laughter as he replied. "It's an institution founded for the emotionally unstable. It's an outlet valve."

"Am I emotionally unstable? Quit your nonsense and tell me what it really is."

"Well, one time when I was visiting my aunt—she lived in Tennessee then—there was a camp meeting nearby. We—"

36

"What's a camp meeting?"

"I didn't know that myself until Uncle and Aunt took me. There was a tent with folding chairs, a rattly old piano, and a preacher that yelled. There was a long bench in front of the platform. At the close of each sermon everyone who had been sufficiently convicted of his sins went up and kneeled down, and the preacher and some of the other people would pray with them until they felt that they had been rescued from the clutches of the devil."

"That all sounds goofy."

"I thought so myself, but when with my fifteen-year-old audacity, I told Aunt Anna so, she rebuked me and said the day might come when I'd want to kneel at a mourner's bench myself. So here I am."

"Here *we* are. But will it do us any good?"

"What do you mean by that?"

"I'm wondering what I do mean. I'm still frightened. Would religion help us, do you think?"

"What kind of religion? There are several."

"Any kind. I'd turn into a yogi if I thought it would help."

"You'd make a better yo-yo."

"Be serious, please, Tony. Would religion help?"

"I don't think so. To accept any philosophy of religion is a sign of weakness. The fellow that does it is acknowledging that he is insufficient in himself and is trying to enlist occult, or what he calls divine, powers in his behalf. I looked them all over in college and discarded the whole mess of them."

"So did I. And one summer while we were touring the South, I found the funniest hymnbook that someone had left in a dressing room. I took it to school with me that year and my roommate and I had lots of fun reading it. There were the most absurd things in it. There was one that spoke of a Sovereign giving His life. I think it meant Jesus. We'd studied about how He died for what He thought was right. But He

37

certainly was no sovereign. The song went on to question, 'Could He devote that sacred head to such a worm as I?' If that isn't getting rid of your sufficiency, I don't know what could be. To call yourself a worm!"

"That's the way I feel. I've heard that song. I'm no worm. You and I have approached this by different roads, but we both have arrived. I came by a road cluttered by forced church and Sunday school attendance, and lined on every side by the failures of those who claimed to believe Christianity. You came by a clear way with no such obstacles. You never had to go to Sunday school, did you?"

"No. We never stayed in one place long enough for me to even go to day school. Daddy taught me until I was about twelve. Then I went to boarding school. We had to go to church there. But I didn't mind it. I found I could switch off my mind and not listen, so it didn't hurt me."

"Well, however we got here, we *are* here—together. I think we are sufficient for our own problems. We don't need any religious crutches. It's all right for some folks. Aunt Anna gets a lot of pleasure out of hers. She's just naturally a dear. But Mother doesn't enjoy life in spite of her faithful church attendance. That proves that it's just what a person makes of it. We don't need it."

"Tony, who is your Aunt Anna? Is she the one that sent the Christmas card to you and 'Patricia'?"

"Yes, but don't hold that against her. Mother told her that was your name, I'm sure. That's Mother's interpretation of 'Pat.'"

"I know it, and I just don't like it. My name is Linda, except to you. That's why we should have sent some formal wedding announcements. Then the name Linda would have been planted in your relatives' minds before they heard 'Patricia.'"

"Mebby so. Mebby so. But we didn't. It would be a bit anticlimactic if we sent them now, wouldn't it?"

Linda laughed. "Well, rather. But some day I'm apt to write somebody a letter and tell 'em off."

"Don't let it be Aunt Anna. She's too sweet. I hope you'll meet her sometime. Just now, let's try to get a nap before morning. And here's a thought to go to sleep on. In spite of everything, Pat, I love you with every atom of my being."

"Oh, Tony, I love you!"

"Then everything's all right. That's all we need."

Chapter Five

As THE FALL DAYS SPED PAST with Indian summer changing to crisp frosty weather, Linda began to believe that she could learn to love the small house as well or better than she had the apartment. It was exhilarating to go for long walks through the tree-lined streets with the babies bundled into warm suits and their faces glowing with the cool air. She found a neighbor, Ruth Hayes, who had two small children, "one rider and one cycler" as she said, and they spent many hours together in the autumn sunshine. It was fun, too, to leave the supper in the oven and meet Tony at the station at the end of his day's work. Sometimes she lingered behind the clump of evergreens at the corner of the station lawn on purpose to see him look eagerly about for the buggy, and then laugh in sheer joy when he saw it with its load of chubby babyhood. Best of all was, after he had kissed the babies, to have him turn to her and, looking deep into her eyes, ask,

"O.K., Pat?"

"O.K., Tony," she would answer, and they would turn toward home, with Tony pushing the buggy and Pat carrying his brief case and paper.

Those were good days, but there were things to learn as they passed. Even with no dreaded rent payments to make the first of the month, they discovered that a family of four could spend a lot of money. As the cold weather came on, the fuel bills ate up much of the gain. The railroad was granted an increase in commutation rates. Tony found a group of neighbors using the same train schedule as he did and was taken into their daily card game. This brought about an invitation from one of the wives for Linda to join the club that met weekly in the homes. It seemed good to them to have friendly neighbors and to share in the community life.

But these pleasures demanded a price. When Tony received a ten-dollar raise, he decided that it was only fair for a fellow to have a little money to spend—or lose—as he saw fit. So five dollars each week went into his pocket, and the family budget received the other five. Linda knew nothing of this arrangement Tony had made with his conscience, but she welcomed the extra bit of income and thought gratefully that it would come in very handy in paying for a baby sitter on club afternoons. There would be refreshment expenses when her time to act as hostess came around. Surely no five-dollar bills were ever more welcome.

For some reason which she could never figure out when she wanted those bills, they had always been spent for something else. The telephone and light companies seemed to have entered into a conspiracy to see which could get more each month. Grocery prices rose each week. And even when several of the women went together to hire a dependable sitter for the children, the cost mounted beyond Linda's budget.

The club started out with a plan of serving afternoon tea and cookies, but before many weeks had passed, a friendly rivalry over refreshments had grown into an expensive race for culinary leadership. Linda was aghast when she realized one day in the middle of December that her housekeeping money for the month was almost gone and that she was to be hostess for the Christmas party. She just *had* to have more money.

She looked anxiously at the bank book. The balance was small, for somehow there was always some emergency to keep it drained. She wouldn't dare check out more than twenty dollars. If that wasn't enough, she'd borrow from Edna Barrow next door. Edna always seemed to have more money than she needed.

But she hadn't counted on the car needing repairs. Who *could* have anticipated it? She didn't even know about it until Tony burst into the house one night and thrust a letter into her hand.

"Look at that!" he cried. "The check I wrote to the garage bounced! Not sufficient funds. Why didn't you tell me when you took out that money? And what did you need it for anyway?"

"Don't yell at me. I needed it for food! And how did I know you were going to have the car fixed? Couldn't you read the balance before you wrote that check? My arithmetic was all right, I'm sure."

"I didn't look at the balance. You've never done such a thing before so why should I expect it now? It's that silly bridge club of yours."

"It's not silly. If you had to spend your days shut in the house with two babies and washing and ironing and cooking and cleaning all day long, you'd need a club, too."

"Sometimes I think I need a club anyway—a great big one."

He stalked out of the room. When she entered the living room after putting the children to bed, he was writing at the desk. She went to the kitchen to finish putting the dinner on the table. She felt sorry, not only for speaking so sharply but for having been so careless with the money that he earned by long and tedious hours at a desk. Even baby tending and housekeeping were not as hard as that. He was at home only a few hours out of each day. She should make those hours happy ones and do all she could to keep them free from care. So, when dinner was ready, she went softly and bent over his chair with her arms around his neck.

"I'm sorry, Tony. I'm a cross old shrew. I knew I was

wrong all the time, and if you won't get that big club, I'll try not to need it."

Tony, remembering the games on the train and the amount of money that he owed Jack Barrow at the present time, was ashamed of his own part in the quarrel. He pulled her down onto his lap and held her close without speaking. She knew that words did not come easily to him when he was moved, so she accepted this gesture as his apology, and the evening was a happy one with each of them endeavoring, by thoughtfulness and tenderness, to show repentance for the angry thoughts and sharp words.

Several days later an airmail special delivery letter arrived for Tony from Mrs. Bannister. Usually, when he had read the letters, he passed them over to Linda, but this time he put it in his pocket, saying only that his mother was well. Later Linda noticed that a deposit of one hundred dollars had been entered in the bank book.

"That's a low-down trick," she said to herself. "Little Chetwolde wrote to Mama for money. Why didn't he pawn his watch like they do in stories of destitution and hardship. I would have let him have Mom's ring. She said I was to use it if ever I needed something very badly. I'd rather have given it to him than to have him ask *her* for money."

Her resentment over the affair faded, however, as the holidays came on and Tony appeared to be his old considerate and loving self. An unexpected bonus from his employer enabled her to do her part in the club's Christmas party. With it they bought the gifts for each other and the babies. In a burst of seasonal good will Linda insisted that they skimp on each other's gifts in order that they might send a bottle of her favorite expensive perfume to Mrs. Bannister.

"She's the only parent we own," she said when Tony protested. "Perhaps she is lonely so far away on Christmas. Just think of trying to keep Christmas without anything like this to make it worth while." She picked up the baby under one arm and Susie-Q under the other and spun around the room. Tony rescued the children and dumped them onto the davenport, then grabbed Linda.

"Nobody but you could be so decent," he said. "Every day I wonder anew what you were thinking of when you tied up with my family."

"Nothing much. Just you. You, and you alone—then, now and forever."

"Is that true, Pat? Will you always feel that way, no matter how cranky I get or how much Mother bothers you?"

"Of course, it's true. The only thing that *really* bothers me is feeling that I don't measure up to what I should be as your wife."

"You're much too good for me, Pat. I wish I could make things easier for you. I don't like for you to work so hard and not have things."

"Phooey. I'm not working hard at all. In fact, I'm getting fat from *under*work. And who says I don't have things?"

"You don't have new clothes like Edna Barrow, nor new—"

"I have other things. I have babies. Why, I got a new baby when the old one showed hardly any usage at all, and I didn't trade in the old one either. I kept both. I wouldn't swap my babies for all Edna's two dozen pairs of shoes."

So the gaiety and good cheer of the season pushed into the background the problems and differences. But the money question refused to stay out of the center of the stage. It was an ever-present source of concern. Something had to be put away each payday in anticipation of taxes. The plumbing became clogged, and it required two days of costly digging before it was discovered that a root had broken the drain in the garden. A heavy snowfall revealed a leak in the roof.

"Oh, for the good old days in the apartment when we paid

our rent on the first of the month and had thirty carefree days ahead of us," Tony sighed.

On an evening in January after an hour of figuring what the club was costing her, Linda was aghast to discover that she was spending three times as much as they had budgeted for it. Smitten with remorse, she went to Tony as he worked in the basement and offered to resign from the club. For a moment Tony felt a wave of relief at the suggestion. Then he remembered her outburst of a few weeks before and began to doubt. She was willing now, but wouldn't she regret it later? Then, too, he had a guilty recollection of his own careless expenditures and the unpaid debt to Jack Barrow.

"Don't do it, Pat," he said, working carefully on the set of steps he was making for Susie-Q. "I'll think of some other way. What do you think of these? Will they be high enough?"

"Fine. With them she will not only be able to get into her crib, and to wash her own hands, but she can get into fully one hundred per cent more mischief than before."

"Ha! That's what I was hoping. There's the telephone. Run along, Mommy. I'll paint this and be up later."

When he came up a half-hour later, he had decided on his course of action. Near his office was a firm of public accountants who were always in need of men. He could get in a few extra hours each evening until the budget got back into a healthy condition. Neither of them liked the idea, but neither did they want to break off their friendly social relations with their neighbors. And it wasn't as if they expected it to be permanent. In a few weeks they would be all right again. It was not easy, however. After working all day in one office, Tony would eat an unsatisfying supper of hamburgers, coffee, and a doughnut, then work until ten in another office. It would be midnight before he could get to sleep, and when the alarm rang at six-thirty, he felt as if he had just gone to bed. He went forth to another day, illy prepared for the duties it held.

Linda, after she had put the babies to bed, ate alone, making herself keep to the unappetizing diet of hamburgers and doughnuts that comprised Tony's evening meal. Then she spent the long evenings in reading and feeling sorry for herself. She could not go out, for she could not afford a sitter for the children. She wanted to knit a sweater for Susie-Q, but had no money for the yarn. She remembered the hairpin lace Aunt Lucy, the wardrobe woman, used to make. It had seemed to her that there was a mile of lace hidden in each spool of thread. And thread was only ten cents a spool.

"But I don't know how to do hairpin lace—for which I'm thankful. What would I do with a mile of it?"

She borrowed jigsaw puzzles from the neighbor's children and labored at them until she was thoroughly cross and disgusted. She would not go to bed before Tony got home, for during the lunch they ate together before retiring, they had their only moments of fellowship in the day. But when the body is overweary and the nerves are taut with strain, the fellowship is not always happy. Such conditions do not lead to harmonious living. Tony was too tired, even on Sundays, to remember the gallant attentions that Linda loved, and she, resenting it, found it easy to answer sharply if he criticized some small deficiency in her homemaking.

"What do you do all day?" he queried disgustedly as he trimmed the fringes from the cuffs of a shabby shirt which he must wear because there were no others ironed.

Linda's conscience reminded her that there was really no excuse for a two weeks' supply of shirts to be lying unironed —except, of course, that she hated to iron shirts and put them off as long as possible. In this unsatisfactory way of life that was theirs at present, she had lost such system as she had built up during the past years of housekeeping, and the days had slipped away without her realization that the pile of shirts in the dresser drawer had disappeared. She knew that she had grown careless with Tony away all the time. She could have kept up the ironing if she had wanted to. But because she knew she was guilty, she spoke defensively, trying to build up a case against Tony.

"Did *you* ever try to run a six-room house and do all the cleaning and the washing and ironing for a family of four, and care for two teething babies at the same time?"

"No, I didn't. But I think I could manage it if I put my mind to it."

"Then maybe you'd better. I could make as good a living as you do, I'm sure."

Tony gave her a long look, unsmiling and full of hurt. Then he turned again to the mirror and busied himself with his tie. A commotion from the nursery demanded Linda's attention, and when she returned, the bedroom was empty. She hurried to the window just in time to see Tony's tall figure turn the corner. He had gone to work without telling her good-by!

She peeped into the nursery to assure herself that all was well, and that Susie-Q showed no signs of waking. Then she grabbed her coat and scarf, putting them on as she ran from the back door and across the garden. There was a place where the fellows often took a short cut through the lawn of a deserted house. If she ran down the alley, perhaps she could reach there first.

Her feet flew over the frozen ruts, and when she came out on the side street, Tony was coming out of the gate of the old yard. Without a wasted moment she walked straight into his arms.

"I'm a lazy, no-good loafer Tony. I'm a worm—a fat, 'squishy' one. Why don't you step on me instead of holding me like this."

"Guess I just love you, Pat."

"Tony, don't you ever believe a word I say when I get ornery. I can't be trusted then. But believe me *now*, Tony.

47

Please do. I love you. I think you're the best husband and dad anybody ever had. Say you forgive me and run on. The train won't wait."

He held her close, and as she saw that his eyes were tear-filled, she realized how deeply he had been hurt.

"I'm sorry, too, Pat. And if you'll forgive *me*, we'll work this out together. We've *got* to. Now run along, honey, you'll catch cold."

One more kiss and he was gone, running for the train.

As soon as she reached home, she set up the ironing board in the middle of the kitchen floor. Before the babies wakened to demand her time, two of the shirts were done. All day long, between other tasks, she ironed. When seven shirts were finished, she looked at the ones remaining in the basket and groaned.

"If I had done last week's when I should have, I'd be ready to quit now. That's what you get for your lazy procrastination, Linda Lou."

Edna Barrow came in and wanted her to go to the Thrift Shop to look for finds. The Thrift Shop was run by the women of the community. It provided a medium of exchange for the furniture, china, glass, books, and clothes that one family had grown tired of and another might want. The proceeds went to keep up the community playground, so one always had a feeling of virtue when supporting it either by giving or buying. It was Edna's favorite haunt. She had an unusual knack for remodeling furniture and making some clever gadget out of a hopeless-looking wreck. Her house was unique in its furnishings, and she was always looking for some new idea. Tony said the Barrows' place looked like the Old Curiosity Shop, but Linda loved its brightness and warmth which were in great contrast to her own impeccably furnished home. Several times she had gone with Edna and succumbed to the temptation to buy something. But in her brain and fingers dwelt no such magic as in Edna's, and the things she bought did not seem to fit into the rooms Mrs. Bannister had furnished. It had been fun to go with Edna, but it was really a waste of time and money, so today she shook her head resolutely.

"No can do, Edna. I'm disciplining my soul, and I'm going to get this ironing done today if it kills me. By the time my husband gets home I expect to be a reformed character. But try me next week. Maybe I'll have the ironing done ahead of time that day—if my virtue holds out that long."

Edna laughed. "You're good to labor like this over a man's shirts. I wouldn't iron Jack's if he had to go to work in a T-shirt."

"It isn't a case of my being good. It's just that Tony has no T-shirts. No—that isn't it. I might as well tell you the truth. We had a big blow-up over unironed shirts this morning, and I'm feeling meaner than dirt. So run along and let me do penance."

Edna left, and Linda fixed Tony's favorite cocoanut dessert. While it baked she ironed and mused.

"What *is* the matter with me? I thought it was all because of Tony's mother, but she's been gone for weeks and weeks, and I'm getting crankier every day. I've got everything in the world to make me happy. I wouldn't trade Tony for any other man I ever met. I love him so much that I know I'd die if anything ever happened to him. I have the two sweetest babies in the world, and a dream of a house. I'm surrounded with kind neighbors and friends. All of these ought to add up to happiness. Why don't they? What ingredient is lacking? Did I leave out the baking power or didn't I bake it right? There ought to be something that could serve as a—as a—oh, what is that chemical term? Is it a precipitant we need? No-o, I don't think so. Oh, what is it? It's a catalyst, I believe! Oh rats! I've forgotten enough chemistry to fill ten textbooks.

Anyway there ought to be *something* in the world that would take Tony's and my love and our babies and our home and bind them together into real happiness. But I don't know what it is."

What did they lack? Was it a background of similar training and experience? She didn't think so. Their backgrounds were too much separated from them to affect their daily living.

"It's the foreground that makes the trouble."

Was it money that was needed? Well, they could use more money, lots of it. But if they had it, would that insure peace?

"The Hunts up on the hill fight like cats, Edna says, for all their big house and three cars. And the Taylor family around the corner with seven of them crowded into four rooms and no money *at all* are happier than we are. It isn't money we need."

It wasn't love either. In spite of the quarrels she knew that she and Tony had never doubted each other's love.

Could it be religion? She didn't think so, but was willing to consider it. And what kind of religion was needed? She thought of Mrs. Bannister with her strict adherence to her code of church attendance, systematic giving, and formal liturgy. Would that offer any peace or joy? Linda didn't think so. She thought of a time in college when she and her roommate had decided to investigate the claims of the various religions. Their first object of study had been the cold, self-centered church they had attended under the watchful eye of their dean.

"Thumbs done on *that* kind of religion," Marty had said.

Catholicism and Judaism had seemed full of dead ceremonies and superstitions. Theosophy, Mohammedanism, Christian Science, Mormonism—the girls had read books on all of them, and with the arrogance of youth had cast them all aside to issue their fiat, "Religion of any sort is just an opiate used to deaden the mind and soul, if any, to the pains of reality."

As Linda folded the last of the shirts, she thought of that decision and nodded her approval of it.

"No. There's no help there. All religions are the same. They may deaden some of the pain of life but the cause of the trouble is still there. Folks just fool themselves when they go off the deep end over religion of any sort. Neither Tony nor I could swallow the stuff. There ought to be *some* way, though, that lives could be welded together so there wouldn't be so much conflict between the atoms and molecules."

She folded the ironing board and stood it in the closet, set the table with the best china, and put her blooming begonia on for a centerpiece. When the dinner was in the oven and the dessert cooling on the table, she bundled the children into their wraps, and with Little Brother cooing in one end of the buggy and Susie-Q laughing in the other she hurried down the street toward the depot. She could just make the five-twenty train.

As Tony came across the platform, he did not notice her, for she stood out of the wind in the shelter of the group of evergreens. His shoulders were drooping and his face troubled. Her heart smote her.

"Poor guy! He deserves a better break than I'm giving him. I've *got* to do better. I don't want to break his heart!"

She whistled, and noted with joy how quickly his smile flashed.

"Pat! This is great! What you got in the buggy? Groceries? No? Why it's Tarzan and Titania!"

He lifted out his small daughter and carried her on one shoulder. With the other hand he pushed the carriage that held his sturdy young son.

"Now this is what I call 'the berries.' It's worth a million to get this kind of a welcome."

51

He smiled down into Linda's eyes, the shadows of the morning gone and forgotten.

"It's up to me," she thought as she smiled back at him. "There's nobody to help. I've got to do the job myself. But I can, and I *will*."

Chapter Six

For weeks after the good resolution was made there seemed to be real joy and peace in the little house. Frankly telling the other women that she could not afford to keep up with the club, Linda offered to resign. With a sigh of relief at hearing this suggestion, Ruth Hayes did likewise. But Edna Barrow would not have it so.

"Not on your life. We can't spare you. It wouldn't work out right for a single thing we want to do. You two take turns caring for each other's children. That will leave one of you free to come each week. And we'll invite that new woman who moved into the Terry place to make the eighth. No, gals. You can't get away so easily."

"But the baby sitting isn't all of it," wailed Ruth. "I spent over ten dollars the last time I entertained. George was furious. I just can't afford it!"

"We can take care of that, too," Edna assured her. "We're all a bunch of heavyweights, and don't need a big feed. Jack told me last night that I had all the grace and charm of a dressed-up pillow in my new suit. Let's make a ruling that we can serve only one kind of cookies and tea."

As with all of Edna's suggestions, this one went over enthusiastically, and Linda went home feeling as if the weight of a good portion of the world had rolled from her shoulders. When she told Tony what she had done, he made his own contribution to the improved schedule by telling his friends that only once a week could he join them in the game in the smoker. On other days the hour's train ride would have to be spent in studying.

Spring came early and one morning as Tony stepped from the back door, he called,

"Come smell this air, Pat. It's good enough to eat!"

She came out, and they walked down the garden path together. Here and there tiny shoots of green had pushed through the dead leaves to give hint of what lay buried under the ruins of last year's foliage. Tony stooped and uncovered some of them and pointed to a bit of purple.

"There'll be a crocus there in a couple of days," he said.

"How do you know about crocuses? I don't."

"One thing I was allowed to do—there were very few—was to watch our gardener. He taught me about all the flowers and vegetables. I'd love to put in a vegetable garden out behind that hedge. I think that is what was planned."

"For you to plant a garden?"

"No, for the man Mother hired to plant one. Mother doesn't even know that I could, and she wouldn't believe it if I were to tell her."

"Why don't you do it and surprise her."

"Mother doesn't like that kind of surprise. She and the man probably made a chart last fall, and some day soon he will be here with his seeds and rake and hoe, and we'll have the finest garden in the village."

The note of bitterness in his voice irritated her.

"But it's *your* place, Tony. She gave it to you. You should be able to do what you want with your own things."

"Yes, I know, but tell me honestly, Pat. Do you feel as if it were ours to do with as we please?"

"No-o. I guess not."

"Neither do I. It's ours to live in, and we've had a grand time lately. But I wouldn't dare even redecorate without Mother's approval. And she'd never give that unless she had initiated the plan. Some day, Pat, I'm going to buy you a house all by myself. And you can do exactly as you please with it. But as long as we live here, I think **we'd better let Mother** keep up the place and fix it as she wants it."

He kissed her hastily and was gone. But as she put up the clothesline, rejoicing in being able to hang the baby things out in the fresh breeze and sunshine, the irritation persisted.

"It's *awful* for her to be able to run our lives even when she is a thousand miles away. When I get to be a mother-in-law I hope I have sense enough to untie the apron strings, or that my youngsters have gumption enough to cut them!"

But there was a bird building a nest in the tree by the garage, and down in the corner of the garden she could hear the brook gurgling over the rocks. The children in their buggy were laughing at the antics of two dogs who were racing over the lawn. It was not the time to harbor any unhappy thoughts. She found some pussy willows and put them in a yellow bowl, and made even Edna admit that they gave just the right touch to the dining room. When Tony came home, he brought a box of daffodils.

"I just had to," he said. "They will look so springy on the piano."

The warmer days helped to cut down that bugaboo, the fuel bill. Looking at the checkbook one night Tony announced that soon they would be able to do what they had thought would be easy when they moved into the house; that is, put an amount equal to the rent of the old apartment into the bank each month.

"We're getting out of the woods, Tony," said Linda when she heard it. "Can't you catch a glimpse of clear sky ahead? Maybe soon we'll be able to buy you a—"

"We're not going to buy me anything. We're going to get you a new hat. And we're going to do it right away."

"Well, listen to the man! How do you know I need a hat?"

"Because we've been married three years, almost, and I've never bought you one. The hats you have are becoming, and you look better in them than any other woman looks in *any* hat. But every woman should buy a new hat every three years, even the Back Bay ladies who 'have their hats.' Anyway, the hats you have were bought for a schoolgirl. You need a more matronly model this year, what with your two children approaching maturity."

She give a hoot of derision. "Maturity? With twelve and two teeth respectively?"

"I said approaching maturity. I didn't say how near they are. And I say again, I want you to get a hat—a wow of a hat that will make all the men want to whistle and the women want to kill you."

He laid a ten-dollar bill on the table, saying self-consciously, "This is extra special money, Pat. I worked like the proverbial beaver on a set of papers for the boss. He had lost the original ones and needed them for a conference yesterday afternoon. I gave up my lunch hour to do it. He was much embarrassed at his carelessness, so when I finished he insisted I take this. It's mine to spend as I please, and I want you to buy a hat."

She placed her hand on the bill but she did not pick it up. Her eyes, raised to his were full of the love she could not voice. When she spoke, her words were husky with feeling.

"That's about the nicest thing that ever happened to me, Tony. I ought not to spend the whole ten dollars on a hat, but I'm going to. It will be the most beautiful hat to be found in the city. And every time I wear it I'll be remembering how you earned it for me. Lean down a minute, darling. I want to kiss you. You're the nicest husband I ever had."

She took the whole day off to go to the city to buy the hat. Ruth Hayes was keeping the children, and she had a long carefree day ahead of her. Not for over two years had she been able to do such a thing. With a whole ten-dollar bill in her purse—all hers to buy one dream of a hat—she felt like an adventurer indeed. When she first reached the shopping center, she was so excited that she could not settle down to the search. For an hour she window-shopped, buying in her imagination all the little brother and sister outfits she saw. Then she wandered through the toy departments trying to decide on the play-yard equipment that she would like to install in the space between the garden and garage. From there she went to the men's stores, and picked out the necktie she was going to buy for Tony if she could find the right hat for eight dollars.

She roused herself from this pleasant pastime when an accidental view of a clock showed eleven-ten. So, having taken a bit of the edge off her appetite by these preliminary meanderings, she began the real quest of the day. It was not as easy as she had expected. She soon discovered that ten dollars would not give her the choice of all the beautiful hats in the city. After several unfortunate experiences when she was disappointed by finding that the hat she desired was beyond her price, she learned to ask about the price before trying on the hat. Time after time she thought she had found the dream hat. But each time there was a reluctance to buy. What if she bought one and then saw another that was more desirable? Better to look a bit farther. She could come back later to the one she liked best. So the quest went on, and at last she found *the* hat. And—unbelievable luck—it was in exactly the soft rose color that was Tony's favorite for her. If she bought it she could not get the tie for him, but he wanted her to spend the money on a hat. Perhaps she could save enough out of the household bills to get him a tie. But caution still held her back. Ten dollars was a lot of money to spend on a few square inches of hat. Maybe she had better have some lunch and think it over before letting go of that bill.

She was returning from lunch, hurrying along that she might get the hat and catch the three-ten train. That would get her home in time to bake an apple pie for supper. Then she saw the figurines. They were in the window of an antique shop and were almost unnoticeable among the vases, platters, and colonial glass with which the window was filled. But they caught Linda's eye, and in a moment she was lifted from the busy street and set back in a big room in an old house on a hill overlooking a western city. That was the nearest to a happy memory of her childhood that Linda had. Her mother had sprained her ankle and could not dance for several months. The troupe was playing the West Coast at the time, and often her daddy had come to spend a day with them. They had pretended that the house with all its old-fashioned furnishings had belonged to them. The two queer, ugly little figurines stood on the mantel, and Daddy used to make up stories about them. Every time he came he had a new one, a droll tale that made Mother and Linda laugh until they cried. To the little girl that had been the best time of her life. She had no foreknowledge of the bitter friction that was already building up between her parents and was soon to separate them. To her, it was a time of happiness and laughter, and the sight of the figurines brought it all back. If only she could buy them! It would be wonderful to own something that came to her from her own family, something that gave her a feeling of having a background of her own. Of course, these couldn't possibly be the same figures, but that made no difference. They had the same fat little bodies, the same laughing faces, the same quaint clothes.

"I've got to have them," she whispered as she turned toward the door. "They can't cost more than a dollar apiece."

But when the clerk turned the little man upside down, Linda saw the price, "ten dollars" on his foot. She gave a gasp, then shook her head. She was sick with disappointment, for already she felt a sense of possession. But it was beyond thought.

"I'm sorry," she said. "I didn't realize they were worth so much. I couldn't possibly pay twenty dollars for them."

"Oh, they go together," said the clerk. "They aren't priced separately. It is ten dollars for the pair."

Linda looked at them longingly. She *couldn't* buy them, and yet she couldn't make herself leave them. Then a daring thought came. She could buy them instead of the hat.

It was a foolish idea. She did need a hat, and she certainly did not need two homely, squat little china figures. But she *wanted* them—wanted them more than she had ever wanted any material thing in her whole life. She wouldn't mind fixing over an old hat, although she had her doubts as to her abilities along that line. She wouldn't mind going without any hat at all if she could just have these little folks to laugh with her when things went wrong and to remind her of that winter in the big house on the hill.

But what would Tony say? Could she make him understand what they meant to her? Would he see any sense at all in such a purchase? Would he think her ungrateful and selfish, to buy them rather than the hat with this special gift which had cost him such hard labor?

"He wanted me to have the money for something I needed," she thought. "And I do need these. I need them to build up my morale and sweeten my disposition, and to teach me how important it is to give children a happy home to remember. Oh, I know Tony will understand."

But as the train sped toward home, her assurance began to fade. Would Tony understand and laugh with her? Or would he be hurt that she didn't have the hat? She wished she had waited until he could hear her story and know why she loved the figurines. But it was too late now. She would just *have* to make him understand.

She put them on the mantel and realized with dismay that they were entirely out of accord with Mrs. Bannister's carefully chosen treasures. She wrapped them up again. It would be better to tell Tony first and show them to him afterward. As she baked the pie, she planned the approach she would make. She would tell him first of all of that happy winter and give him a glimpse of the childhood she seldom mentioned. She would show how the little pair were vitally linked with that happy memory. When he had heard the story, he'd understand why they meant more to her than a hat.

But it didn't work out quite as she had planned it. Tony came bursting in just before six, demanding to see the hat. Her plea to wait until after supper seemed unreasonable to him. So, when she began her story it was to an audience that was a bit alienated by her refusal to show the hat at once. She thought in a panic of how her mother used to say she couldn't dance unless she "had the audience with her."

"I know just how she felt," thought Linda. "Tony's miles away from me, and I can't think of a thing that will bring him back."

She chattered away with her story until they finished eating. Then she said with a smile that she hoped would win Tony's sympathy, "Go into the living room. I'll show you what I bought."

She came slowly into the room with the box in her hand. Tony looked on expectantly as she opened it, then removed the figurines and set them on the table.

"What are they, Pat?" he asked in bewilderment. "Something for the kids? They're homely things."

"Yes, but aren't they *dear*? Oh, I want you to understand, Tony. They *are* ugly, but they're a symbol to me. I don't care about a hat if—"

"A hat? Do you mean to say you didn't buy a hat?"

"No-o, I didn't. I really meant to, dear. I even had it picked out. Then I saw these—"

"Pat, are you trying to tell me that you gave up the hat to buy those things? What did they cost?"

"Ten dollars."

"Ten dollars? You spent all the money I gave you to buy this ten-cent store junk?"

She looked into his angry face and her own temper flared. He hadn't even listened to her story. He didn't care what she wanted. He just wanted his own way.

"Yes, I did," she answered defiantly. "And they are *not* junk. They are valuable or they wouldn't have been in that antique shop."

"Oh, wouldn't they? They probably cost twenty-nine cents apiece to begin with. And won't Mother be pleased when she sees them among—"

"I don't care whether she's pleased or not. After all, it *is my* home, Tony, not your mother's. If I want them here, I'm going to have them."

"You're not going to put them on that mantel."

"I am so."

She placed them at one side of the exquisite vase that had been Mrs. Bannister's pride. This afternoon Linda had conceded to herself that they looked incongruous there, but now she was determined that they should be on that spot. Perhaps she was blinded by the tears that she was trying to keep back. Perhaps her hand was unsteady. She never knew how it happened, but she touched the vase, and before she realized what was happening it lay in fragments on the floor. She stared at it dully thinking that it reminded her of the happy plans she had made a few hours ago. Then Tony's angry voice chilled her.

"You did that on purpose. I can play at that game, too!"

His hand swept across the mantel and the little figures crashed to the floor by the side of the vase. She gazed at them for several minutes, then, without speaking stooped and gathered the broken bits into her apron. Tony watched her shamefacedly, but she did not look up. She went into the guest room and closed the door. On the shelf of the closet she found a silver and white box that had held one of her Christmas gifts. When she had wrapped the pieces of china in tissue and tied the box with the white ribbon, she thought heavily, "It looks like a casket. I wish I could bury them, but they're too common for that high class lawn and garden. I'll hide them, and when I take the babies for a walk some day, I'll find a place where I can dig a deep hole and put them in it. Then, *perhaps*, I can forget it all."

She heard Tony leave the house, probably for one of the long walks he would take if an unhappy mood were upon him. Usually when he did that, she would spend the time in restless waiting, trying to plan some pleasant surprise or bit of interesting chatter that would lift his spirits. But she did not do that tonight. She wrapped the box in paper and carried it up to the attic. Back under the eaves behind some heavy cardboard cases she pushed it, feeling sick of the whole incident. As she turned away she thought of laughing little faces and wondered if they had been broken. She had not noticed when she picked them up. Back downstairs, she flung herself across the bed and cried until she was exhausted.

"I hate cry-babies," she said as she sat up and wiped her eyes. "But I can't walk out of the house as Tony does when things don't suit him. I have to stay on the job. Crying is my only way of 'compensating' as my 'psych' teacher would say."

Tony was still absent, so she washed and wiped the dishes, inspected the sleeping babies, and went to bed, too low in mind to read or knit.

Chapter Seven

IT WAS LATE when Tony came in, and he did not turn on the light in the bedroom. Linda lay still hoping he would think she was asleep, for she was not ready for any discussion of the unhappy incident. It was hours later before she did go to sleep, and when she wakened, Tony had already gone from the house. She could hear him outside working with the garage door which had been giving trouble. She hurried so that she might have breakfast ready when he came in. She wondered what his attitude would be. Would he still be sulky, or would he put his arms around her with some loving, foolish remark and expect all to be right between them again?

"If he does, I *must* have backbone enough to let him know I'm not going to be coddled out of my hurt. It was a mean thing he did. That vase might have cost ten times what my little folks did—I don't know—but it didn't mean a thing to anybody. His mother can buy another any time she wants to, but I can *never* find my dear little figures again. Anyway, I didn't mean to break it, and he smashed mine on purpose. But it's awfully hard for me to stay mad at Tony. If he puts his arms around me, I'll probably forgive him before I think."

But Tony didn't put his arms around her, nor did he appear to be seeking forgiveness. He passed through the kitchen without speaking, then, having washed his hands, returned to find breakfast waiting. It was a silent meal, and he arose from it to make an equally silent leave-taking. Linda watched him out of sight. He did not turn at the corner for the customary wave, and she turned back to her work with an angry flush.

"Let him sulk! If he had been spanked a few times twenty years ago, it would make life a lot easier for me now."

In this mood she administered a sound spanking to Susie-Q who had climbed from her crib and was enjoying herself with a box of face powder and a bottle of cologne she had found on the dresser. Combined, they made a lovely, fragrant mess! Even the baby did not escape the maternal wrath, but received his share of chastisement when he threw his bottle at his sister. It was made quite plain that this generation would profit from early application of the rod.

"I hope my children-in-law appreciate what I am doing to make life easier for them," she muttered grimly.

However, as the day wore on her mood softened.

"It *was* wrong for me to spend that money on something else when Tony wanted me to buy a hat. Somehow I'm going to get another ten dollars and buy that hat or one as much like it as possible. It wasn't nice of him to break my figures, but he didn't know how I loved them. He can't help being the way he is. He got a lot worse deal in life than I did. Even with my folks divorced they were better than that mother of his. I'll just remember that, and forgive him, and keep on trying to teach him to grow up."

With this high purpose in mind she prepared an especially good dinner and put on a fresh gingham dress that she knew Tony admired. The babies looked like pink and white cherubs in freshly ironed brother and sister suits. It was a setting to assure any recreant husband and father of forgiveness.

But it did not go quite as planned. Tony kissed her formally, rather tenderly, but with none of his usual zest. Then he turned eagerly to the children. During the meal he was courteous, most attentive and full of polite interest in anything she had to say. She found herself chattering nervously of the doings of the children and the news of the neighborhood. Several times he smiled at her in a gracious way that was no kin at all to Tony's usual happy-go-lucky manner with her. The smile seemed to be a surface one only, designed to cover a broken heart.

"So that's the way it's to be," she thought. " 'Sad and sorrowful' is to be the theme of our relations. And how polite we can be! Tony has vanished from the picture and I find myself in the company of Chetwolde. What a perfect lady he is!"

After the little ones were in bed, they sat at each end of the davenport, Tony with the evening paper, Linda with her knitting. Tony wasn't sulky. She had to admit that. He was just polite and gracious and casual—and at least half a world away. Linda having resolved to be forgiving, met him with equal politeness, grace, and casualness—and with equal distance of spirit. As her fingers busied themselves with the yellow wool that would eventually be a sweater for Susie-Q, her thoughts raced along a different track.

"H'm. So that's the game, is it? He thinks *he's* forgiving *me*. Why, he's exactly like his mother. She's *always* forgiving me in that patient way of hers. I *hate* that kind of forgiving! And now it's Tony. That's too much! I don't *want* to be forgiven. He's forgotten all about what he did to hurt me. I'm going to figure out how to get ten dollars and I'll buy that hat, and he'll find out who's forgiving whom!"

After she had gone to bed, her mind was busy with the problem, and at last she reached a decision. *This* was the place where Mom would want the ring used. In the morning she would go about selling it and get the money to make things right between her and Tony once more. She wasted no time in carrying out that resolution. As soon as she could get away the next day, she took the children to Ruth again, promising a double return favor sometime, and took the train once more to the city. It was not an enjoyable day as the other one had been. It was made up of hours of going from one place to another, of facing suspicion, of experiencing disappointment. When she was ready to give up in despair, she remembered the name of the lawyer who had handled her father's affairs. To him she went and was recognized and greeted cordially. With his reference in her purse she went again to a jeweler who had turned her down earlier in the day. It was only a matter of minutes until she had three hundred dollars in her pocket. It made her rather sad to think she had given up the ring her dad had given to her mother twenty-five years before. But the thing the ring stood for had not survived, so its symbolism was lost. What better purpose could the diamond serve than to bring her and Tony together? That was what Mother would have wanted her to do in this circumstance. She had mailed it to Linda the day after the divorce became final.

"I don't want to see it again, ever," she had written. "Keep it until you need some money sometime. It will always be worth several hundred dollars. Or have it reset if you want to. It could be made into a gorgeous dinner ring."

Linda had never worn it, for the sight of it always brought pain. Anyway, what could she do with a "gorgeous dinner ring"? She never wanted to wear any diamond except the one Tony had given her. If this money could just mend the relations between her and Tony, mother's ring would have served the best purpose anyone could desire. By this time she was thoroughly sick of the whole childish incident, and was anxious to get home and back to the shelter of Tony's love and care.

"Next time I'll think first and act later. Every trouble I get into comes from impulsive thoughtlessness. From now on I'm working on developing some thought habits!"

She hurried to the shop and found to her joy that the hat was still there. It was even more beautiful than she remembered it. No husband, not even one who thought he had a real grievance, could resist it. Then she went to the great store where she thought Tony's mother had bought the vase. She could not duplicate it exactly, but she found something so near like it that she believed it might pass inspection from Mrs. Bannister's nearsighted eyes. The cost of it startled her, but she bought it and bore it off with her. She could not wait for delivery. She must have it in place tonight when Tony came home. When it was in its place on the mantel, she would breathe more freely and be ready to live again.

"It really is a good substitute," she assured herself as she put it in place and stood back to note the effect. "If Madame Bannister isn't *too* alert, I think it will pass."

She laid the hat on the bed where it would be the first thing Tony would see when he entered the bedroom. Then she ran to Ruth's to collect the children.

"You're an angel, Ruth. You may have saved my marriage today. If yours is ever heading for the rocks, signal me and I'll plunge to the rescue."

The phone was ringing as she entered the door again, and Tony's voice inquired petulantly,

"Where have you been all day, Pat? I've tried a half-dozen times to get you."

"I had to go to the city."

"Again? What now?" Then without waiting for an answer, "Listen, I have to hurry or I will be late. Mother sent a message saying that she will be in on the six-thirty-five. I'll meet it and bring her out."

Linda stared dully at the telephone after she had replaced the receiver. "If ever I had a good fairy or guardian angel, he's lain down on the job. There will be no reconciliation scene tonight. Oh, what's the use? Nothing ever works out right. This mess shouldn't happen to a dog!"

Chapter Eight

Linda always felt that she could have closed the rift between herself and Tony that evening if his mother had not been there. There was no chance for any sort of conversation except such as Mrs. Bannister directed. Whenever she was about, Tony was nervous and temperamental, conciliatory to her and irritable with Linda. He seemed to forget his usual chore of dish-wiping and left the kitchen to Linda while he followed his mother into the living room. When she spoke, which she did almost continuously in soft, rather sad tones, Tony hastened to agree with her. He moved quickly to perform any little task that might please her, and accorded to her many courteous attentions. He never argued with her, no matter what theories she might advance or what criticisms she might make.

Of those criticisms Linda had always been the target. Had they been straightforward, she might have been able to meet them. But they were usually implied rather than stated. To answer the implications was to call forth a plaintive lament about how hard it was to be so unloved and so easily misunderstood. Linda resolved many times each day to remain silent and let the challenge go unaccepted. But it often came at an unexpected time and in such a subtle way that she was in the battle before she realized it.

If only Mrs. Bannister hadn't chosen this particular time to appear! Linda had planned exactly how she would show Tony the hat and tell him how sorry she was for her impulsive thoughtlessness in buying something other than the gift he had wanted for her. He would understand when he saw the hat and the vase that nothing else in the world meant as much to her as his love. Perhaps, when he did understand that, he would be ashamed for his part in the quarrel, and in the spirit of mutual forgiveness they could reach a new realization of the value of their love. Much as she had wanted the figurines she did not yearn for them as she now did for Tony's nearness.

But the opportunity for this scene did not come. All evening they sat listening to the account of Mrs. Bannister's disappointment in the companion of those weeks. It was exactly what Linda had expected of the vacation, but she did not say so. She sat quietly and managed to express appropriate sympathy.

"Oh, it's so nice to be home. I don't think I'll ever want to leave," said the traveler looking about the room. "This is such a beautiful room. I grow more proud of this house every time I look at it. There are several incongruous items I have noted, but those can be easily corrected. I can't expect everyone to have a feel for the right thing, and I don't want you to think I am too critical of these little touches you have added, Patricia. Unless one has had the right background it takes a lifetime to acquire good taste. But tomorrow we will go over the house and I'll show you what I mean."

Again she cast her glance around the room, bringing it to rest at last upon the vase Linda had placed on the mantel only a few hours before. The puzzled expression on Tony's face showed that only this minute had he discovered it. The silence in the room might have presaged a thunderstorm of destructive force. Then Mrs. Bannister spoke, and Linda's breath came back with a gasp.

"That vase looks especially lovely in the glow of the lamps. It grows upon one as time passes. It never looked so beautiful before. It is quite the nicest thing in the room."

Linda remembered in panic that she had forgotten to wash

the small price label off the bottom and silently hoped her mother-in-law would not inspect it more closely until tomorrow. This danger was averted as the talk drifted to plans for the garden in the approaching spring. Linda's heart lightened. She had noticed a twitch at the corner of Tony's mouth which told her of laughter held in check, and she knew that the humor of the situation had not evaded him. When they were alone, they could chuckle together over the narrow escape. And all would be well with them again. Together they could face the problems of the days ahead, no matter how trying.

When she went to their room after giving Susie-Q the customary midnight drink of water, Tony was standing with his hands on his hips looking at the hat. He was plainly embarrassed as he noted this gesture of reconciliation. But all he said was,

"Did you sell the crown jewels?"

"No. Only my mother's engagement ring."

His face reddened, then he said huskily, "Will you put it on?"

She adjusted it in front of the mirror, then faced him, knowing that never had he seen her in a hat so becoming. He gazed speculatively for so long she became fidgety, then he spoke with a self-conscious grin.

"It's the prettiest hat I ever saw. Almost as pretty as the face beneath it. But take it off now, won't you? I don't want it to get smashed when I kiss you."

Tears of happiness came to her eyes as she placed the hat in its box. But as she turned to him a knock on the door was accompanied by a plaintive voice,

"Chetwolde, will you come and sit by me while I go to sleep. Your father often did, and I'm lonely tonight."

Tony stood for a minute looking first at the door and then at Linda. His face was troubled as he hesitated in indecision. But the call came again, more insistently, and he answered,

"Coming, Mother." He turned to Linda and started an apology, but she pushed him toward the door.

"Run along, Chetwolde," she said contemptuously.

When Tony came back an hour later, she lay quietly on a pillow that was damp with the tears she had shed before she went to sleep. Her despairing conclusion had been,

"It's no use. I shall quit trying. He can't be her Chetwolde and my Tony at the same time, and he made his choice when she called him tonight."

But with morning came a more optimistic attitude.

"All this must be just plain torture for Tony," she mused as she set the table for breakfast. "He didn't leave me last night because he wanted to. He was so thoroughly cowed by his mother when he was small, that he can't get over it. I'd rather be the gal that he wants to stay with and can't, than the one that takes him away by force. I'll be good for a change, and he won't be able to resist me. Maybe she won't stay long, and after she's gone, he will tell me how he appreciates me."

Tony's appearance twenty minutes later dampened her spirits somewhat. He came in hurriedly, saying shortly, "If you'll fix up a tray I'll take it in to Mother. She is worn out from the trip." He forgot the kiss with which he usually preceded his breakfast, and after he had delivered the tray, ate abstractedly with one eye on the clock. He did kiss her good-by, however, and she, with her new resolutions in mind said smilingly,

"Have a good day, darling."

To which he replied gruffly, "I'll try. I wish I could hope for as much for you."

She accepted that as an effort at an apology, and turned to the work of the day, determined that all her powers should be used to the one end of preserving the peace. She succeeded so well that there were no unpleasant incidents to report on Tony's return, and another evening was passed in quiet acceptance of Mrs. Bannister's place as head of the house.

That day became a pattern for many that followed it. Linda's veneer of patience wore very thin in places, but by dint of constant effort, open friction was avoided. In any place, under any circumstances, the two women could never have been compatible. In temperament, background, and training they were completely inharmonious. There was never between them the companionable chatter that even casual acquaintances usually indulge in. During most of the time of Tony's absence from them, Mrs. Bannister discussed at great length all the affairs of her own life, her early hardships as the eldest of a large family, the struggle to maintain the necessary social contacts without the money that should have been the accompaniment of such "background" as her family possessed, her marriage to a man who could provide her with those things that were hers by what Linda inferred was "divine right," Tony's birth, and the death of his father soon afterward.

"That was too bad," sympathized Linda. "It must be very hard to be left with a little child to rear."

"It was, of course. But all things have their compensations. By being alone with Chetwolde I was free to rear him by myself with no interference. His father was a good man, a most estimable one, and he left me enough money to do well, very well, for Chetwolde, and still be able to live in comfort for the rest of my life. In a way, it was not too hard for me to see why it had to happen. My first husband was, as I said, a good man. But he lacked some of the refinements that have always been very important to me, and it was for the best for Chetwolde, I am sure. But it *was* hard." She raised her handkerchief to her eyes.

"Chetwolde was in college when I married Mr. Bannister," she resumed. "He was a wonderful man, and of a *very* fine family. He and Chetwolde were the best of friends from the first time they met. I had always thought that we would have an ideal life together, Mr. Bannister, Chetwolde, and myself, and to that end I obtained a very fine position for Chetwolde with some friends of mine. But—oh, why should I talk? Other influences came in, and Chetwolde came to the city. It is too late now to change. One just has to go on and make the best of things. But I've always felt that it was grief over the fading of that happy dream that made Mr. Bannister ill."

Linda remembered the encouraging talk from Dad Bannister that first Christmas and was not disturbed by these remarks.

"It's the smartest thing you ever did, Son," he had said. "Your mother will resent it for awhile, but give me a little more time and I'll have her thinking that it was her own idea, therefore a very fine one."

But Dad hadn't had much more time with her, and apparently she had never admitted the worth of the move.

"And she doesn't try to hide the fact that Tony's marriage was a mistake, in her opinion. She probably thinks I am responsible for all her troubles. She doesn't realize how much reason she has to be thankful. If I were to get really angry and set my mind to it, I could show her what real trouble is— trouble with a capital T."

When she talked to Edna Barrow on the street one day, Edna urged her to a more aggressive attitude.

"Why don't you tell her off?" Edna said. "After all, it's your house and your husband, and you have a right to them. She's had two men of her own. Tell her to leave yours alone."

With the determination in her mind that she would win Tony's approval of her patience and forbearance, Linda did not follow Edna's advice. But as the days wore on in a never changing pattern of criticism, misunderstanding, and the perpetual attitude of patient martyrdom, there were many times when she was tempted. There were no evenings of recreation to break the monotony or give relief and fellowship with Tony. All day Mrs. Bannister could lie on her bed with a sick headache and accept Linda's ministrations. But when evening and Tony came, she was always well enough to be the center of the family circle. If Tony suggested that he would like to go out for an evening, it was Linda who stayed with the children. She knew she could go with them of course. In fact, her refusal to do so seemed to irritate Tony. But she was firm in that refusal.

"Nothing doing," she told Edna. "I live with her all day. A chance at a quiet evening at home alone is to me like drink to a desert traveler. I'd like to go out with Tony, just by ourselves, but with her—no thanks."

"Believe me," said Edna, the aggressive, "I'd get rid of her, pronto."

"I'd like to, but I don't know how it could be done."

"I'm going to the library this afternoon. Want me to bring you some 'who-done-its' to read? You might get some ideas from them."

"No, thanks, but I do appreciate your interest. It always makes me feel better to talk to someone. I was thinking of going over to see Ruth Hayes this afternoon. I haven't seen her since the day this earthquake landed. Or do earthquakes land?"

"I don't know. I never met one. But I can tell you about Ruth. She has quit the club and gone in for religion."

"Religion! What's the idea?"

Edna shrugged her shoulders. "I don't know. The last time the club met she called me and said she'd not be coming any more. I thought it was finances or too many babies. But Lillian met her on the street and asked her. She said they had joined that little church on Hill Street. Said she was busy there. What do they do in churches that would keep a person too busy to spend a few hours with friends?"

"I couldn't tell you, never having been interested. I do want to see Ruth, though. Maybe I'll find out."

She did see Ruth a few days later. The day had been unusually trying, and after the dishes were washed she left Tony and his mother playing checkers in the living room, and went for a walk. She knew that Tony had an acute dislike for checkers and it irritated her to see him so meekly play game after game, always managing to let his mother win by such a narrow margin that she could feel that she had been victorious in a stiff battle.

"The poor dope," she muttered. "Why doesn't he give her such a good trouncing that she would never ask him to play again? I don't think she likes to play anyway. I think she just does it to be monopolizing him. She doesn't like any games that three can play. Well, that's O.K. by me. Neither do I— with her as the winning third all the time."

As she turned into Hill Street, she saw Ruth ahead of her and called to her. Ruth's face lighted as she recognized Linda.

"I'm so glad to see you. I've been wanting to come, but I knew you had a guest and I wanted to be alone with you. I've missed seeing you."

"I've missed you, too. And I'm glad you didn't come to the house. I have a guest all right, and she's the best spoiler of conversations that I know. It's my mother-in-law."

"You say much by the tone of voice," Ruth laughed. "But they aren't all that way. I wouldn't trade mine for anything on earth. In fact, she's responsible for what I'm going to tell you."

"I'd hate to tell anyone what mine is responsible for. So if you have a different kind, let me hear about it."

Ruth drew a long breath. "Well, I guess I'll start my story with the club. I love those girls. They are a jolly crowd, kind-hearted and neighborly. But every time I went to the club, I had a guilty feeling. I knew I was out of place. I know now that my husband felt the same way about playing cards with the fellows on the train. But we were new here and rather lonely, and the neighbors were the only friends we had. We knew we were off the track. You see, Linda, we are Christians and didn't belong in those places."

"Why? I don't see anything wrong in what we did. We just had a good time, and goodness knows, we needed it. I know it was good for me to get away from the house and babies for awhile, and I think you were just as glad as I."

Ruth walked along in silence for a few minutes as if pondering her answer. When she spoke, it was as if she were weighing each word to be sure that it was the right one.

"It's going to be hard to make you understand, Linda. I want to have a long talk with you as soon as you can manage it. I'd even cancel this meeting I'm going to now, if you'd be willing to give me the time this evening. I've been a Christian for years, but I'd been living 'just as if Jesus had never lived, as if He had never died.' That isn't the way a Christian is commanded and privileged to live. When Mother Hayes came last month, she saw what was happening, and we all had a long talk together one night that set us straight. We've joined this church, and we're much happier than we were before. But we'd be happier still if we could see our friends here walking in the same way. I really could talk for an hour, Linda. Can you give me the time? I'll drop in at the church and excuse myself to the others, if you'll let me talk and tell you all about it now."

"No. I'm sorry, but I must be getting back now," said Linda hastily. "Some other time. 'By now, Ruth. Glad I met you."

"I doubt that," thought Ruth, looking after her as she ran back down the hill. "You don't want to let me talk to you, so I'll just do a lot more talking about you on my knees. You're going to hear the story that will change your life some day whether you know it now or not."

Chapter Nine

IF LINDA HAD HOPED the visit would be a short one, she was disappointed. As each day passed the situation became more tense.

"Why can't you play up to her a bit, Pat?" asked Tony despairingly after an evening when Linda had thrown back a verbal missile that brought forth an hour of self-commiseration from her mother-in-law.

"Because I don't want to, I'm afraid," came the answer. "You seem to have the method down to a fine point, but I can't do it. I'm just not that kind of a sheep."

"I know you think I'm a sheep," he said defensively. "But you haven't lived with Mother as long as I have. You can't win with her, so why try? It only makes things more unpleasant."

"I may not win, but I'm not going down without trying when it's the care and discipline of my children that she's interfering with."

"You don't have to let her boss you about the kids, Pat. I won't stand for that. They're ours, not hers. But do you have to get so fresh as you do at times?"

"Such as—what?"

"Such as telling her that you were going to put Susie-Q in a barrel and feed her through the bunghole, just because she tried to keep her from making such a mess when she eats."

Linda giggled reminiscently. "That was a clever idea, I think. I found it in a comic strip. It seemed to be just what was needed to protect the kitchen from a two-year-old's efforts at self-feeding."

"And *why* did you tell her that you look at the weather reports every evening to see if you're going to have to dust next day."

"Because I do. There's no use in dusting if it's going to be cloudy."

"I know all about those ideas. But why tell Mother? With her nearsighted eyes she'd never know whether you dusted or not."

"Oh, wouldn't she? She can't begin her daily headache until she has seen me make with a dust rag. Anyway, why does she worry? Why doesn't she just laugh and forget it?"

"She doesn't think it is funny. It's never good to answer Mother, Pat, and you might as well give up now as later. You'll have to, eventually."

She did not dispute this nor argue further with Tony. She felt sorry for him. It must be pretty tough to be in between two women who so thoroughly disliked each other. No wonder he was crabby at times and took his long walks more frequently in the evenings. How she wished she might go with him! If they could stroll together through the quiet darkness of these tree-lined streets they might forget the troublesome problems of the day, and absorb some of the peace of the night. But she was not asked, and she sensed that if he took her along he would have one of his problems with him. But why did she have to be a problem? She was trying as hard as she could to keep sweet and patient. *Sometimes* she succeeded. But she could use a little help from him. Why didn't he stand up to his mother and let her know that Pat was the mistress of this home and was to be treated and respected as such?

"I know she bought this house for us," she said to Edna one day, "but we didn't ask her. It was her own idea. And she does just as she pleases with it. She has discarded every single thing that I had put in while she was away. Last week she took down my plastic kitchen curtains and put up some frilly ones that will take an hour to iron."

"Didn't she even ask you if you wanted them changed?"

"She did *not*. She said she knew I meant well in putting up the plastic, but that it lacked atmosphere, and she wanted our little home to have the *best*."

"Phooey! I'd like for anyone to try to treat me that way! I'd show her. I'd let *her* spend that hour ironing the 'atmosphere.'"

"Oh, no, you wouldn't. You just think so. She can't be shown. She's so *right*. She's *always* right."

"Folks that are always right are a great big pain in the neck. If you know what's good for you, you will make things so uncomfortable for her that she will head for home, *but fast!*"

"She calls this 'home,'" said Linda wearily. "I doubt that she will ever leave."

"She will if you manage it right. Think up a few new ways of making life miserable for her. You've got a good brain for that kind of thing, Linda. Use it."

Linda could not bring herself to do that, however. After all, Mrs. Bannister was Tony's mother and anything said or done against her would hurt him. Linda's heart ached for Tony. He had lost weight she knew. He was quiet and moody most of the time. If only she could go to him and put her arms around him and pour out to him the love that was in her heart. If they could have just one evening alone in their home. She'd sit on the davenport and Tony could lie with his head in her lap as he used to do when he was tired or troubled, and she would rub away all the wrinkles and pain. But she couldn't do that. This moody, irritable man did not seem to want any demonstration of affection from her. Not once since the incident of the broken figurines, had the "wall" between them been taken down. Once, the night she tried on the hat, it had seemed to be toppling, but a word from Mrs. Bannister had reinforced it and it was stronger than before. Occasionally they touched hands or exchanged glances. But it was still there, and as long as Mrs. Bannister stayed with them, it would remain.

One morning in early June the postman brought a letter which caused a great uplift in Mrs. Bannister's spirits, and brought forth a dismal groan from Tony when he came home that evening. A cousin with her son had returned from a prolonged stay in France and would be at home for the summer at their country place on the North Shore. Mrs. Bannister was immediately full of plans for their entertainment.

"Lydia was always dearer to me than my own sister is," she said. "And her Miles was *such* a nice companion for Chetwolde when they were little fellows. They were *so* congenial."

"Oh, yeah?" muttered Tony in a voice that he knew could not reach his mother's ears.

"They went to the same preparatory school, and we even sent them to the same college so that the companionship would not be broken. They were *so* close. But somehow, since Chetwolde married, they have drifted apart."

"For all such blessings the gods be thanked," whispered Tony in Linda's ear, and the camaraderie in his tone brought a lift to her heart. Maybe Cousin Miles, whom Tony appeared to dislike, would be the means of breaking down the wall!

Mrs. Bannister began enthusiastically to plan a dinner party as a reception for the travelers. That would call for a trip to the city to buy just the right linens and china for such an occasion.

"But you gave us some dishes when we moved here."

"Oh, that stuff! It was just for you to use casually with *your* friends. I want something better for Lydia. If I were in my own home, I'd have my choice of several lovely patterns. But it is all packed away now and I haven't time to go and see to it. So I'll go in tomorrow and get the dishes. I'm so glad I gave you that set of sterling. And for the tablecloth—"

"*I* have a tablecloth."

"You have? A suitable one?"

"Sure. Most suitable. One that those playful little boys, Miles and Tony, can spill their gravy all over and it won't hurt a particle."

"I'm sure it's a very nice cloth, Patricia. And please don't think I'm critical. You do wonderfully, considering your background. Some day you are going to be a most successful wife and mother. But we will save your little cloth for another time. This time it must be *just* right. Lydia does have a most appraising eye, and we must not be at fault in the tiniest matter. A real lady is known by her table appointments."

"Then we *must* be exactly right," said Linda grimly. "Let's start out with names. My name *isn't* Patricia, even if Tony does call me Pat. It is Melinda Louise, commonly called Linda Lou."

"How quaint! But I don't think I could ever call you that. It sounds like the name of a hound dog that my father used to have."

"It's my name, so why not use it?"

"Chetwolde doesn't use it."

"And I don't call him Chetwolde. The 'why' of that is our own little secret. But my name is Linda and I'd like to be called so."

Mrs. Bannister appeared not to hear her as she busied herself with preparations for the trip. As she was leaving she said sweetly,

"I'll try not to be late, Patricia. Do be careful about the children. They're at an age when they need most constant watching."

"As if I didn't know," thought Linda, watching the dainty little lady go down the street. " 'Patricia,' she says. Oh, phooey, what's the use?"

*　　*　　*　　*　　*

Miles Walcott proved to be a very ordinary and, to Linda, a very unattractive young man. He was always immaculately groomed and seemed to have no other occupation than escorting his mother about and furnishing her with a sounding board for her incessant chatter. At first Linda felt only a sense of disdain for one so aimless and idle. Tony's hesitating diffidence was more appealing than Miles' suave assurance, his four-year-old suit more attractive than Miles' tailor-made outfits of which there seemed to be a new one every time she saw him. However, as the acquaintance progressed she saw that back of Miles' lazy dalliance was a keen wit and a mind that could have coped with major business or intellectual problems had its owner desired. At times when the two older ladies were chatting together during the afternoon visits that had become a regular part of the schedule, Miles would saunter out to the kitchen to watch idly while Linda prepared small sandwiches and tea.

"Where did old Chetwolde find you?" he asked one day.

"Want to go and see if there are any more left on the parent bough? There aren't. Fortunately, I was an only."

"Oh, I don't want a wife. One woman is enough for me. I can't help but wonder how Chetwolde manages."

"Hang around awhile and you may see some fun."

"Yes? Do you feel an eruption coming on? I've been wondering how long you could take Cousin Alta and her possessive ways. I've a bet on with myself as to who will blow up first, you or Chetwolde."

"You'd better bet on me. Tony hasn't it in him to blow up."

"You think not? That just shows how much you don't know. Some day little Chetwolde will blow the lid off, and there'll be one grand explosion. It takes that guy so long to get really mad that folks think he can't. But when he does—gal, you'd better look out!"

"I don't believe you. Did you ever see him real angry?"

"Yes, once. And he has never gotten over it. When he hates, he hates. And woe betide the object of that hate!"

"You frighten me."

"I don't mean to. He would never be angry with you. Come on, Linda Lou, let's go build a castle in the sandpile. Susie-Q looks lonesome out there."

"You go on. I haven't time for sand castles. Don't you ever do any work? Do you play all of the time?"

"I never work if I can find anything else to do. I consider it too strenuous. When someone finds me a job that pays the maximum of salary for a minimum of effort, I will talk to them about it if they come to see me. But I doubt that I would take it. Any job would be too cramping to my abilities."

* * * * *

"Soft living has made him soft in character," she told Tony in their room one night.

"Yeah, soft like a cornstarch pudding," grunted Tony wrestling with a knotted shoestring.

"You don't like him at all, do you?"

"I do *not*. I never did, even when our mothers made us have our pictures taken with arms entwined. He was a baby snake then, and he's full grown now. That's the only difference."

"I don't think he's so bad. He's fun when he wants to be."

"He always has been. But most of the time it has been at my expense, and I don't care for any more. *You* can have him for *your* Cousin Miles as far as I'm concerned."

He put on his old sneakers and went out to sit in the garden. Linda turned off the light and stood at the window watching him. He was on the bench under the apple tree, his attitude bespeaking weariness and dejection.

"Poor Tony," she whispered. "I wish the world would leave us alone. If we were here by ourselves, just us and the babies, we'd fix things up all right. But there's a wall between us almost as high as we are. Every time we tear down a few bricks

83

so we can think about getting together, someone comes along with a whole *load* of bricks and builds it up higher."

That really seemed to be what was happening. Linda would promise herself each morning to be sweet and patient. She would keep her hair curled and wear her most becoming housedresses. She would plan pleasant topics of conversation for the breakfast table, that Tony might go to his day's work with only happy thoughts of his home. But before the meal was over some remark, some jest, or even a failure to cook the morning egg just right, would reduce Mrs. Bannister to wounded tears. With brimming eyes she would look at Tony and smile bravely.

"Don't mind me, darling. I don't mean to be so much trouble. It's hard getting used to not being wanted. I—I—"

She would disappear into her room, and Tony would say reproachfully,

"Can't you learn not to stir her up, Pat? What did you say this time?"

"I didn't say *anything*. I just *failed* to say something she could be grieved about. So she's grieving about *that*."

"How ridiculous!"

"Yes, isn't it?"

He would slam out of the door, and Linda would go about the day's work with heavy heart and cheeks flushed with anger. The daily repetition of this scene was becoming unbearable.

"Tony knows I am not to blame. But the poor guy is afraid to breathe when she is around. How in the world did he ever get backbone enough to marry me? I wish I had a mother or a sister or even a forty-second cousin. I'd pick up the babies and leave here for awhile. H'm—I wonder if Aunt Lucy still lives where she did when I stayed there that summer. Where's the directory? Oh yes, in the hall closet where it won't spoil the atmosphere. Now, let's see—h'm—here it is! The same address

—4538 Argyle Street. I've a notion—I've a *big* notion—to go and visit her. She'd be tickled pink to see me, and she'd love the babies. She doesn't even know I'm married, I guess. Shame on me. But she'll welcome us anyway. I'll just—no, I *won't!* That would be exactly what *she* wants me to do. So that's what I *won't* do under any circumstances. This thing can't last forever, and if it's going to be an endurance test, she'll find out who can last the longest. I'm going to be in there fighting when she goes down!"

Chapter Ten

Cousin lydia was giving a dinner party in honor of a visiting celebrity who had been the speaker at the Kenilwood Garden Club that afternoon. The day had been one of the worst of the summer. An argument at the breakfast table about Susie-Q's milk had widened during the morning to include everything Linda mentioned. There had been a lengthy dissertation on the necessity, if one were to expect to be received into desirable circles, of a long line of ancestors distinguished for their cultural, intellectual, and financial standing. Linda, worn out with the effort to maintain an appearance of amity in the household, had replied pertly that ancestors, in her opinion, were only biologically useful. In other respects, each person would be better off had he been found under a cabbage leaf as was sometimes supposed. Mrs. Bannister had retired to her room with a headache and Linda, in exasperation, had told the tale to the interested Edna, who was finding these confidences more thrilling than a best-seller.

"No one is worth her notice unless he swam over ahead of the Mayflower. It makes me sick! What difference does it make who my grandfather was? It isn't he nor my grandmother either that is married to Tony. It's me, myself and I. And if she'd leave us alone, we'd make him a good wife. She's so sore this morning because her favorite candidate has been found guilty of malfeasance in office, that she can't stand it. He isn't bad. He has just been the victim of the 'skulduggery' of *my* candidate."

"*Your* candidate?" laughed Edna. "You don't know nor care a thing about politics."

"Oh, yes I do. I am unalterably lined up on the other side, whatever its name might be. And if this thing goes on much longer, I'm going to hunt me up an opposing church to belong to. If she's determined to fight all the time, I'm going to have some fun out of it."

"Go to it, Pal. And if you need help, call on me."

After lunch, while Linda was ironing, Mrs. Bannister came into the kitchen.

"I have been wondering. Do you have a suitable dress to wear tonight, Patricia?"

"Oh, sure."

"What is it? I am most anxious that it be right. I don't know why I didn't think of it sooner. We could have gone in to the city and bought you a new one. I do hope yours is suitable."

"Well, what do you want? There's my taffeta, my blue, my rayon and my spotted one."

"I'll have to see them on you. Could you let the ironing wait and model them now so I can decide?"

"Sure. Oh, sure."

She finished the little dress then put the ironing board away and started for her room.

"Which do you want first?"

"Let's try the blue. It's better for your complexion than those off shades you often wear."

Linda slipped the blue dress over her head and eyed herself in the mirror.

"It looks almost as well as it did the other forty 'leven times I've worn it," she said with a giggle. "This is going to be good. I hope she gets so mad at me that she will tell me to stay at home."

She walked majestically into the living room, her white anklets and brown loafers making an incongruous note beneath the blue dress. That, of course, was the first thing her mother-in-law spied.

"Oh, dear! Get on some other shoes. I can't judge at all how the dress looks with those old things. You do have some good shoes, don't you."

When Linda had returned with a pair of high-heeled pumps she was given a critical inspection.

"That dress isn't *bad*. It's a bit—oh, not this season's model."

"That's right. It's three years old. I got it before I was married."

"Well—it isn't bad. And the shoes are good except that they look so large. But I guess—with your height—"

"Yes, you'd better leave them alone. With my height, as you say, a number four would look pretty silly. Anything less than a number eight would pinch. Let's concentrate on the dress."

"This is rather becoming. It *may* do. But let's see the others."

Linda disappeared into her room to return a few minutes later and again turn slowly for Mrs. Bannister's inspection.

"This is the taffeta," she said soberly.

"But—but—I don't understand. It *looks* like the same dress."

"It is. It's my blue, and my taffeta. It's also my rayon."

"Then let's look at the dotted one. Though I don't as a rule care for anything but plain colors for a dinner dress."

"Don't worry. We can fix that. This is the spotted one, too. Susie-Q decorated it at the last club party, and I forgot to clean it. But ten minutes and the bottle of Energine will make it O.K."

The silence in the room became ominous to even Linda's rebel soul before Mrs. Bannister spoke plaintively, "I never get used to your odd sense of humor. Well—if it's your *only* dress I guess you'll have to wear it."

"I certainly will—if I go."

"You will go, of course. The dress isn't *too* bad. Be sure and air it well after you clean it. And I do wish your shoes weren't *quite* so large. Nothing so denotes the real aristocrat as dainty feet."

"I like my feet. I think they look fine alongside of Tony's oversized extremities."

"Yes—Chetwolde's feet *are* large. His father had very large feet, and Tony is built just like him."

"Oh! Then Tony isn't the only one in the family who made a mesalliance?"

Linda was sorry and ashamed the minute she had spoken. This was no way to create an atmosphere that would be restful to Tony when he came home. But she had no opporutnity to apologize, for her mother-in-law hastened out of the room with her handkerchief to her eyes. She was seen no more until time for departure when she appeared looking like a courtly little queen. As Tony assisted her down the steps, Linda looked at his oft-cleaned wedding suit and her blue rayon dress and thought that they, she and Tony, might well be footman and personal maid for this grand personage. At that moment the baby sitter called for some last instructions that had been forgotten, and when Linda reached the car, Mrs. Bannister had appropriated the front seat by Tony, and she was left to sit alone in the back. Her mood was not improved when the older lady turned and spoke apologetically.

"The dress doesn't look bad *at all*. But—I hope you will forgive me—I meant to tell you this afternoon that a seam is pulling out on one armhole. I don't think it will get too bad if you're rather quiet. I'm so sorry I forgot to tell you. I hope you won't be *too* uncomfortable."

"I won't," promised Linda airily. "I'll just be uncomfortable enough, just as uncomfortable as my worst enemy could wish."

She could see Tony's face flush and knew she had irritated him again.

"Fine start for a bang-up evening," she thought. "Why

can't I keep still? I want so badly to smooth things out between Tony and me, but instead I just keep stirring them up."

As they rode along, however, the joy of being out in the country, of breathing the air fragrant with odors of cut hay and wayside flowers, of having freedom from care of the babies began to quiet her.

"If only I were up there by the side of Tony I could ride and ride and never want to go in to a stuffy old dinner party. But the evening air smells just as good back here as it does up there, and I'm going to enjoy it all by myself."

The last few miles led down a side road through the woods. The birds were already nested for the night and from either side came sleepy chirps. Through the trees a small creek could be seen flowing between banks lined with moss-grown rocks and drooping ferns.

"Oh, I'm so glad I came! I'm even glad I'm back here where I can't talk. I feel like all my kinks were straightening out, and the Pat whom Tony loved is coming back."

As they came out of the woods, they faced the last rays of the setting sun. Dusk was stealing over the land, but the western sky was still aflame with color. Unbidden to Linda's mind came the words of a song remembered from college days. At vespers they had sung it:

> Day is dying in the west,
> Heaven is touching earth with rest;
> Wait and worship while the night
> Sets her evening lamps alight
> Through all the sky.

"I could almost worship at a time like this," she mused. "Only I don't know what to worship. There *must* be a God some place to have made all this beauty and to be able to keep the earth in order. *Something* or *Somebody* is back of it all. I wish I knew. Any power that could control all the forces of nature ought to be able to manage Tony and me. I've tried and tried, and we get no place. And I'm so *tired* of trying. There might be something to this religion business after all. I'm going to ask Ruth Hayes to take me to church with her. If there *is* anything to Christianity, I'm going to find out about it."

* * * * *

At the long dinner table in the dining room of the great house, Linda was seated between a very deaf elderly man and a very greedy young one. This gave her plenty of time to look about her at the beautiful table which glittered with crystal and silver.

"Perfect!" she thought. "Very, very perfect. Cousin Lydia must rate A1 as a lady, judging by her table appointments."

She was glad to have no part in the conversation. She was tired, and it was much easier to sit and listen than to try to carry on a conversation with either of her neighbors. From one side she could hear a discussion about a new book, while across the table there was an argument as to the expediency of trying to cultivate the local wild flowers in a garden. Farther down she could hear a woman holding forth on a new dahlia she was developing.

"I hope no one asks me any questions about books or dahlias," she mused. "I haven't read a book in two years, except on baby feeding, and I wouldn't know a dahlia from a sunflower. I'm certainly in the wrong crowd. Well, Daddy used to say that anyone could pass for a wise man if he just kept his mouth shut and listened with absorbed attention to others talk. So here I go to give an impression of great wisdom."

As she lifted her eyes she met the puzzled stare of the man across the table. His gaze was so intent that she flushed in embarrassment. Could it be possible that he knew her? He certainly acted as if he did. Yet he wasn't sure about it, for that baffled look came every time she met his eyes. She could not remember having ever known him. Could he be one of the trustees of the college? They were always under foot, and perhaps he remembered her face from some meeting there. In no other place could she recall having met any elderly businessmen. Maybe he was the clerk who had filled out her marriage license. Her lips twitched at the thought of such a lowly person in this august gathering. Far down the other side she could see Tony in an animated conversation with a young woman who was seated between him and Miles. It had been a long time since she had seen Tony enjoy himself as he appeared to be doing now. This was the sort of thing he had been accustomed to all his life. Perhaps he had been missing it. Maybe he was homesick for all the things he had left behind when he married her. She had forgotten her surroundings, and it was only when she caught Miles' amused glance and a mischievous wink, that she realized she had been staring. With a flush she turned back to her partner.

Later, in the library where the party had gathered to look at Cousin Lydia's collection of photographs of colonial gardens, Linda found a quiet corner and sat listening to the talk going on around her. She gazed in wonder at the shelves of books.

"Think of having time to read, and a place like this to do it in!"

She met once more the gaze of the man who had given her such perplexed attention at dinner. It made her uncomfortable to know that whenever she turned her head she met his intent stare. Nearby Mrs. Bannister and Cousin Lydia were deep in conversation with the celebrity. Miles and the beautiful young lady were talking to Tony, whose eyes were restlessly roving over the crowd. She realized with a feeling of joy that he was seeking her, so she stepped out of the shadow. But before Tony could reach her, a loud voice interrupted all the conversation.

92

"Oh, now I know!"

Everyone turned and Linda felt her face grow hot as she realized that the man who had been staring was now pointing his finger at her.

"Look, you folks! I've been wondering all evening where I had met this young lady. I was sure I had seen her some place. And now I know. She's the image of Mary Mitchell, that dancer we were all so crazy about ten years or so ago."

There were laughs from several of the listeners, and Mrs. Bannister tried to divert attention by asking about a painting she had not seen before. But the man had had his glass filled too often at dinner, and he would not be silenced. He crossed the floor and, taking Linda's hand, drew her with him into the center of the room. She knew her face was flushed, and she wondered frantically if the pulled seam of her dress would show. Tony started forward, but the man pushed him aside.

"Now look at her. Did you ever see such a remarkable likeness? It's amazing!"

Linda drew a deep breath. "Not so amazing as you think," she said with a catch in her voice. "I think it's very natural. Mary Mitchell was my mother."

As she said the words a hush fell over the room. She looked straight ahead into the angry blue eyes of Mrs. Bannister. Oh, what had she done? Was it wrong to tell about Mother? She looked for Tony, but he was moving toward his mother. She was all alone. She stepped back to her chair and stood wondering what to do. If Tony would come, she would ask for the car keys and go sit in the car until they were ready to go. But as Tony reached his mother's side, her high, sweet little voice cut the silence.

"Did she go out? Isn't she dear? She is *so* sensitive about her background, but her strong sense of loyalty made her speak up. We never mention it before her. Poor child, she can't help it."

For a moment the room swam before Linda's eyes. She drew a deep breath and steadied herself against the wall. Someone asked a question about an antique clock on the mantel and attention shifted to that center. Turning blindly she stumbled through the first door she saw, then down a long hall, and out onto a terrace. She did not see Tony coming toward her, and before he could reach the door, she had disappeared. From the terrace, steps led down to a walk which disappeared among the trees. She found a bench behind a clump of shrubbery, and here she sat lifting her hot face to the breeze that whispered through the woods.

"Oh, I hate her! I hate her! Why can't she be just a little bit like a mother should be? I try, and try, and every time she spoils it. I don't want to come between her and Tony, but neither do I want her to come between us. She's Tony's mother and he loves her, I guess. And I'd *like* to love her. But it's no use trying any longer. If there's a God any place I'd like to get Him to help me. But I don't know how."

She heard Tony calling from the terrace, but she did not answer. She was not yet ready to meet him and try to go on with the business of living. When she had gained a bit of control over the tumultuous hatred in her heart, she would go back to the house and try to be a gracious guest for the rest of the evening.

A step sounded on the walk, and Miles came around the turn. "I saw you leave and decided you were going out for a solitary hate-fest. Can I come along?"

"Whom do *you* hate?"

"Oh, everybody sometime, and somebody all the time. Just now it's dear Cousin Alta. She ought to be choked. Why doesn't Chetwolde do it?"

She laughed scornfully. "He? He's afraid to."

"Yes, I think he is. He may bust loose some day, but the time hasn't come yet. I think occasionally that I see signs, and he's been edgy this evening. He's tuning up for a real show, I think. But as of now, he's still an obedient son."

"Well, I'm fed up! If they knew how mad I am, they would be afraid to have me in the back seat on the way home for fear I'd slug them!"

"Honest, do you have to sit in the back while Mama rides with Chetwolde?"

"Honest."

"Rotten. Absolutely putrid. Hey, I have an idea. What say I take you home? You don't want to go back to that stuffy party, nor do I. Is it a deal?"

"What will Tony say?"

"I'll fix it with him."

He was off before she could object further. She saw him talking to someone on the terrace, but could not see whether it was Tony. In a few minutes he was back bringing her coat, and led her to the low, rakish, open car that stood in the drive. In answer to her question as to whether he saw Tony, he replied carelessly that he'd fixed up everything and she was to forget it. As they turned into the highway, he shifted the car into higher speed and laughed as she drew in a sharp breath at the skidding curve he made.

"I'm going to take you for a real ride. We need to have the cobwebs cleaned out of our brains. Nothing like a night ride in a good car to do that. You're going to see something, lady, that you will remember. This car is vastly different from that quaint model Chetwolde drives."

"But I want to go home."

"I'll get you there before the folks arrive. We're just going to take the long way round. We won't be late."

It *was* good to be out in the night air flying through the darkness in this powerful car. If only it were Tony beside her, she could be *very* happy.

Chapter Eleven

THE FIRST HALF-HOUR of that ride was very enjoyable. The clean evening air was a refreshing contrast to the smoke-laden room they had left behind. Miles was in a gay humor and regaled her with stories of his and Tony's childhood and the escapades that their mothers never knew about. But after a time she became anxious. A high-powered car, driven by one who has no regard for speed laws, can cover a great deal of distance in thirty minutes. She was not sure of her directions, but feared that they were not going toward home. Tony and his mother might reach there before she did, and then there *would* be fireworks.

"Let's turn back, Miles. I *must* be home soon. We promised the sitter we'd be there before midnight."

"Oh, let Chetwolde worry about the sitter. You and I can't be bothered."

"But I *am* bothered. Please, let's turn at the next road and go home."

"The next road has an all-night stand on the corner. We'll stop and stoke up."

"Oh, no, let's not. I really want to go home, Miles."

"And I really want to stop. So stop we do. Next ride we take you can have your way."

They drew up in the lot and a uniformed youth took their order. Linda did not want anything but saw that argument would only prolong the delay, so ordered some lemonade. In spite of Miles' urging she could not take more. She was extremely weary and sat listlessly while he consumed two hamburgers and several drinks. She was disturbed at noticing that he poured something from a flask into his glass.

"Miles, *please* don't drink any more. We have to get home."

"Why do we have to?"

"You know why. Come, let's go. You promised me we'd not be late."

Sulkily he complied, turning the car and whirling out onto the highway with a screeching of tires. For a few miles he pouted and they rode in silence. But his mood of gaiety returned, and he began to recount again the episodes of prep school days. But it was no longer amusing to Linda. She noted to herself that all the stories made quite a sport of Miles and put Tony in a role that was not at all to his credit. Dully she resented this, though she had suspected ever since she met him that Miles had been the leader in the exploits and Tony had been only an acquiescent partner. Now, as Miles grew more talkative and more reckless, she shrank back in the corner of the car, completely miserable. Oh, why had she come with him? She suspected that his increased hilarity was due to the drinks he had taken, but she dared not mention it nor question when she observed the speed go up to eighty-five. Several times she tensed and grew cold with fear as they passed some other car and got back on the road with only inches to spare in the face of oncoming traffic.

"I'd better not look or I'll scream and that would make him worse. I'll just close my eyes and think. I've got plenty to think about."

She wished she weren't so tired. All she wanted to do was to get home and go to bed. Even the differences with Mrs. Bannister didn't seem important. Tomorrow she would go to Ruth Hayes and ask her about her religion, and if it were responsible for the quiet good nature that made Ruth loved wherever she went. If religion could help to bridge the chasm between Tony and herself, she would try even that in spite of her resolution to have nothing to do with it. For she knew with no shadow of doubt that she could not go on in the strained, unhappy relationship that had existed for these last weeks. What mattered hats, or vases, figurines, or even Mrs. Bannister, so long as she and Tony met life side by side? And if they could not do that, life was not worth living.

She sat with closed eyes, feeling the cool night wind against her cheeks. Miles was singing now and she listened with revulsion to his nasal tenor voice singing a medley of silly songs. She knew he had taken several more drinks from his flask, and all she could do was to cower in her corner of the seat and wish fervently that they would soon reach her home.

After what seemed to her another hour of riding, she sat alert. On each side stretched the darkness of forest trees. This was no place near home!

"Miles, where are we?"

"I don't know. But the scenery is beautiful, the night is young, and we're having a wonderful time."

"We are *not*. And if you don't take me home I'm going to yell for help at the first car we meet."

He laughed loudly at that. "Do you think anyone will pay any attention? Sit down, Linda, and enjoy the ride."

She had risen in the open car and was looking back over the deserted road. As they rounded a sharp curve at high speed she swayed and fell against the door. In panic, Miles clutched at her, and the car, out of control, swerved from the road. Linda, struggling to regain her balance, was conscious of a tree trunk looming before her. There was a jolting crash, then blackness. She wakened to find Miles bending over and frantically splashing water in her face. As she attempted to rise he spoke, hysteria in his voice.

"Linda, are you hurt?"

"A little. What happened?"

"We hit a tree and you were thrown out. I told you to sit down!"

She tried again to sit up but fell back dizzily. "My head! And this hand."

"Guess you whacked your head. Here, let me get more water."

He dipped his handkerchief in the ditch at his side, and in spite of her protests swabbed her face and hands. Her head ached intensely, and whenever she moved waves of blackness threatened to overcome her again. One hand was cut and bleeding profusely. But the thing that bothered her most was her desperate desire to get home as quickly as possible.

"Is the—car—wrecked?"

"I don't know. Let me wrap up that hand with a clean handkerchief and then I'll see to the car. If it won't go I'll have to flag another car to send you home."

She lay in dumb misery, hearing as if from a distance his efforts to get the car to start. After a time he returned and asked anxiously,

"Can you get up if I help you? The old bus got a nasty knock and looks a mess. But she will run O.K. Come on, easy does it."

At last she was back in the car, her head aching furiously, and her left hand throbbing and smarting under the clumsy bandage of Miles' handkerchief. Miles was sober now and very anxious to get her to her home. He drove as rapidly as he dared with a crippled car, and she sat, mutely miserable. Her dress, coat, and hair were soaked with the water Miles had used so liberally, and the wind chilled her. Through her chattering teeth she spoke.

"It's just around the next corner and—I want to go in alone—please."

"Can you make it?"

"Yes."

He helped her from the car. As her feet touched the ground she swayed and would have fallen had it not been for his arm. She leaned against him and the blackness crowded around her. Miles spoke hastily, "Here take this." A stream of fire seemed to choke her as he forced her lips open with the flask. She straightened with a jerk, and pushed him away.

"I don't *want* that. Go—please—I'm all right."

She started up the walk a bit unsteadily but very resolutely. He climbed into the car and sat watching her. Slowly she mounted the steps. When she stood in the lighted doorway, Miles drove off.

"She's all yours, Chetwolde," he muttered. "You can have her. I don't want her. And what Mother will say about this car will be plenty!"

*　　*　　*　　*　　*

Tony was pacing restlessly up and down the living room. Mrs. Bannister sat in the big chair that faced the front door. To her son in his overwrought condition she seemed a bit like a cat waiting to pounce on a mouse. He was ashamed of the thought but it persisted.

"Why don't you go to bed, Mother?" he asked irritably. "You can't help things by sitting there. That won't bring Pat home."

"Well, since you insist I am to blame for her leaving Lydia's so rudely, the least I can do is to wait to greet her."

"I don't want you to wait. What has to be said here tonight should be between Pat and me—*alone*. You *were* to blame and you know it."

Her handkerchief went to her eyes as she said with a sob, "You never spoke that way to me before."

"Maybe I should have. I've been a coward to keep still all these weeks you've been heckling Pat. And that show you put on tonight was the limit for me. I made up my mind on the way home that Pat shouldn't be asked to have you in the house any longer. After all, it's *her* home. She's the mistress of this establishment and—"

"Who bought it for you, Chetwolde?"

"You did. But no one asked you to, and I wish you hadn't. Things have been wrong ever since we moved into it. When Miles delivers Pat here tonight, I am going to break his head. I've wanted to for over twenty years. Then tomorrow Pat and I are going to look for an apartment I can afford. And we are going to furnish it ourselves as we please and as we can. And *no one* is going to interfere."

She was crying softly, and Tony's heart smote him. But his anxiety for Linda came back sharply and he did not weaken.

"Are you sure she went with Miles, Mother? Who said so?"

"I told you before. Lydia's maid came to me and said that Miles had come into the kitchen and asked her to tell us that he was taking Patricia home. That's all I know."

"There's one thing you'd better learn then. From now on her name is Linda, to you. Don't let me hear that Patricia business again. She's asked you a dozen times to stop it. Now I'm telling you. Why didn't Miles say something to me, I wonder."

"How can I know? You blame me for everything. I'm sure I didn't know she would act so childishly."

He turned wearily away from the window. The clock on the mantel said two o'clock. For almost three hours he had been pacing between the window which looked out over the road that wound into the hills and woods, and the door which gave a view of the long village street. Over and over again he had reviewed the events of the evening. He burned with resentment, first with his mother, then at Pat for being bothered and hurt, and at Miles for going off with her and staying until this unreasonable hour. He had hurried home as soon as the message was delivered, believing that Pat would be there and

101

he could apologize for his mother's inexcusable rudeness. But a sleepy sitter assured him that she had not been there.

As the minutes had grown into hours his impatience and resentment had increased. Mingled with this was fear that clutched at his heart, and a sense of guilt for his own part in the unhappy situation. He knew that a man with more courage would have taken hold weeks ago and, in some way, made his mother give to Linda the respect due her. If his mother had fought openly and honorably, it would not have been so hard to meet her. But her clever insincerity, her sweet helplessness which was not helplessness at all but efficient hardness, had long ago defeated him. He never had been able to stand against her. His only attempt at breaking away had been when he married, and now that marriage was in danger of shipwreck. His resentment overcame him once more and he spoke angrily,

"Please go on to bed. Pat and I will settle this tonight and we'll talk to you in the morning. I'm not going to—"

A stumbling footstep was heard on the porch and they turned. Linda stood there with one hand in her coat pocket and the other supporting her against the door frame. Her dress was torn and wet, her face streaked with mud and water from the roadside ditch, her hair tangled and damp. At sight of her Tony's hours of anxiety were forgotten in a burst of anger.

"You're a pretty sight. Where have you been?"

"Riding—with Cousin Miles."

"Why didn't you come home?"

"I did. I'm here."

Tony started across the floor, but Mrs. Bannister's gently rebuking voice stopped him.

"We've been terribly worried about you. Couldn't you have thought of us?"

"Didn't have time. Wait till next winter. More time then," she said thickly.

She was swaying as if she might fall. Tony took her roughly

102

by the shoulders, then as he caught the smell of the liquor that Miles had forced through her teeth, he drew back, his face white with disgust and anger.

"You—you—" he choked. "You're fit to be neither a wife nor mother!"

She would have fallen had he not caught her. He carried her into the bedroom and dumped her with no gentle touch on the bed. Closing the door behind him he went back into the hall and faced his mother.

"She's been drinking. I hope you're satisfied. You have accomplished what you set out to do. Get into your room and stay there. Don't go near Pat. I'll take care of her when I come back." His voice was harsh with anger and pain.

"Where are you going?"

"It's none of your business but I'll tell you. I'm going to wring the truth of this night's doings out of Miles. After I do that—I don't know. I'm done with both of you. You've managed to kill the only happiness I ever had in all my life. And I'm quite sure I'll never forgive either you or him."

He slammed the outside door, and a few minutes later she heard the car back out of the drive. She turned, and through blinding tears felt her way to her room.

Chapter Twelve

LINDA LAY ACROSS THE BED where Tony had thrown her and shook with a nervous chill. She had never seen such anger in Tony's face before, nor heard such harshness in his voice. His words were still echoing in her ears,

"You're fit to be neither a wife nor mother!"

What had she done to make him so angry? Couldn't he understand that she didn't want to stay out so late with Miles? Her head ached so blindingly that she could not see the objects in the room although the moonlight made it almost as bright as day. But there was one thing she *could* see—Tony's white face with its blazing eyes, as he had uttered that blasting condemnation. And behind him was Mrs. Bannister with a smug expression of rebuke on her countenance.

"They think I'm bad. Oh, what can I do? I can't stay here when they hate me that way. Tony says I'm not fit to be his wife. Maybe he won't let me see the babies. What *can* I do?"

Her hand throbbed and the rings cut into it. She crept to the bathroom and bathed it in warm soapy water. When she had, at last, coaxed the rings off, it felt better. But her head was getting worse. She found the bottle of aspirin and shook out several of the tablets.

"One won't be enough for a headache like this. I'll take three. That ought to do it. But it hurts—oh, it *hurts*."

She crept back to bed and tried to lie quietly, hoping the pain would subside. Her thoughts turned to her mother and father. It had been long since she had felt a need for them, but now there swept over her a heartsick longing for them. They would love her no matter what she had done. What *had* she done? She could not remember clearly why Tony should be so angry, but the memory of his anger remained and made her feel lost and alone. It was hard not to have anyone left who cared for her. She hadn't minded not having any relatives as long as Tony loved her and she had the babies to cuddle. But if she had to lose them she would be all alone. Dad and Mother were gone, and there was no one else. Yes, there was one who might care. It was old Lucy, the wardrobe woman in the troupe. Just the other day (was it yesterday or last week?) she had thought of Aunt Lucy and wished she could go to her. That would be one place where she would not be doubted or criticized. Aunt Lucy would forget everything else in just loving her. And a little bit of love was what she needed now.

"I'm going there," she said weakly. "I've got to go some place and rest until this headache stops, and I can think things out. I *can't* stay here."

She had to try several times before she could stand, for every movement brought increased intensity of the pain and nausea. But this condition only served to increase her determination to go as quickly as possible. With great effort she managed to get off the bedraggled blue dinner dress and to replace it with a dark suit. Her hair was matted with mud from the roadside ditch, but when she attempted to brush it the pain was too sharp to be borne. She found a scarf in the drawer and tied it over her head. She felt all over the drawer but could not find her billfold. Nor could she remember where she had put it. She couldn't go without money! Her head was pounding worse than ever as she hunted frantically, fearing that Tony would return before she could leave. As she turned in despair to look through the drawer again, the sight of her rings on the dresser reminded her of her mother's ring. The money from the sale of that was in an old purse in her closet. She didn't need her billfold!

"I'm a mess," she whispered to herself as she crept from the room, "but Aunt Lucy will fix me up."

As she stood for a moment in the hall steadying herself for the tiptoed journey to the front door, a whimper from the nursery came to her ears. As softly as she could she crept in to lean for a moment over the restless two-year-old. Under her hand the little girl grew quiet. Then she turned to tuck the light cover over the spread-eagle baby boy.

"Be good babies," she whispered. "I've got to go away until this headache quits. Then I'll think things out and come back to you."

She stole around the side of the house lest she rouse the Barrows' dog, then through the alley to the station. She did not know when a train was due, so she lingered in the shadow of the shrubbery lest she be recognized. She was shaking from the exertion of the walk and the headache was so bad that she took some more of the aspirins which she had put in her bag. She *must* retain consciousness until she could get to Aunt Lucy. She could not see the hands of her watch in the deep shadow, but it seemed to her that it had been days ago that she had fled out to the terrace and Miles had followed her. After a weary time of waiting, the whistle of the train aroused her. There were no other passengers, and the conductor helped her up the steps, looking intently at her white face. She paid her fare to the city and sank back into a seat. Now all she had to do was to remain alert enough to get to Lucy Haines' door. Dear old Aunt Lucy! She had retired when Linda was twelve and had opened a little dress shop. Two years later when the troupe toured Europe and didn't want to be bothered by having a temperamental adolescent with them, Linda had had a wonderful summer with her. But she hadn't heard from her since.

"That was an awful way to treat her. Mother should have made me write. But she will be glad to see me anyway. That's the way she is."

The train sped through open fields and suburban villages. With every turn of the wheels Linda's head beat with a throb that brought waves of dizziness. There were minutes when she hardly realized where she was. Then the jerk of the train as it started away from a station would arouse her, and she would sit upright and struggle to remain conscious.

"I must get to Aunt Lucy before I get so bad I can't talk. What *would* happen if I fainted? I'd better write down what I want."

She found a stubby pencil in the purse, and tore off a piece of the newspaper that lay on the seat beside her. In writing that was almost undecipherable she put down Aunt Lucy's name and address and a request that she be taken there. She pinned this on her lapel where it would be seen if she fainted. This done, she sank back in her seat and concentrated on drawing one long slow breath after another. By remaining quiet she might retain consciousness. Each click of the wheels over the joints of the rails sent a throbbing pain through her head. The lights of the car moved crazily before her eyes. The few passengers seemed to be swimming in air before her. She closed her eyes to shut out the glare of the lights, then was frightened when she found that she had to struggle to open them. She dare not go to sleep! On and on they went, the train swaying and clicking, and Linda's head pounding like a huge trip hammer.

How she got off the train and into a cab she did not know, but at last she found herself being driven through the streets. The driver had her bit of paper and had assured her, with an anxious look at her face, that he would get her to her destination as fast as possible. The pavements were rough, the turns sharp, the traffic heavy. The honking of horns seemed to be

107

the pounding of sledges on her aching brain. When the cab stopped in front of the shabby apartment building, the driver helped her up the steps and waited until the door opened. The plump, white-haired woman who answered the bell stared unbelievingly for a moment then reached out her arms.

"Linda Lou Mitchell! Why, what's the matter with my little girl?"

Linda saw the outstretched arms and all her strength left as she fell into them. "Aunt Lucy, I'm sick," she gasped.

Somehow they managed to reach the bed and Aunt Lucy's hands began to prepare her for rest. The pillows were soft and it was wonedrful not to have to stay awake any more. The blackness crowded around her again. She had almost let go completely when panic seized her and she struggled up.

"Aunt Lucy, I'm going to be terribly sick. No matter *what* I say, don't tell anyone. Promise me you won't."

"Of course, I won't, you poor little chicken. What you say now or any other time is just your own business, and I'll keep my old mouth shut."

Then Linda did let go, and the black velvet curtains that had been pushing closer around her all during the ride, closed in smothering folds over her.

Chapter Thirteen

THE YOUNG DOCTOR WHO CAME in answer to Aunt Lucy's call looked down at the unconscious form on the bed. For an hour he had been working. With the help of the old lady he had bathed the muddy hair and found the ugly bump underneath. The hand had been washed, some small bones set, and the gash across the palm sewed up. During the entire ordeal there had been no quiver from the girl. Now, shaking his head as he watched, he said,

"She should be in a hospital. But we haven't a bed. There was an explosion over our way tonight, and there are people even in the halls. Anyway, I hesitate to move her. Think you could watch yourself until I can send a nurse? It's almost six now, I could have one here at nine I think."

"Of course, I can watch her. I've done it many a time."

"Probably not when she was as sick as this. Is she your granddaughter?"

"No kin at all. Her parents were my friends, and I used to take care of her."

"And you don't know what happened to her tonight?"

"I don't know a thing about it. I hadn't seen her for ten years until I opened that door about four-thirty this morning. And she didn't tell me a thing. She just dropped on this bed and was gone. She's in trouble of some kind, I know, or she wouldn't have come like that. She knew where to come. I always would take care of her."

"Well—we will see what the day brings forth. When she

recovers consciousness, go easy. Don't question too much. I'll send the nurse. If you need me call me."

That day was the beginning of a long hard battle. After the first few days, the nurse was dismissed as Aunt Lucy insisted she wanted to do the nursing herself. Extracting a promise that she would call for help if she needed it, the doctor let her have her way. Day after day Linda lay, unheeding both the doctor's visits and Aunt Lucy's care. The hair had been clipped away from the bruise on the head, and the hand had been saved from infection. But she did not rouse. The doctor frowned as he watched the slow rise and fall of the light cover over her.

"Someone gave that child an *awful* whack. I am sure there's no fracture, but there's a great deal of concussion. She should be in the hospital, but there's still no room and I'm afraid to move her. Even an ambulance ride could be dangerous."

"Let her alone," commanded Lucy. "She's better off with me. She came here because she wanted to be with me, and I aim to be right by her bed when she wakes up."

"It's going to take some close watching for an indefinite time. Can you get any relief?"

"I won't need much. May Hansen across the hall will come in every afternoon while I get a spot of sleep. Don't you worry. I'll manage."

And manage she did, somehow. She left the bedside only long enough to prepare simple meals for herself and to make the broth which she had to administer a few drops at a time, through unresponsive lips. The delirium Linda had feared did not come. Instead there was a deadly stupor which lasted long past the time the doctor had set for its departure. Sometimes there would be a slight moaning and a restlessness that seemed to be a struggle to waken to consciousness. But it would pass, and that unnatural sleep would continue. After a week had gone Aunt Lucy asked the doctor a troubled question.

"Do you think she will *ever* wake up, doctor?"

"Oh, yes. She's coming along. But don't try to hurry her. Perfect quiet is her best medicine, and she can do nothing better than sleep."

During the second week the moaning and restlessness increased, and the doctor had to give a sedative to help her obtain the needed quiet. Once, Lucy, after taking an hour of rest on the cot in her living room, returned to the bedside to find her patient's face wet with tears. But when she spoke, there was no answer. The fever was gone, however, and there was more response to the efforts at feeding.

"When she wakes up, don't let anything startle her," cautioned the doctor. "Is there anyone who should be allowed to see her?"

"Not that I know of. Her parents are both dead and she had no brothers or sisters. I'm the only one that's interested."

"I'm interested. I'd like to know where that young lady came from, who gave her that bump on her head, and why no one is looking for her."

"I never thought of that. Maybe someone is worrying right now."

"Not much—at least not enough to inquire about her. I found the taxi driver who brought her here. He picked her up at the station just after a suburban train got in that morning. There aren't many trains at four o'clock, so I'm convinced she came from one of the suburbs. Yet there has been no advertisement for her. Nor have the police been questioned. I found that out."

"Well, she's here with me, and I aim to keep her. She's nobody else's business."

After he had gone she talked to herself as she moved about her kitchen.

"And that's the whole truth, I reckon. She always was my

baby, and if she has come to me in any kind of trouble, I'm not going to say anything until she tells me all about it."

She thought back over the years when she had traveled with the troupe, and how often she had put the tired little girl to sleep on a trunk in the dressing room of some small theater. She had made doll dresses out of the scraps of discarded dance frocks, and had taught the little fingers to embroider sunbonnet babies on small quilt blocks. When she had retired to open the shop for which she had been saving, the twelve-year-old Linda had cried stormily to be "retired too." It had been a great joke to the heedless parents, but to the woman and the little girl it had been tragedy. There had been one bright summer two years later, when, for four all too short months, Linda had been left with her and they had pretended that it was to be permanent. It had been a time when Lucy Haines had forgotten all the loneliness of forty years of living alone and had reveled in the pretense that she had a family— just one ill-poised overgrown adolescent, to be sure, but nevertheless a family that she loved. Linda had been allowed to have all the things which her parents' vagabond career had denied her—a puppy, a kitten, a canary, a tank of goldfish. Perhaps the shop had suffered a bit of neglect that summer, but Lucy had never regretted it. She had acquired some memories that had become like jewels to be taken out and loved in the years to come.

"That's ten years ago, and she's not changed at all. She's still got Eddie's build and Mary's pretty face. If her disposition is as mixed up as her looks are she couldn't help having trouble. I haven't heard from any of them since Mary and that second husband of hers were killed. That must be four or five years ago now. And Eddie went soon after. I saw that in the *Stage News*. I wonder where the poor child has been since then. Well, I'll not ask any questions. When she wakes up and gets good and ready, she can tell me. Until then, not even the doctor can make me talk."

There came one hot August night when Lucy heard a movement in the bed and wakened instantly. Linda was sitting up in bed, looking sleepily around the dimly lighted room. When she saw Lucy she cried out in wonder.

"Where am I?"

"Here at my house, honey child. Don't you know me? It's Aunt Lucy."

"Oh—how did I get here?"

"You came because you wanted me, dearie. You've been sick."

"I'm—so—tired."

"Well, just you lie back down and rest. Here, I'll get you a cool drink and you can go back to sleep. We'll talk in the morning."

She lay on the pillow obediently and was soon breathing regularly in what was apparently a natural sleep. Lucy watched her anxiously, fearful lest there be some ill effect from the exertion by one who had lain in complete helplessness for almost three weeks. Would Linda waken again soon or would she sink back into the coma? Would she remember then how she came to Lucy in her hour of need? Would she want to tell the story of her injury? Were there anxious friends some place who were looking for word from her? Lucy had looked in the papers every day to find some clue, but there had been no lost girls described. Perhaps it was best that she did not know anything, she reasoned. She had promised not to tell anything, and she meant to keep that promise. Well, it was almost morning, and a new day might tell the story. She must get a few hours of sleep.

For several days there were increasingly long periods of consciousness. When Linda was awake, she seemed sluggishly uninterested in the life around her. She ate when told to, answered sleepily when spoken to, and for the rest of the time lay watching the shadows on the wall and listening to the noises from the street, with no apparent interest in either.

Lucy was preparing breakfast one morning when she heard a smothered sound of sobbing from the bedroom. Hurrying in, she found Linda with her head buried in the pillows and her shoulders shaking. She sat down on the side of the bed and drew the thin figure into her arms. Linda clung to her convulsively, and the sobs increased. Lucy held her close murmuring tender words of comfort and reassurance. When the storm was spent, the girl looked up into the kind face and cried piteously,

"Mother was killed. Did you know it, Aunt Lucy?"

"Yes, I did, darling, and my heart ached. The poor, pretty thing!"

"I almost went on the trip with them, and when I heard it I almost wished I had. But Daddy says he can't spare me yet, and that's why I wasn't taken."

"None of us can spare you, darling."

"Is Daddy here, Aunt Lucy?"

"No! Oh—er—no."

"I guess he had to go back to Eloise. I can't remember. When did I come here?"

"Some days ago. You've been very ill."

"Am I all right now?"

"You'll take a lot of building up, but you'll be fine when you get a little flesh back on your bones."

Quite suddenly she was asleep, to waken a few hours and return once more to the subject of her mother.

"How long have I been here?"

"Over three weeks, dear. You've been very ill."

"Then mother is buried. I can't remember her funeral. Did you go to it?"

"No. They were buried in California."

114

"That's why I can't remember it, I suppose."

Lucy held a troubled conference with the doctor. "She seems to have forgotten everything since her mother's death. That was over four years ago."

"Well—she had a nasty blow, and the concussion may have blocked off a part of the brain. It will clear up eventually, I am sure. In the meantime, protect her from shock."

"That's a big order," whispered Lucy, watching him drive away. "She's already wanting her daddy. How can I tell her he's been dead three years."

She turned from the window and went heavily about her work. She was weary with the long hours of watching, and her heart was heavy with this new burden of apprehension.

"I wish I could remember how I got here," said Linda, when Lucy took her lunch in to her. "It's so strange. I can remember the dean coming to me to tell me that mother had been killed. Then Daddy came and I cried so hard that they gave me some medicine and I went to sleep. That medicine must have had a *real* punch. How *did* I get here, Aunt Lucy? Did someone bring me in an ambulance?"

"Oh no. You came in a taxi. The driver helped you in. And you've been here ever since."

"I guess I was too sick to remember. But it's queer that no one came with me. Daddy will be furious if he finds the school let me go off alone when I was sick."

Poor old Lucy did not know what to say. Linda's father had died in September three years ago. It was the day the Weinberg baby was born. She had seen the news while she was waiting with Mrs. Weinberg for her husband to come and take her to the hospital. And just today she had heard Mrs. Weinberg say that she was going to have a party on Maxie's third birthday. How could she tell Linda that her daddy couldn't come to her? How could she avert the panic that she knew would come when she realized that he was gone? The doctor said she must not be excited, but who could prevent it when the girl discovered that the father she was expecting would never come?

Lucy drew a sigh and wiped away a tear. "I've lived this long by just taking life a day at a time, and I guess I can continue to do so. But, Lord, I'm needing your help pretty badly this time."

Chapter Fourteen

FOR SEVERAL DAYS they were able to keep away from the question of the father. Linda wept for the loss of the lovely mother she would never see again, and apparently accepted her father's absence in a matter-of-fact way.

"He can't come now," she said once. "He has to do just as Eloise says, and she never has liked me. But he will find a way sometime soon. He always manages eventually. He'll come slipping in some day."

She spoke once of college. "I have only one more year and then I'm going to teach kindergarten. I majored in education. I want to teach oodles of little youngsters to make up for the brothers and sisters I never had."

After a long silence she spoke again. "In one way I'm glad I was sick. Daddy had it all fixed up that I should go to camp again, and I didn't want to. I'm so sick of summer camps. They're all the same and nothing ever happens. I'd *much* rather be with you. I've been wanting to ever since that other summer when the folks were in Europe."

When the doctor said she could be dressed and venture out into the living room, she looked with perplexity at the cotton dress Lucy brought her.

"Where did that thing come from?"

"I—I had a neighbor buy it for you."

"Where are my clothes?"

"You didn't bring any."

"How silly of me to come without any luggage! Where's the clothes I came in? I was dressed wasn't I?"

"You—you had on a suit, a blue one. It's in the closet."

"But I don't own a blue suit. Somebody has been pulling some mighty funny stuff. I'm going to call the college and find out what it's all about."

"You mustn't. The doctor wouldn't like it. Wait until he comes and ask him what you can do. Now get into this dress, dear, and then we will have lunch."

Meekly she yielded, and when the white organdie belt was tied in the back the effect was not bad. She was very thin, but the crisp print dress gave her a fresh look, and when Lucy tied her hair with a ribbon, she looked like the fourteen-year-old that had lived here once. But the effort and excitement had tired her and she lay back on the bed, pondering with troubled brow the mystery of a blue suit and a trip without any baggage.

Lucy waited the coming of the doctor with heavy heart. In some way Linda had dropped four years out of her life. Where had she been during those years? Why was she in this condition now?

"I'm sick with it all," she said to the doctor. "What will happen when she finds it out? She's grieving now over the death of her mother, and when she realizes her father is gone too, it will be awful. I won't know what to do."

"Don't cross that bridge until you get there, Mrs. Haines. Some morning she will waken and the calendar will be in place again. That may be tomorrow. No one knows, but we will face it when it comes."

He walked into the bedroom where Linda was lying with half-closed eyes. In her hand was the red purse that she had brought with her when she came. As he neared the bed, he saw that she was trembling, but he only asked casually,

"How goes it today? Feeling better?"

She ignored the question and held up the purse.

"See this, Doctor Page?"

118

"Yes. It was a beautiful purse once."

"And now it looks as if it were several years old and had been dragged around and maybe used for a weapon of defense. It's a wreck!"

"Admitted. Do you need a new one?"

"Let's stop talking around the subject. My father gave me this purse a few weeks ago—at least that is what it *seems* to me. I can't remember using it more than three or four times. Now it is worn out."

"Well—"

"And what about this?" She held out to him the empty box that had contained some of her medicine.

"That date is right, isn't it, Doctor Page? Please answer me truthfully. I've forgotten about four years, haven't I?"

Soberly he answered. "I shan't try to deceive you. The date on the box is correct."

"Can you tell me how it happened?"

"I only know that you came here to Mrs. Haines, and she called me to see you. You had a nasty knock on the head, and it's not all cleared up yet. Don't let it worry you. You'll wake up some morning and it will all come back. Until then don't think about it."

"Doesn't anyone know where I came from?"

"No, and we haven't tried to find out. We want to leave that to you to tell us when you remember. Now try to rest. I want you to take two of these tablets and then go to sleep. When you wake up, you can talk to Mrs. Haines. You are all right as long as you're with her."

She did sleep, but the waking on the morrow brought no lifting of the veil.

"Hasn't anyone tried to find me?" she asked Lucy. "Haven't you tried to get in touch with Daddy? He'd know all about me."

At the sight of the **distress on Aunt Lucy's** face she cried out in alarm.

"Aunt Lucy, what's the matter? Is Daddy—is Daddy—oh, I can't stand it!"

She buried her face in the pillow, and Lucy hurried from the room to hide her own tears.

"Poor little girl! She's having to grieve for them all over again, and it's a double blow this time, both at once. I don't know what to say to her. Dear Lord, You've *got* to take over. The job is too big for me."

Poor old Lucy felt that her Lord had really taken over, for when she went into the bedroom, Linda was lying, her cheeks wet with tears, but her body relaxed in restful slumber. When she wakened again, she did not speak of her parents nor ask any questions. She set about the business of getting well as if that were all she had to think of, and Lucy co-operated, thankful to avoid the painful subject.

When she had become strong enough to walk around the block twice a day and to help Lucy with the housework, the doctor came again.

"You're beginning to look like something besides a picked chicken," he said, smiling. "When your hair grows out you might even be pretty."

She laughed shakily. "I doubt that. I do feel lots better. But I still can't remember. I keep trying and trying, but I get only a headache out of it."

"Don't try, *please*. When it comes, it will come, and you can't hurry it. I feel sure of that, but just to avoid any mistakes, I want to take you to the hospital tomorrow to get some X-rays and tests made."

At the hospital the picures revealed no injuries. For a week she was put through various tests and answered endless questions. When the doctor took her home he gave her a parting admonition.

"You are well now. You can go about normally. Get a job, take plenty of exercise, mix with other young people. Lead a normal life. Above all, don't try to remember. You will only delay things if you do. Some day that memory will come back with a snap, but you can't hurry it. Think of Mrs. Haines. She isn't well, and she needs someone to care for her. You turn the tables on her and show her who's boss."

Lucy wasn't well. Linda saw that when her attention was called to it. She reproached herself for not noticing it before.

"You've worn yourself out on me," she mourned. "And you've probably spent hundreds of dollars on medicine and bills. And I just let you do it."

"No, I didn't spend anything. The doctor wouldn't let me pay him even for the medicine. He says he allows himself one case just for fun whenever life gets dull. And you've hardly eaten anything."

"Maybe I didn't at first, but I'm like a—a—starved refugee now, which of course, is just what I am. And I'm going to pay for it."

"No, dear, please don't think of it."

"Oh, yes, I am. There was over two hundred dollars in that old purse I brought with me. I don't know where I got it so it must be mine. I don't remember having shown thieving tendencies, so I don't believe I stole it."

"Of course, you didn't. You never would."

"I don't think so myself. So I'm using it. From now on I'm carrying my share of the expenses here. Doctor Page says I can go to work in two weeks. So I'll be the man of the family and support us so you can rest. Those fingers of yours are too sore to make all those alterations."

Lucy had not realized that Linda had noticed her growing inability to do the sewing that had been her livelihood since she had been unable to keep the shop. Now she looked down at her hands with their enlarged joints and said,

"I think my hands will be better when I take the new medicine the doctor is ordering. I don't want to stop sewing. But I can't tell you how glad I am to have you here. Do you remember how we wanted that a long time ago?"

"Yes, I do. And I still want it. When I remember, it won't make any difference. We have just each other, no one else, and I'm never going to lose you again."

Chapter Fifteen

Linda tried to carry out the doctor's orders. She found a place as filing clerk in the office of a nearby factory. She joined the recreation club and spent two evenings a week in the fellowship of other young people. She took long walks, and when the winter months came, she skated on the lagoon in the park. And she tried faithfully not to wonder about those four lost years. Occasionally, however, the subject was bound to recur.

"Didn't you ever hear of *anybody* looking for a stray girl, Aunt Lucy? Were there no advertisements in the papers or human interest stories that might suggest me?"

"No, not a thing. I looked every day for all those weeks. The doctor wrote to the college but no one there remembered where you went after graduation. They said they would make some inquiries, but they haven't reported anything. I asked the doctor yesterday when I went to his office."

"Maybe I should go to the college myself."

"He doesn't think so. He wants you to just wait and let things happen naturally."

"I'm glad. I didn't really want to go. I have the *funniest* feeling when I think of it all. I feel as if I were standing on a cliff and someone is urging me to jump, assuring me that I won't be hurt. But I am so afraid that I can't."

"Don't think of it then."

"I try not to, but it sneaks up on me. It's so *queer* that no one ever tried to find me. Someone must have been very glad to get rid of me. Wonder why they didn't throw me in the river instead of knocking me on the head. It would have been surer."

"Oh, don't say that. That's *awful*. I think you were living alone and it was nobody's business where you went."

"My landlady probably thought I eloped, and my boss was glad to be rid of my never efficient services. I wonder if I would recognize them if I met them."

"Don't wonder about anything. Doctor Page says you mustn't. It will come some day and you can't hurry it."

"I don't want to hurry it. To be real honest, Aunt Lucy, I want to dodge it. I just love living here with you. If I remembered, I might find a lot of responsibilities that I don't want to go back to. I'd rather let well-enough alone."

As the winter wore on, Lucy became increasingly helpless. It was hard for her to care for the apartment, and she worried because Linda had to help after her day at the office.

"I'm just a burden on you," she said. "I'm going to have to be cared for like a baby before long, and you can't do it. I'm an old nuisance."

"You're nothing of the sort, and don't talk that way. You're my Aunt Lucy and I'm taking care of you. We will work this out, some way."

She went to the doctor for advice, for the burden *was* heavy and she felt at times that she was not giving her old friend the care she needed.

"What can I do?" she asked. "If I pay a woman to stay with her she would be unhappy. Anyway, I can't afford it and she knows it."

"Has she ever spoken to you of going to the Chandler Home?"

"No. What is it?"

"A home for elderly people who need just such care as Mrs. Haines requires. She has known for several years that this condition was coming, though we did not expect it to accelerate as

124

it has done these last few months. She has been preparing. She has enough money in the bank to enable her to get in, and if she will sign over her equity in the apartment building, they will give her good care for the rest of her life. I investigated them for her, and they are thoroughly reliable. She has planned for several years to go there when she needed care."

"Why hasn't she mentioned it? Why shouldn't she go at once?"

"Don't you know why? She won't leave you alone."

"But she must!"

"I think you will have a hard time convincing her of that."

It did indeed prove to be a difficult task. Lucy was torn between her reluctance to permit Linda to care for her and her even greater reluctance to leave the girl alone.

"Some day you might need me. I can't go off and leave you until you are more settled."

"Until I remember, you mean. Well, six months have passed, and I'm as far from it as ever. I don't think I will find those four years, and what's the difference if I don't? I can go on from here just as well."

But Lucy was adamant, and Linda realized that the only way she could effect the desired result would be to find herself another home. But where? She turned again to the doctor. He seemed to be her only real friend and adviser.

"H'm," he said thoughtfully. "That will take some thinking about. I'll admit your need for a place, but I want to pass on that place. It must be one where you will feel at ease and happy, and where I can keep in touch with you. You aren't dismissed as my patient yet, you know."

A week later he called. "Would you be willing to work in that home we are looking for?"

"What kind of work?"

"Well—act as a mother's helper, do some of the lighter housework, help with the cooking occasionally."

She laughed. "I'd be *willing* enough, but the other fellow would surely get the worst of the bargain. I never was around children in my life, and my cooking experience is limited to dishing up after Aunt Lucy cooks."

"You could learn. Would you be willing to talk it over if I get the other party in here?"

"Yes—if you think I should. I'm frightened at the thought, but I have to find a place so Aunt Lucy can be relieved of me. But I feel as if I were going to be thrown to the lions."

"It won't be that bad, I'll promise you. It will be a place where you can fill a real need for several weeks, maybe months. And you will find the people to be very pleasant and easy to live with."

"I'm not afraid of them. I'm afraid of me and what I might do, or not do."

"Let me worry about that. Just come on over this evening."

Linda approached the interview in the doctor's office with real trepidation. She felt more lost and helpless than she had told even the doctor. Lucy's home had been a refuge to her, a haven where she could be out of reach of the storms that she had no power to meet. If she went to a strange place to live with people who did not know nor care about her, she would indeed be all alone. There would be no one who really cared what happened to her. This strange woman might be hard or unkind. She might think Linda had some mental disease. Perhaps she should yet call the doctor and ask him to cancel the engagement.

But Lucy's desperate need drove her on. The dear old friend had sacrificed too much already and must not be allowed to do more. So, in spite of her pounding pulse and clammy hands she went resolutely to meet her fate, as it seemed.

"Here we are," said the doctor heartily. "Linda, this is one of my best friends, Mrs. Scott Willis. She also happens to be the wife of a cousin of mine but that's of lesser importance.

Marion, this is Linda Mitchell. I want you two to get together, for I think you can do for each other just what the doctor thinks needs doing. I am going to leave you alone, for there are a dozen other people out in the waiting room who need me worse than you do. Go to it, and God bless you."

Linda wished she could grab him and hold him and tell him she couldn't go through with it. She and Aunt Lucy would just have to battle it out together. But the doctor hurried off, and she was left with the other woman. Before she could do more than wonder how she could tell this stranger that it was all a mistake, a laughing voice spoke.

"Why, I believe I'm as frightened as you."

She looked up to meet a friendly smile in the warm brown eyes of a young woman only a few years older than herself. She laughed nervously.

"What are *you* afraid of?"

"Of you. Bill (he's the doctor) has told me all about you. He thinks you are very smart and very capable, and can do wonders for me. That's what he said."

"Did he tell you *all* about me? Did he say that I can't remember?"

"Oh, yes. He said you'd had an accident that hurt your head. I've had one that hurt my back. He thinks we will both be O.K. soon. In the meantime, I need someone to help me run the house and care for three wild youngsters. Would you be willing to try it out?"

"Do you think I could?"

"Of course. Let's sit down and talk. I do need someone very badly. I've tried out several, but no one wanted to help with the baby. But that's where I need help the most. He's a big chap for his age, and I can't lift him since my back was hurt. Do you like babies?"

"I don't know. I never was around where there were any.

I'd like to *try* to like them if you know what I mean. But I'm very ignorant."

"I'm sure you will do nicely when you get used to it. I hope you will come. I know the children will love you, and we will try very hard to make you happy and comfortable. Do you think you could try us?"

"Oh, I'd be happy just to have a good place to stay until I get—until I remember. I hope I can be worth something to you."

They sat side by side on the davenport and for almost an hour they discussed the plans for their work together. Mrs. Willis, or Marion as she insisted she be called, had slipped on the ice some weeks before and severely sprained her back. She was still in what she called a "strait jacket" and was much limited in her activities.

"I have a woman for the heavy work, but she is a miserable cook and she doesn't like children. You say you can't cook, but I am sure you can learn and we will do it together. The baby is my worst problem. I just *can't* lift him. Bill said he was sure you would be handy with a baby."

"How did he get such an idea? In all my life I never held a baby."

"Really? Then you have a thrilling experience ahead of you. Holding a baby in one's arms is life's choicest experience, I think. No, it isn't. It's second. The very *best* thing is to be held in the arms of the man you love, the one God made for you."

Linda looked up in astonishment at this remark. Marion's cheeks were flushed and her eyes shining. She laughed at Linda's expression and said smilingly, "You'll agree with me some day. I'm not ashamed to admit I'm still in love even though I've been married eight years. Just wait until your time comes and you'll find out how it is."

"I hope it makes me as happy as you are. But who'd ever

want a wife who couldn't remember? He might wake up some morning and find I'd forgotten him."

"When you meet the right man you'll never forget him. Anyway, you're going to be all right. Bill said so, and he knows."

"Of course, he does," came the doctor's voice from the doorway. "Or if he doesn't he just looks profound and makes folks think he does. Well, ladies, how goes it? Are we all set? Good. And if you don't both live to thank me for this day's work, you'll be a pair of ingrates."

Chapter Sixteen

IT WAS A WINDY MARCH EVENING with the air full of the promise of spring when Linda drove out with the doctor and his wife to the place where she was to live for many months. Aunt Lucy had been left at the Home that day. Linda had gone with her and helped her to get settled. When the clothes had been placed in the closet and dresser drawers, and when the few keepsakes and books had found their places on table and shelf, Linda had put both arms around her old friend. "I have to go, Aunty. But I'll be over every week to see if you are behaving. Be a good aunty, and don't forget your child. Send me a thought wave occasionally."

"I'll do better than that. I'll pray for you."

"O.K. Let's hope it does some good. Anyway, I'll be back Saturday."

As they drove along the highway that evening, Linda thought of the old lady and felt a glow of warmth at her heart to know someone cared enough to pray for her. Of course, it was all a psychological illusion, this prayer business, but it was nice to know someone cared for her.

The brooks and the roadside ditches were running bankful of icy water. The last snow had gone from the fields although patches of white on the distant hillsides showed where a few drifts remained. Dr. Bill, and Mrs. Bill as he called her, were chatting together in the front seat of the car, and Linda relaxed in enjoyment of the fresh, clean air and the beauty of the twilight. Aunt Lucy's apartment shared common walls with the apartments on either side, and there had been all too little of either sunshine and air. How glad she was that Aunt Lucy was settled out at the Home where she could enjoy some of the pleasant things that had been so scarce in her life!

The road wound through a stretch of woodland, and suddenly Linda felt a sense of depression. She didn't like these dark woods. They were reminiscent of something, some book she had read or some play she had seen. She felt almost a sense of panic at her need to get to the place she was going. But in a few minutes they came out again between open fields and tidy farmsteads. Her depression left, and she had a lift of spirit. Spring was a wonderful time of the year. It was a beginning all over again for everything green. It was the time when birds came back and built nests in the trees. It was the time that gave promise of all that the year was going to be. Was there any significance for her in that? Was this day the beginning of a new life for her? Would she ever remember those four years, or would she just go on without them?

The doctor's voice roused her. "There's Sunnyknoll, just beyond that clump of trees. That's where the Willises live."

The stately colonial house stood on a hillside among great forest trees. A long avenue of pines led up to it, and at one side a noisy brook chattered over the rocks.

"What a lovely place! Am I to live there?"

"I hope so. It *is* beautiful. Scott's great-grandfather and mine built it over a hundred and fifty years ago. We all love it, and I am sure you will."

Linda did love not only the house, but the family of which she soon found herself a busy part. That first evening she was introduced to Scott Willis, a friendly fellow who looked so much like Doctor Bill that it would have been easy for a stranger to become confused. Then Marion brought in her two older children, seven-year-old Dick, and five-year-old Jane.

"You can meet the Big Boss of the family tomorrow," said Scott. "He is in his crib now and if anyone wakens him before morning the guilty party will have to pay the fiddler's bill."

Linda saw a new side of her doctor's character that evening. She had known him only as an overworked, abstracted young man who had been very kind to her, but who, she was sure, thought of her just as another "case"—a most interesting one which he liked to study. Here in this home he was relaxed and full of fun, romping with Dick, going with Scott to see the new puppies, strolling through the pantry to help himself to a handful of cookies. Later when they were all seated at the table for the dinner Marion had saved until they could arrive, there was a short silence, and all of them bowed their heads. Linda did likewise, remembering how much it seemed to mean to Aunt Lucy to have grace at each meal. She expected to hear Marion's or Scott's voice, but it was Dr. Bill who prayed, thanking God for the food and all the rest of His provision for their needs, asking Him to bless that food and those who partook of it, then adding a special prayer for Linda as she began her life in this place, asking too, for healing for both Linda and Marion and a blessing on all of them "as we strive to serve Thee, each in his appointed place. In the name of our precious Saviour, present Lord, and coming King. Amen."

Linda lay awake for several hours after the house had become quiet, thinking of all that had happened since that day she had wakened in Aunt Lucy's tiny bedroom. It was a queer turn her life had taken. Through three years of college she had played a lot, studied a little, and had no thought for the future. After that, nothing, until that day last August when she had become aware that her whole world was changed. Her father was gone, but she could not remember about it.

"I suppose I suffered and grieved for both Mother and Daddy once and then gradually grew accustomed to life without them. Then I had to go through the same shock and grief again. I wonder what else I missed? What other people were there in my life that I've forgotten about? I'm sure I didn't go through all those years without making some friends. What kind of a job did I get after Daddy died? Where did I go when I left college? Where was I for those three years after graduation, and *why* doesn't someone try to find me? I must have been an unfriendly soul, or I lived hundreds of miles from here. Or maybe I walked out of a situation that was better for my leaving it. I wonder—but the doctor said not to wonder.

"That was queer, that prayer he said at the table. It didn't sound like the grace Aunt Lucy says, and it didn't sound like the prayers in chapel. It certainly wasn't something he learned out of a book. He made it so—so—personal as if he believed he just had to ask for something and he'd get it. It's funny that such mature and well-balanced people as the Pages and the Willises could believe in such things. It seemed all right for Aunt Lucy. It was a comfort to her. But these folks don't need comfort. They have all the best things life could give anyone —plenty of money, lovely homes, darling children, and happiness with each other. It must be they are just interested in it as a hobby, something new and diverting when they're bored with life.

"That was a funny way the doctor ended his prayer. It was sort of threefold. I remember we used to have a threefold Amen in the choir at school. 'Precious Saviour'—and he sounded as if he really meant it. 'Present Lord'—that would mean that He is now the doctor's Master. That's a big order and I doubt if he meant it. 'Coming King'—what *was* the sense to that? If the doctor meant Jesus, well, He's already been here once and certainly isn't planning a return engagement. It all seemed rather childish, and below the intellectual level of such people as these.

"Oh, well, why should I worry? I suppose most folks have to go through some spiritual and emotional splurges sometime in their lives. They will get over it after awhile, and it needn't affect me while it lasts. I am thankful for such a good place to stay until I'm well and can take up my life where it was broken off. I'm sure I'd never find a place or people nicer than these."

Chapter Seventeen

A SUMMER SUNDAY AFTERNOON in a quiet country home is an experience that anyone will long remember. To Linda, who had never known such contentment and peace, it was a rich experience, one whose memories would remain with her always. The only sounds that invaded the silence were nature's own—the splash of the brook as it tumbled over the rocks, the soft fall of a piece of bark brushed from the tree by an active squirrel, the scolding of a pair of blue jays in the tree by the porch, and the drowsy cut-cut of the hens in the chicken yard. The trumpet vine over the west end of the big porch shaded it from the heat of the August sun. In the porch swing Linda sat enjoying the sounds and the silences and, at the same time, trying to write a letter to Aunt Lucy. Although she went over to the Home once a week, she always tried to send a letter or card in between the visits. Mail meant much to the old lady who was trying to adjust to idleness after a life of activity. The letter-writing did not progress very swiftly, however. The writer's eyes were more prone to wander to the fields and to the hills and forests beyond them.

"Oh, what's the use of trying to write?" she said at last. "I can do better at night when I'm dead tired. I'm just too lazy today."

The screen door opened, and Linda looked up to greet Marion Willis with a smile.

"So here you are! I looked in the living room and the library, but I should have known you would be here. I think I shall name this porch Linda's Lair, or some such thing. Are you alone? I thought I heard you talking."

"Not talking. Just thinking out loud about how lazy and happy I am out here. It's so lovely. I just like to sit and sit and think and dream."

"What do you dream of, little sister?" and Marion seated herself in the other end of the swing.

"H'm. It's funny, but I can't tell what I dream about. It just won't go into words. The sound of the brook always affects me queerly. For some reason I'm very happy when I hear it, and sometimes when I sit and listen, I get a picture of water flowing over a dam and of someone with me as we watch it. Then quick as it came, it goes, and I'm alone again and very sad. Oh Marion, *why* can't I remember?"

"Don't you worry. You will. Even such a small snatch of a picture as that shows you are improving. And don't forget that Bill said not to try, for the trying would confuse you."

"I know. But it's *so* hard not to try."

"Do you ever get any other pictures?"

"Once in awhile. When I'm holding little Billy, or feeding him, I feel that he's someone else. Once I called him 'Little Brother.' "

"He is little brother to Dick and Jane."

"But I wasn't thinking of that. When I said it, something slammed shut like a door that I had almost seen through but was shut in my face. What does it mean? I never had a brother."

"I don't know, dear. But little by little the curtain is lifting, and some day it will be light again. Just as my back is going to get well, so is your head."

"But it's so slow for both of us. Don't you get tired of waiting?"

"Yes, a bit. But Bill says we are doing as 'well as could be expected.' And we're not to worry. Those are his orders."

"How can one help it? He says we must be careful. You can be careful with your back, but how can I protect my mind?

136

How can I make it behave? I can't turn it off like a light."

"There is One waiting to help you. He can 'turn it off' as you say. All it needs is for you to accept all He is offering you."

Linda said nothing, but sat watching a bee that was circling around the verbena border. Her face was sad, and there was a dejected droop to her shoulders. Marion, watching her and praying silently, thought that after all the weeks of witnessing and explaining this surely must be the moment of decision. But Linda shrugged her shoulders impatiently and spoke.

"Honestly, Marion, I can't. It isn't that I won't, it's just that I do not believe it. There's something in me that can't accept it all. I'm not against it as I used to be. No one who has lived in this home and seen the working out of your faith as I have seen it could ever say it wasn't good. But it's not for me."

"It is for you as well as for me, if you will only let go of self and let Christ do for you what He has done for me."

"You talk as if I were deliberately rejecting it. That isn't true, Marion. I'd love to believe as you and Scott and Dr. Bill and Rosanne do. It would be a tremendous relief to know there was Someone who could do all you claim for Him. If ever a human being needed such a One, I do. If there *is* a Saviour who bore all our sins, or a Burden-bearer who wants our load, or a Lover who could love me in spite of my un-loveliness, I'd give my hope of remembering to have Him. But I *can't* believe, and nothing you say convinces me."

Marion's face was full of joy as she cried, "Do you mean that, Linda? Do you really mean it?"

"With all my heart. But I can't."

Marion stood up and drew Linda after her. "During all these weeks when we have been praying so hard for you, we've been waiting for this time—the time when you would ac-knowledge that you needed and wanted a Saviour. Come with me, honey. We're going to your room. We're going to ask

God to take away all the barriers, and I know He will for now you want Him to. His promise is for 'whosoever *will*,' and He will keep that promise. There's another that proves it, 'Though we believe not, yet He remaineth faithful. He cannot deny Himself.' "

Up in the bedroom they knelt together. Linda was skeptical as to any results that might be obtained, but she was lonely and heartsick, and felt that any experiment might be worth while. Marion prayed. At first Linda hardly heard her. Then the earnest entreaty in Marion's voice began to touch her. This was no idle flow of words. It was desperate pleading for the soul of a loved one. It was a matter of life or death, of Heaven with Christ or an endless eternity without Him. Only one who loved much could plead so earnestly. And Marion wasn't talking to an abstract idea or a mythological figure. She was talking to Someone real, Someone she knew and loved dearly. And she knew He was hearing her. It was true. He *was* real!

Then Linda's tears came, and through sobs of real repentance and acceptance she acknowledged Jesus Christ as Saviour and Lord. As they arose Marion put her arms around the radiant girl.

"You're really my little sister now, my little sister in Christ. I must call Bill and Rosanne. They made me promise to tell them at once when it happened. You see we *knew* it would come if we just held on. I won't have to tell Scott. He will know the minute he sees you. Your face fairly shines!"

"I feel shiny. I want you to know, Marion, that I wasn't pretending. I really couldn't believe before, even when all of you would tell me what Christ had done for you. I thought if it would make me as happy as you are, I would be willing to try it. I even tried to make a bargain with God by telling Him I'd believe if He'd give my memory back. But no matter how hard I tried, I *couldn't* believe. Then while you were praying,

I just quit trying and let Him take over. And all at once I knew it was true—all that you folks had said."

"Can you let Him take the worry now?"

"There isn't any worry. It's so wonderful to know that I am Christ's forever, that I can't think about anything else."

The next evening when Dr. and Mrs. Bill came, he greeted her with outstretched hand. "I hear you are my little sister now. I've been praying for you for a year. Do you realize that it's just about a year since Mrs. Haines called me in to care for that forlorn little 'niece' of hers?"

"Did you pray for me then?"

"I surely did. I wouldn't dare prescribe for a patient without praying. They all get their share of it. But from the first you got a double portion. And I got the rest of my family in on it. You've been our pet prayer project all these months. And I'll say it has paid off. Both in body and soul you are a different girl."

Then while the others chatted together he took her off to the den where he questioned her closely. To all his questions she gave only a shake of the head.

"It's just as dark as it ever was. I can't remember one thing from the night I got the telegram about my mother until I woke up in Aunt Lucy's bedroom. It's just gone."

"No traces? No unexepected little recollections?"

"Well—sometimes I *almost* remember. But when I try to focus on it, it's gone. There are some things that puzzle me. I had never been in a kitchen in my life, except at Aunt Lucy's, and I did nothing there. But when I came here, I knew how to cook lots of things. When I stop to think, I get confused, but when I forget myself, I go about it as if I had cooked for years. There's another thing. I can't remember seeing a certain set of nursery books Janie has. But one day I was reading to her and without turning the page I kept on repeating it. And yellow roses bring a picture of a small room with a big basket of them on a chair."

"Are you afraid of anything?"

"Yes—cows," she said with a shamed laugh.

"So am I—the ornery beasts. That's why I'm a doctor and Scott gets to live on the ancestral home. Even with an office in town as he has, I couldn't enjoy the cows and other adjuncts of a farm. But that's off the track. Is there anything else you're afraid of?"

"Marion's mother-in-law."

"Aunt Jessie? Of all the people to fear! Why, she wouldn't hurt a worm, let alone a husky like you."

"I know that. And I really love her. The fear is terribly silly. But the first time Marion told me that her mother-in-law was coming, I got almost sick with fright. When she came and proved to be such a plump, grandmotherly dear, I was ashamed. But that sense of fear comes back every time we anticipate her coming. Don't tell any of the folks that, please."

"Certainly not. Is there anything else?"

"No other definite fears. Often there is a sense of concern as if I should be doing something, and I can't think what it is. And often I find myself doing, subconsciously, something that I didn't know I could do. The other day when the baby was sick and you told us to change his food, I found myself preparing the new formula without reading the directions. And I was doing it right."

"Sounds as if you might have been a nursemaid."

"That's what I think. But I surely was not a very good one or they would have hunted for me. I think that is the hardest part of all this—that I didn't mean enough to anyone to even be inquired for."

"Don't you worry about that. You're coming along fine. This country life has made a different person of you. And when we get the whole picture of those lost years, I think we will understand them."

"It isn't the country air that has made me different, Dr. Bill. It's the thing that happened here yesterday. I don't just *look* different, I *am* different, and I'm sure the friends of the old Linda will never recognize the new."

Chapter Eighteen

O<small>N A BEAUTIFUL</small> O<small>CTOBER</small> <small>DAY</small> Marion wanted to drive to the small town forty miles away where her parents lived. Dr. Bill had not yet given her permission to drive the car after the severe back sprain that had kept her rather inactive for many months, so Linda accompanied them as driver. They stayed later than they had expected, and as they passed a filling station where a clock showed in the window, Marion uttered a startled exclamation and looked at her watch.

"Why, it's five-thirty. The stores will be closed by the time we reach Williston. I think we'd better stop in this town we're coming to and get some bread and fruit."

"O.K. What will you have?"

"Oranges and apples. And a loaf each of white and whole wheat."

"And some bubble gum," said Dick.

"No sir! You can get some animal crackers, Linda, but no gum."

Linda found that they had no fruit in the store, so handed in the bread saying, "I'm going down this street to another store. You wait here. I won't be five minutes."

She was coming out of the store with the bag in her arms when she collided, in the dim doorway, with a man who was entering. The bag of fruit was overfull and several apples rolled onto the step. The man stooped, picked them up, and put them in the bag. Looking up to thank him she was startled at his white face and blazing eyes.

142

"You—you—" he gasped as his hands reached for her. In panic she fled, hearing behind her a frantic cry,

"Pat! Oh, Pat!"

She was shaking as with a chill when she got into the car.

"A man chased me," she whispered to Marion under the noise of the starting engine. "He tried to grab me. I think he was crazy."

"How terrible!" said Marion in dismay. "Why, it's still daylight. Isn't the world getting to be a terrible place, where a woman isn't safe in a small town like this at five-thirty?"

All evening Linda was distrait. While her fingers were busy with the doll's dress she was remodeling for Jane, her mind kept reverting to the scene at the door of the small store—the wild look in the eyes of the young man and his almost hysterical voice calling after her as she fled down the street. She seemed to recall a glimpse of him staring after them as the car drove away. After the children had gone to bed, she spoke to Marion about it.

"I can't forget that man. You know, as I look back on it now, I wonder if he thought he knew me."

"Perhaps he did. Was his face at all familiar to you."

"I didn't think so then. But it keeps coming back."

"It may be someone who knows you and was surprised to see you. You've been absent from your old associates for over a year, and they haven't heard from you."

"But if he really knew me, he'd know my name. He called me Pat."

"Pat?"

"Yes, as I ran away he called after me, 'Pat, oh, Pat!' in the most frantic tones. Then I thought I heard him behind me, and as the car started off, I caught a glimpse of him staring after us."

"And you didn't know him at all?"

"Not at all."

"Then just forget him. If he were anyone to whom you meant much and lived in any of the suburbs, he could surely have found you. We watched all the ads for months. Long before you knew we existed, Bill had us hunting for any clue. Anyway, your name isn't Pat. So just forget him."

But that proved to be a difficult thing. At most unexpected moments the white, distraught face would appear before her, and the voice calling, "Pat! Oh, Pat!" came often to startle her from some reverie. Then it began to disturb her dreams. Her sleep became troubled and unrestful. After a long night which left her unrefreshed, she would waken with a half-memory of dreams, of confused happenings—of laughter and tears, of happiness and sorrow, of pleasant fellowship and angry quarreling. It was all so chaotic that she could retain no orderly sequence of the dream events. Nor could she remember the characters who moved across the dream stage. Except one. That one, the man whom she had seen that October evening, was always there, and he was always hunting her. She began to lose the look of health and vitality that had been a source of pride to all of her friends. Her cheeks grew pale and thin, and Dr. Bill worried.

"Can't you just let go and live like you did last summer?" he asked. "You were doing so well that I saw complete recovery just around the corner. Now you're getting yourself all mixed up again."

"I know it," she confessed. "And I *do* try. But I can't help it. When I go to sleep, I start to dream, and the dreams make me 'mixed up' as you call it. Sometimes we're happy and we laugh and play together, and then awful things begin to happen again and—"

"What awful things? And who are 'we'?"

"I can't remember either the faces or the things that happen. I just know when I wake up that it has been dreadful."

"Haven't lost that joy you had a few weeks ago, have you?

144

God still cares for you, you know, and you're still His child."

"I know that, and I just hug the thought to me. It's all that keeps me from losing my balance completely. But there's something about that that bothers me, too. Maybe if I remembered I wouldn't want to be a Christian anymore. Or maybe I'd forget all this, and you folks would be strangers, and I wouldn't even know that Jesus died for me. I couldn't stand that!"

"That's something you won't have to stand. God hasn't brought you this far to turn His back on you now. And if you should forget, we'll all be here to tell you the old story again. Don't forget, Linda Lou. You are a new creation now, and God's work won't be undone."

"You're a comfort. I don't deserve such friends as the Pages and the Willises. But I'm mighty glad God gave them to me. There's another thing that has begun to worry me. Suppose there are people some place who need me. Even if they didn't want me enough to hunt me, I'd like to go back and do my work. Maybe there were little children for whom I was caring. They couldn't hunt me. I get to thinking of that sometimes at night, and I ache with loneliness. You are all *so* good to me, but I'd like to know where I belong."

"I'm going to give you something to make you sleep better. And I want you to try to forget it all. Don't worry and think so much about those lost friends that you forget the one Friend who can't be lost. Pretend for awhile that you are Marion's little sister who has always been one of the family and always will be. I know that's a big order, but we will be praying for you. Maybe we've been too sure and haven't backed you up as we should. Or maybe we've grown so used to using and enjoying your services that we haven't been very eager to solve your problems and see you leave us. From now on we will do our best for you, and I want you to co-operate by learning to trust and wait. It will come right, someday, I am sure."

To Marion and Rosanne he said later, "If I could just get her to let go and really *want* to remember, she could."

"Bill Page!" exclaimed Marion. "You don't know what you are talking about. She *does* want to remember. Sometimes she tries so hard that it becomes a physical effort. She's not fooling you. You make me *mad!*"

"No, she's not fooling me at all. But she has herself thoroughly fooled."

"What *do* you mean?"

"Oh, the old subconscious is on the job. She *thinks* she wants to get back her memory, but there is something so unpleasant in that past that whenever she gets near to it, her mind blocks off. I am beginning to have a glimmering of what it is, but don't ask me, ladies, for I won't tell you."

"In that way you can say, 'That's what I thought' no matter what happens."

"Don't have such a low opinion of me. I'm a good guy when you get to know me. And I'll never say 'I told you so.' I'm saying that I've got a hunch and that's all it is. I've added one and one and one and one, and made four out of it and I'm guessing I'm right."

"We're guessing the same way," agreed Marion. "But what I want to know is, what will help Linda. Is she going to get better, or just worry herself sick?"

"She's going to come out all right if her friends don't let her down by forgetting to pray. She's trembling on the brink of recovery, and we can help her if we will. I'm the only one that can prescribe a sleeping pill, but the rest can help as much by praying. Let's win a real victory."

The medicine did quiet her, and her friends did their best to help her. Marion's back was pronounced strong again, but there was still need for Linda. Scott's mother became ill, and Marion spent several weeks with her. The entire care and discipline of the three Willis children were left to Linda, and

146

there was no time for self-pity. By the time she went to bed at night she was too weary to lie awake and brood, and bodily exercise produced a healthy weariness that brought sleep. She loved the care of the fine old house and took great pride in keeping its mahogany polished and its brasses shining. She liked to cook in the big kitchen which fascinated her with its mingling of old and new. In one end was the huge, black-mouthed fireplace where Great-grandmother Willis used to cook over the logs. On the mantel above sat a Seth Thomas clock, and at each end was a lantern of punched tin. An elderly neighbor came down the road to visit one day and told of how, when she was a small child she often saw "Old Lady Willis" going through the woods at night to visit a sick neighbor, a tin lantern in her hand. Linda had thought at first that the lanterns looked crude and out of place here, but as the months had passed, she had realized that they belonged right here with the other relics of a past day. On the walls around the fireplace hung the brass pans and kettles that had been the pioneer mother's pride. A low rocker on a braided rug, and a wooden cradle with its tiny Star of Bethlehem quilt made this part of the room a quaint reminder of the people who had lived and loved here so many years ago.

The other end of the room held Marion's workshop—the cabinet sink, the electric range, and the huge deep freezer into which they had put great quantities of food last summer. Above the sink the windows looked out over the rolling meadows and orchards.

"This is God's own House of Rest for me," mused Linda one wintry day as she looked at the snow-blanketed fields and hills. "I am so thankful for it and for all of these dear folks. But I'm *lonely*. I just don't belong to them no matter how much we all try to think so. I want someone of my *own*. Dear God, if there's someone any place that belongs to me, won't You help me to remember them and find them again?"

* * * * *

Marion was at home again after the weeks of caring for Grandmother Willis. Noting how pale Linda looked, she suggested that the girl take a bit of relaxation.

"I'd like to send you away for awhile, but I've no place to send you. So I'm going to insist that you take it easy here. We've been imposing on you and loaded you down with our own burdens. It must stop. Billy is walking now and doesn't have to be lugged around anymore. With Mrs. Gorman coming two days a week for cleaning and laundry, I can do beautifully."

"If you're well again, you don't really need me at all. I should be getting another place to work."

"Try telling Dr. Bill that. I wouldn't dare release you until he said I should. I don't want to anyway. I'm quite selfish in this so don't worry. I want you to stay here so that you can go east with me in the summer. I should be there to help close up a family estate that has been hanging fire for several years. My dad isn't able to go, so I'm to do it for him. It will take several weeks and I don't want to go alone. Scott can't be away then. So I've got my greedy eye on you."

"But summer is several months away. You don't need me *now*."

"I do need you. But my conscience is smiting me over your paleness and loss of weight. I'd like to see you looking as well as you did last fall. Is there anything you would like to do that you've never had a chance to try?"

Linda laughed. "This will sound very childish. I've always wanted to go into the city and just roam around as I please. When we would go in from school, we would have to go by threes or more. No two of us ever wanted to go the same places, so we just milled around, never seeing what I wanted to see."

"Where would you go?"

"Lots of places. To the Historical Society and the Museum

148

and the Zoo. I'd go to the Zoo first of all. Go ahead and laugh! I never did get to the Zoo. The other girls all thought it was 'kid's stuff' and wouldn't go with me. I've always wanted to see a kangaroo with its babies in its pocket."

Marion's laugh brought Scott from the den. Upon hearing the explanation he joined in, but said sympathetically,

"Anyone who has never seen a kangaroo deserves several trips to the Zoo. Take your lunch along so you can hang around until Mama Kangaroo gets ready for a walk with her babies."

"It will take me weeks and weeks to do the Museum and Historical Society the way I want to. We always went through so fast I only got the most unsatisfying glimpses of things. And I want to eat in a place down under the sidewalk, and I want to see a bridge open for a boat to go through, and I want to ride a pony in the park,—and—I may as well say it—a merry-go-round."

"What a lot of suppressed desires you have!" said Scott. "Why not begin to satisfy them right away? Take a couple of days each week and just go to it. You can get a lot of recreation during these spring weeks that way. Go into town when I go in the morning and come back on the five-eight. That would insure you a ride from the station."

"That's a plan," agreed Marion. "Will you do it? Start tomorrow."

Chapter Nineteen

Linda had spent the day in the Museum. It had been most interesting as hour after hour she had strolled through the great halls, pausing often for a prolonged study of some exhibit that attracted her.

"I could spend a year in here," she said as she moved along looking into the cases filled with thousands of small stones, each one different and each one beautiful.

"How could I ever have studied science and disbelieved in God? There are a lot of science teachers in this world who will have to answer some day for their failure to proclaim and give credit to the Creator. Everything in this mammoth place shouts of His handiwork. What was that Psalm Scott read the other night? The hundred and fourth, I believe. Yes, I know it was, for that one verse at the last hit me so hard. 'I will be glad in the Lord.' And I wasn't being glad at all that day. And the reason the psalmist was glad was because of His mighty works in the physical world. If I were building a place like this, I'd have a verse from that psalm in the stone over the door. And over the Observatory I'd put, 'The heavens declare the glory of God.' There's a verse some place that says He is in all and of all and above all, or something like that. I don't know my Bible as well yet as I should. I find that out every day."

When she became tired, she sat down on a bench in the central hall and watched the people passing to and fro. So many persons, each a different personality, each an individual soul accountable to the God who made him. Were any of them as lonely as she? Did any of them have in his heart such a hunger for love and such a lack of it? Of course, there was Aunt Lucy, but she was safe in the haven of the Home and couldn't go out and face life's buffetings with Linda. And there were the Willises and the Pages. They had all been grand. She could never repay all their kindness and care. As long as she lived, she hoped they would be her friends. But she didn't come first with any of them. They had their own homes and families. At best she was an outsider. She remembered a sparrow that had perched disconsolately on her window sill one snowy day. It had looked so bedraggled and forlorn that she had yearned to take it in. Knowing that to be impossible she had kept crumbs and suet scattered on the porch roof all winter for the pathetic creature.

"That's what the folks are doing for me. They do all they can to help, but I can never really belong to them. I am just a stray whom they have taken into their homes. I want my *own* home. Do I have one some place?"

She bowed her head, and there in the dim hall among the hurrying people on every side, she prayed.

"Oh, Father, I'm so tired of being lost! Won't you help me to remember? And if I belong to anyone, if anyone wants me at all, send me back so I can rest."

It was late when she came out, and she hailed a taxi that she might catch the five-eight. Scott was waiting anxiously at the gate, and they ran for the train. The cars were crowded, and it was only in the one farthest from the end that they found a seat for Linda. Scott stood nearby and drew out the evening paper to read during the forty-five-minute run. They had left the city behind and were streaming through country fields that were beginning to show signs of spring activity, when Linda's ears caught a fragment of conversation from the seat behind her.

"It was a tough break for the guy all right. No one seems to

151

know the whole story. All anybody knows is that she disappeared and that Miles left these regions and only returned last week. I hope he got a good pommeling out of it. He's been needing it for many a year. And if his amiable cousin got mad enough to give it, I can only wish I'd been there to see it."

"Miles is saying that he doesn't know what it was all about."

"He may say so, but unless he has changed a lot, that doesn't mean a thing. He was always the animating spirit in the troubles those kids got into, and when they were caught, he never knew a thing about it."

They roared past another train, and the noise drowned their voices. Linda sat transfixed, cold fear gripping her. She could not tell why, but a nervous chill began to shake her, and her pulses pounded furiously. She looked for Scott, but he had found a seat at some distance away and was not looking in her direction. Then the other train was gone, and the voices were clear again.

"Sure. There was good ground for a divorce all right, and you know there'd be money enough to have it done as painlessly as possible."

"What do you think he will do next?"

"Nobody ever sees him any more. I got all this from Miles. But *he* says there's another marriage in the making. And this time you can be sure Chetwolde will do as Mama says!"

The train was approaching Williston Station, and Scott arose from his seat, folding up his newspaper and picking up his brief case from the floor. He sauntered along the aisle to Linda's seat.

"Williston coming up," he said touching her on the shoulder. As she did not stir, he spoke again.

"Linda, here we are. Linda, what is it? Are you ill?"

She did not look up, and as the train was drawing into the station he knew he had to act promptly. Motioning to the conductor who was standing in the doorway, he said anxiously,

"Clint, this girl has fainted, I think. If you'll help me get her off, we will take her to the doctor's office. She lives with us, and my car will be at the station."

The conductor had known Scott Willis since they had attended high school together, and asked no questions. As they prepared to lift her, Linda raised a face so white and stricken that Scott felt himself grow cold in apprehension. Surely, some terrible thing had happened to her. But how could it with him almost in reach? With Scott on one side of her and the conductor on the platform she was helped down the steps. Marion from the wheel of the car saw them and came running.

"Scott! Linda! Is she hurt?"

"We don't know, dear. She just—"

Linda looked past the men straight into Marion's eyes. "I know now," she gasped. Then as Marion reached her she slumped unconscious into Scott's arms.

When she wakened, it was to find herself in her own room at Sunnyknoll. Marion sat at her bedside, and Dr. Bill stood by the dresser writing something on a pad. For a moment she gazed at them in bewilderment, then recollection came, and she uttered a sharp cry of pain. Dr. Bill turned and hurried to the bedside. Taking one of her hands in his, he spoke softly with his fingers on her pulse.

"How goes it, little sister?"

In answer she struggled up to face them wildly. "I remember! I remember! Oh, Tony, where are you and where are my babies? Can't you find them for me, Dr. Bill? I didn't mean to leave them. I was only going to Aunt Lucy's to think things over. I *must* go home. It's been so *long!*"

"Quiet, now, Linda. Don't you want to go back to sleep and then tell us in the morning?"

"No, I want to go now to see my babies. And I want Tony."

As she spoke that name remembrance came of the conversation on the train, and a wave of dizziness made her fall back on

153

the pillow. She started to sob so hysterically that Dr. Bill spoke sternly to steady her.

"Get quiet now, Linda. You aren't in condition to go. We'll find your Tony tomorrow."

"But we can't. We don't dare. The men said—they said—oh, dear God, can I bear it?"

"They said—what? If we are to help you, we must know."

"They said he has—married again."

Then blackness came once more. Dr. Bill watched for some minutes until he saw indications of returning consciousness. He counted the pulse again, listened to her heartbeat, then pushed back the sleeve and gave an injection in the arm.

"That will hold her for awhile. I'll stay all night. Will you call Rosanne, Marion? If you can stay with her until midnight, I'll take the rest of the night. I want to be here when she wakes again."

In the early morning just as the darkness outside was fading to gray, Dr. Bill wakened and started guiltily when he realized that he had been asleep. He moved cautiously from his cramped position lest he waken the sleeping Linda. But she opened her eyes and smiled at him.

"I'm ashamed. You've been here all night, haven't you?"

"Only since midnight. And it's not four yet. That's not a long watch considering the fact that I seem to have slept through it."

"Only since two."

"Have you been awake so long?"

"Yes, but I didn't want to waken you. I wanted to think a bit before I talked to anyone. I'm sorry I was such a bad patient last night."

"You weren't bad. You had had a real knockout blow, and you hadn't got your breath yet. You're O.K. now. I can tell without asking."

"I hope I am. But I want you to know that I couldn't take

154

the blow at all by myself. I crumpled completely under it. But this morning I turned it all over to the Lord. And He can face with me anything that has to be faced. Do you mind if I talk to you awhile before the others wake up?"

He took her pulse again, then gave her a drink of water and a small tablet. After she had lain back on the pillow, he drew his chair close and said,

"Do you want to tell it all now, or is there anything you want us to do for you before we go into it?"

"I don't want to tell very much until I do some more thinking. But I want you to know what it was that upset me. Then you will know why I don't know where to go or what to do. I heard some men talking on the train. From the time they first spoke I was startled although I couldn't understand why. Then one of them spoke a name, and all of a sudden it was as if a bomb had burst in my brain. It was my husband's name that they spoke. You didn't know I was married, did you?"

"I thought so. And I think you are a mother, also."

Her eyes were swimming in tears, and she could not speak. She reached for his hand and held it in a convulsive clasp. He waited, knowing that it was best for her to talk just as she desired. At last she drew a long breath and went on.

"I have two babies, one and two years old—oh no! I've been away from them two years. And they won't know me!"

"We'll hunt them up as soon as possible," the doctor answered huskily.

"But you don't know all that the men said. They said Tony was married again. So I'm divorced. Oh, it isn't right! I didn't mean to do anything."

"Are you sure of what they said?"

"Yes, I'll never forget it. My brain feels as if it were seared with the words. One man said, 'There's another marriage in the making. And this time Chetwolde will do as Mama says.'"

"You're jumping to conclusions. They didn't say he was

married. They said it was in the making. That could mean nothing more than a lot of gossip."

"But they said he was divorced. I don't think I can stand that. Tony was all I had. And even when we quarreled, we loved each other."

"Do you want Scott to do any investigating for you?"

"I don't want to do anything until I'm not so confused. I feel that I can't wait to see the children, but Tony has had them all these months, and I suppose I have no claim on them. Most of all, I want to do what is right, and I don't know yet what that is."

"Take another drink of this elixir I mixed for you, and try to sleep some more. I will see Scott and Marion before you come down and we will try to help you decide what our first move shall be. Don't forget for one minute that we are all back of you. And you have another Friend who is better than all of us put together. There has never been a tangle yet that He couldn't straighten out, and never a wound He could not heal. So trust in Him and go to sleep."

Chapter Twenty

MARION, SCOTT, AND DR. BILL were in the living room when Linda came slowly down the stairs. As she entered, she looked anxiously from one to another as if fearing to find condemnation in their faces. There was only reassurance, however, in the smiles with which they greeted her. Marion came quickly forward to put her arm around her and lead her to the chair which Scott was drawing up to their circle.

"Good girl!" said Dr. Bill approvingly. "Pretty soon Marion is going to give you some breakfast, a whopping big one to make up for the dinner you missed last night. But because Scott and I have work to do and must get into the city, we'd like to have a conference before we go. O.K.?"

"O.K. Thank you all. You've been wonderful and you deserve a hearing."

"We aren't wanting to interfere or presume to tell you what to do. We just want to know what your plans are and see how we can help."

She drew a long breath, one that quivered a bit as with suppressed emotion. But her voice was steady when she spoke.

"My first impulse when I wakened at two o'clock, was to get up and dress and start for home at once. I felt I couldn't wait to see Tony and tell him that I didn't mean to go off and leave him. And my arms ached with desire for my babies. But I couldn't go in the middle of the night. So I had to lie and think for several hours, and I saw things in a clearer light. I don't even know if they still live there. Tony may have sold the house and gone back to his home town where his mother could care for the children. That's what she always wanted."

"Do you want me to find him?" asked Scott.

"Not now, but thank you for offering. In these hours since two o'clock I've come to a few decisions. May I tell you what they are and see if you approve?"

With their sympathetic attention she continued, "I'll have to tell you a little bit of what happened so you will understand. Sometime, before too long, I'll try to tell it all. I want you to know it. But just now I'll shorten it. Things hadn't been going well with Tony and me for several months. It doesn't matter who was to blame. We both should have done better. But we still loved each other very much. I know we did!" She spoke this as if defying them to contradict her.

"There were several things to disturb us and I had thought I would like to talk them over with someone, and Aunt Lucy was the only one who cared. I hadn't seen or heard from her in many years, but I knew she would remember me. I found her name in the telephone directory, but I didn't go that day. Oh, Marion, I wish I'd known you then. You could have helped me. That last night I was driving home with Tony's cousin from a dinner at his house. We had an accident and I was thrown from the car. My head was hit and my hand hurt. When I got out of the car at home, I almost fainted and Miles tried to get me to take a drink. I wouldn't and he spilled it on my dress and coat. When I got inside, Tony said something *awful* to me. I know now that he thought I was drunk because of the smell of liquor. But, honestly, I never touched a drop. I didn't know why Tony was so angry. He left the house, and I was all alone. My head hurt terribly and my hand was swelling. So I took off my rings and wrapped the hand in a clean towel. I felt I couldn't stay there with Tony so angry. I *had* to talk to someone. I thought of Aunt Lucy again. I didn't intend to stay at her house. I just wanted to talk to her.

When I was little, she always helped me when I was in trouble. I can remember getting to her house, but I can't recall anything else until I woke up about three weeks later in her bedroom. Then I couldn't remember anything that had happened since Mother died. Tony and the babies just weren't there. You believe me, don't you?" she asked, looking pitifully from one face to another.

"One hundred per cent," said Dr. Bill promptly, and the others agreed. Marion reached over to pat her hand in sympathy, and Scott's voice was husky as he said,

"Can't we *do* anything, Linda? Don't you want us to start some balls rolling?"

"No, please. Tony is divorced. I'm sure of that. He may be planning to remarry. Whatever happens I want to do just what is right. I wasn't a Christian when I got my life into such a mess. But I am now, and I truly want the Lord's will. But—"

She hesitated, and Marion's heart was sick at the desolation in her eyes. Her voice, when she continued, was low and shamed.

"I can't find His will now because I'm out of fellowship with Him. The old Linda is very much in evidence this morning. I'm so angry at my—at someone that I can't pray as I should. I'm back in the fit of anger that made me leave the dinner before the rest were ready to go. Until I can get right myself I can't make any right decisions. If you want to help now, pray for me that I can get a real victory over this feeling. It isn't going to be a bit easy."

"You don't want me even to try to locate Tony?" Scott was eager for action.

"I don't care if you find out where he is living if you can do it without contacting him. I'll give you his name and the address of our house, and also his employers. But please don't make any inquiries among the folks who knew us. Let me do it my way. After a few days I'll be able to decide what is right.

159

I don't want to consider myself. I just want to find the best for Tony and the children. I'll let you know as soon as I can."

As Scott and Dr. Bill rode cityward in the doctor's car, Scott asked,

"Have you known any of this before, Bill? It's difficult to think of Linda as a wife and mother. We've known her as a lonely waif for so long. Did you never have any suspicions?"

"Yes, a lot of them. When I first worked on that hand, the marks of rings were plainly visible. I knew there was a man some place who should be hunting for her. But when he didn't, I was afraid to stir up trouble by hunting him. The sight of him might have thrown her clear off balance. You saw last night what the mention of his name did after two years. I didn't dare risk it when she was so ill. Anyway, why wasn't he doing the hunting? I'd like to get my hands on that guy. Any chap who let's his wife, the mother of his children, just disappear without moving Heaven and earth to find her, is a —a—" Dr. Bill stopped for lack of a word.

"But there were the rings left on her dresser," said Scott. "Wouldn't that seem to indicate that she had left her marriage behind her? He probably didn't notice in his anger that she had been hurt."

"He should have told by looking at her. She was a sight when I saw her. Anyway, what kind of a man is he to be dropped so easily? I guess I have a bit of the cave man in me. For I'd have gone after her and found her and brought her back where she belonged."

"Didn't she or Aunt Lucy notice the marks of rings on her finger?"

"By the time I took the bandages off the marks were gone. But there were other things that were clues. She knew exactly how to care for a baby though she said she had never handled one. She knew a raft of nursery stories, little ones such as a mother would tell a two-year-old. She said she did not

160

know how to cook. Yet she did it easily unless someone questioned her. Then she got confused. She told Marion she had never seen a washing machine in operation. Yet when Marion took her to the laundry, she knew what to do. There were a lot of things like that which indicated that she had kept house in a small home where she did her own work. And I think I know with whom she is angry."

"The unpursuing husband? Some other woman?"

"Yes, to the last question. But not what you think. I think it's her mother-in-law. She confessed to me once that she is afraid of your mother."

"My mother! Well!—Why?"

"I suspect because she is a mother-in-law. Did you notice she said this morning when surmising that Tony might have taken the children to his mother's house, 'That's what she always wanted'? And when she was speaking of being angry, she started to say 'with my' and changed it to 'with someone.' "

"Could be a mother-in-law complex."

"Perhaps Tony, otherwise called Chetwolde, was tied to mother's apronstrings. Do you remember what the men on the train said? 'Chetwolde will marry as Mama says this time.' Where do you suppose they got that name?"

"Chetwolde? Oh, it could have come from Back Bay. But why any fond mother should wish it onto her offspring, I can't see. I'm beginning to think you are right about the mother-in-law being the cause of the trouble. You're a pretty good detective, Bill. I'll see about getting you on the force. And I think I'll do a little sleuthing on my own. I want to find out the plain truth about that divorce that was obtained without her knowledge. And if there's a wedding in the offing, I want to do all I can to prevent it."

"Careful. She said no contacts with Tony."

"Nary a contact. I have other ways of working that will get

results. When Linda gets ready to move, I'll have the machinery oiled."

"Well, that's your bailiwick, not mine. But watch your step."

"I will. And now will you put me off at the next station? I don't want to go to the hospital with you, and I hear a train coming."

He jumped from the car as it stopped, and made a dash for the station. As he entered, the doctor leaned from the car and called frantically.

"Scott! Hey, Scott!"

Scott dashed back looking anxiously at the oncoming train. Dr. Bill asked seriously,

"How can you, being a lawyer, be interested in the plain truth about anything?"

Scott stood for a moment in exasperation, but the train was stopping and he had to sprint to catch it. Dr. Bill watched it pull away, then raced it to the next station and waved to Scott as he passed it.

For several days Linda fought her battle in silence. Only by their kindness and patience did the others show their sympathy. But as day after day passed and there was still no lightening of the load, they became concerned for her. When time came for Marion's trip east, Linda went with her, willingly but apathetically.

Chapter Twenty-one

THE BIG WHITE HOUSE at the end of the long village street had been built before the Revolutionary War. When colonial soldiers gathered on the common to meet the men of Britain, the house had looked just as it did now. Some of its furnishings were older than itself. Generation after generation of the same family had occupied it. For almost ninety years Marion's two great-aunts had lived in the house where they had been born, seeing the other members of the family go, one by one, and leave them behind. They would not leave the old place to seek a more comfortable life in some other place. To have uprooted them would have been to kill them, so a woman had been secured as nurse and housekeeper, and they continued on until the death of one so shocked the other that she followed almost immediately. The house was left to a grandnephew, the only one who bore the family name. And to Marion were given all the contents. To remove and dispose of these was the task for which Marion had come east, and it was no light one. Some of the finer pieces were crated and shipped back to Sunnyknoll where they would become a part of the gracious setting of Marion's own home life. Other pieces were to be sold, and the young women spent several days at polishing and preparing them for display. When they had finished this, there were bundles of documents, old letters, and papers which only Marion's father, the sole survivor of his generation, could sort and evaluate. These were boxed and shipped to him. There were trunks of clothing, drawers of linens, chests of bedding. Marion counted eighteen quilts that bore no evidence of ever having been used. The great cupboards on each side of the fireplace were filled with dishes and glass, and the pantries were stocked with ancient cooking utensils and accompanying paraphernalia, the uses of which the girls could only guess.

"I'll just send it all home," said Marion as they stood in bewilderment before the pantry shelves. "I'll probably have to charter a whole freight car, for I am certainly not sufficient for the job of deciding which must be kept, which are of great value as antiques, and which should be thrown on the junk pile. If that cousin of mine who gets the house wanted this stuff, I'd leave most of it for him. But he doesn't. So it's up to me. I want to give some of the nice things to Bill and Rosanne. They're so good to us. Bill never will take a penny for all the care he gives our family. All we've ever been able to do for him is to supply them with eggs and garden produce, which doesn't count since we have more of everything than we can use, and it's too much trouble to try to sell it. And I'm going to give you some of it. Be thinking what you want."

As the young women worked at sorting, selling, and packing they felt the spirit of another day around them. The ones who had lived and loved and toiled in this house had "one by one been gathered to his tomb by those who in their turn should follow them." But the things that had shared the home with them were still here and could, had they been able to speak, have told many a thrilling story of what had gone on under this roof in those vanished years.

"I used to think it was foolish to cherish such things as this furniture and these lovely dishes," said Linda one afternoon as they packed dishes for shipment, under the direction of the local expressman. "Furniture was furniture to me, and dishes were something to eat from, and why should anyone want old stuff when they could get new? But I am learning that there is something in it that I never understood before. There is a

164

value in having a heritage one can be proud of and a home that holds memories and traditions. I'll never get over being glad I came with you. The experience has given me a perspective that I needed."

"May I say I'm glad to have you? I never would have been able to do all this alone. I've enjoyed your company very much, and oh, how I've appreciated the elbow grease you've expended on this furniture! We are about done now. I signed the last papers yesterday, and all these crates and boxes will go tomorrow. We can leave the next morning. I had a letter from Scott today, and he suggests we take another ten days or two weeks for a real vacation and just bum around New England for awhile. Were you ever in the East before?"

"Yes, but we never stopped at any one place long enough to do any sight-seeing. We traveled so fast that the scenery was a blur. And we were not interested in historical remains—but definitely."

"Do you want to go now? I don't want to urge you. I know that you are eager to get to doing something about your own affairs, and I want that for you more than I want a trip. So you do the deciding."

Linda sat silent for a few more minutes, then spoke slowly, "Every nerve in my body and mind is crying out to go back and get busy at finding Tony and the children and determining where I stand with them. I see a lot of things in a different light after this opportunity for quiet reflection. But there's one thing I haven't settled yet, and until I do, I can't feel that I'm in God's will in acting. Let's start out on our jaunt. I'll tell you when I'm ready to go home. I promise not to tarry too long."

They drove up into the mountains and spent a restful weekend in a cabin where a rugged peak loomed on one side and a river tumbled over rocks on the other. They took pictures of old covered bridges, of tiny white churches, and of farmsteads where house, shed, chicken house, and barns were all joined together. They went to Northfield and bowed for a few quiet moments of prayer by the graves on Roundtop. They stood on a busy wharf and watched the fishing boats come in. They slept at Wayside Inn, and visited the homes of poets and authors whom they had loved, and who, for the first time, seemed now to have been real men and women toiling, rejoicing, suffering as is the common lot. With tears in their eyes they read the inscriptions on the monuments at Lexington and Concord, and realized as never before what a price had been paid for the liberty they enjoyed.

They spent several days in Boston, and left resolving to come again when they could take more time for the innumerable things that attracted them. They stood on the stern and rockbound coast at Plymouth and imagined how it must have looked on that day over three hundred years before when the small band of exiles first saw it. Then on up the wind-swept cape to a place where the waves of the Atlantic Ocean pounded against the rocks on one side of them and the breakers of the Bay rolled on the beach at the other side. Here, on an afternoon when a summer storm held them in their tight little cabin, Linda's reserves broke down, and for the first time since the evening when Scott had carried her to her room in a state of collapse, she began to talk freely of the things that were heavy on her heart. Outside, the waves were beating angrily against the shore, the stunted trees were twisting in the wind, and the rain dashed in sheets over the windowpanes. Inside, two easy chairs were drawn up before the little oilstove that had been lighted to counteract the cool dampness. Marion sat in one of the chairs, but Linda, after trying the other, took a pillow from among the luggage and placed it where she could look into the flame of the little stove. From that place she could look up into Marion's face when she desired, or, if the telling were hard at some point she could stare into the pseudo-fireplace. Once or twice she stopped in her recital and for many minutes buried her face in her hands. Marion did not hurry her nor interrupt.

"I'd like to tell you all about it, Marion, and then tell you what I've decided to do. First of all I want to thank all of you dear folks who have held the ropes for me during these two years, and especially this last month. I never knew the meaning of the word friendship before. And if I'd had a real sister, she could not have been to me what you have. It's been wonderful of you to keep quiet and let me think this thing through without being confused with all sorts of well-meant advice. I couldn't talk before, for I hadn't been able to leave it with the Lord and be calm about it. I was so terribly angry that I knew I could not talk about it sanely. And I couldn't pray as I should and ask God's forgiveness for my part in the awful mess until I had forgiven someone else.

"I'm going to start back at the beginning and tell you about my childhood. I know now that much of the trouble lay there. I never had a real home until I was married. That was probably why I was so jealous about it. During these weeks we've been working and traveling here I've learned the value of good deep roots. I never had any. We traveled all the time, so I grew up with only shallow ideas of homes and heritages. I keep wondering how anybody could grow up with as little thought for any of the serious things of life as I did. I used to wish for a home that was our own, but I never gave a thought to where or how I might spend the time after I left this life. I loved my parents devotedly, but I don't know whether or not they were Christians. My mother used to get up real early and go to church every Sunday. Daddy used to make fun of her for it, but she went anyway. During the rest of the week she was just like all the rest of the troupe, and never once did she try to explain to me what it meant to her. Daddy's parents had been quite religious. For some reason he had turned against it all. Once Mother wanted to take me with her, and he refused to let me go. He said no one should go to church until he was twenty-one. Then he was old enough to decide for himself. I think perhaps Daddy changed before he died because Eloise, my stepmother, said she'd had a hunch he was going to die because he'd turned religious and had been going to church lately. Maybe both my parents were Christians who had gotten onto the wrong track some place. I don't want to judge them. Only God can. But I hope I'll see them again some day. They made some terrible mistakes, but so have I. I've done a lot of thinking, and you have been a peach to have so much patience with me. When I've felt like chattering, you have chattered with me, and when I wanted to keep still, you've let me alone. God has had patience too, and has at last brought me out into a place of peace where I can talk about it and try to make some plans. Do you want to hear it all?"

Marion did want to, of course, and as the day faded into a windy, gray twilight, and that, in turn, gave way to a starless night, Linda told her story—the frustrated childhood, the rebellion at being put in boarding school, the shock of her parents' divorce, her resentment at the second marriages, the growing feeling that she was not wanted by either couple. She spoke of her feeling of desolation at being sent to summer camp after her mother's death when she longed for her father's comforting presence. It was at this camp that she had met Tony, and her voice grew warm as she told of his immediate attraction to her and of the courtship and marriage that followed. When she told of the births of her babies, her tones were tender as if she were speaking to, rather than of, them. She laughed as she recounted some of her early efforts at cooking and homemaking in the small apartment. The move from the apartment to the bungalow seemed, to the listener, to mark the beginning of confusion and trouble. Linda tried to speak without bitterness of her mother-in-law, but the story must be truthfully told, and Marion received a fairly accurate picture of the domineering little lady.

"I'm trying very hard not to be unfair to anyone, even myself. Tony was to blame for fearing her so much that he let her take over our lives as she did. But he had been so thoroughly dominated by her for so long, that he could not stand up to her. She was always having 'attacks' when she was opposed, and I think Tony was afraid she would die, and he would feel as if he had killed her. I was to blame, for when I found out she looked down on me and wanted to make me all over, I got just as contrary as could be. Tony reproved me for being 'fresh' to her. In fairness to myself, I'll say that I tried desperately to please her, for I was afraid she would come between us. But when I failed, I shouldn't have said and done the things that I knew would irritate her. And she was to blame in wanting to hold on to Tony after he was grown and married. I have more sympathy with her ideas and ideals than I used to. I can see now that there is a great deal of real value in those customs and traditions she held on to so rigidly. She put too much emphasis on the tangible, material symbols of that quality rather than on the quality itself, but I am trying to believe that it was because she loved us that she wanted us to conform to her standards.

"Tony used to beg me to be more conciliatory and not quite so pert. For days at a time I would behave, and things would go along nicely. Then she would say something that angered me or would get Tony to go out with her and leave me at home, and I'd think up some new way to annoy her. It wasn't that I minded things for myself, but I feared that she was trying to take Tony and the babies from me. I don't believe, as I think of it coolly, that she really wanted to do that. She just wanted to run our lives. But I was sure she wanted them and did not want me. All my life I have had to give up the things that I prized. Once when I was a tiny girl the staff of the hotel where we were staying one Christmas time gave me a doll house. I loved that little house more than any toy I ever had. I can see it yet, with every chair and bed and table in place. It had small rugs that two of the maids crocheted, and ruffled curtains at the windows. There were pictures on the walls, and the cunningest little stairway ran up to the second story. For two weeks I was the happiest child in the country. Then we had to go away and mother wouldn't let me take it. I'm not blaming her. A doll house of that size just couldn't be dragged about the country at the pace we traveled. But I cried until I was sick. The maids promised to keep it for me, but we never did go back to the hotel. That has been the way with everything I've ever had. One summer I stayed with Aunt Lucy and she let me have a kitten and a puppy and a bird. Daddy told her she spoiled me. But she said I needed such an experience. Then when the folks came back in the fall they made me leave them behind. So you can see a bit of how I felt about Tony and the babies. They were *mine*. And from Mrs. Bannister's first visit I began to feel like they might be snatched away from me."

She went on to tell of the growing tension in the home and the arguments over trifles, of the different reactions and of the inability of both to see the other's viewpoint. When she came to the incident of the figurines, her face flushed in shame at the recollection of the childish quarrel and the unkind remarks that were flung back and forth between them.

"We were a pair of badly spoiled children. Tony had been pampered all his life, and I had been allowed to grow up with no real discipline at all. Each of us was an only child and used to having all the attention. But please believe, Marion, that I never intended to go away as I did. That last night we were invited to Tony's cousin's house for dinner. Mother Bannister made me angry before we started by making remarks about the clothes I intended to wear and by comparing my feet with

170

hers. She is very small and dainty, and her feet are her pride. I've never thought much about feet. Mine are fine for carrying me about, and that's what I thought they were for. But she inferred that the size of them was some indication of my lack of the quality that she had a right to expect in a daughter-in-law. Then, as usual, I became 'fresh' and gave her a saucy answer which hurt her feelings. When we started, she pre-empted the seat with Tony and left me to ride alone in the back. All at once I knew I'd had enough. I had reached a point where I had to do something. Both Tony and I had coolly dismissed Christianity from our thinking. We were too self-sufficient to even think about it. But that night I came face to face with the fact that I needed help from a higher source. One of the young women I'd been friendly with had recently tried to talk to me about her faith. I wouldn't listen, but that night when I was feeling so low, I resolved to go and see her the very next day and find out what made her so happy. Then when we got to the dinner I was bored by it all and didn't pay much attention until one of the men who had been drinking too much made a remark about my likeness to a dancer he used to know. I answered that she was my mother, and at once I realized that I'd committed an unforgivable sin in Mrs. Bannister's eyes. I wanted Tony to come and take me home, but he was across the room and I was all alone. Then Mrs. Bannister said—oh, I don't want to tell you what she said. But she—she—made my mother seem someone to be ashamed of. I ran out of the house and hid in the garden. I heard Tony trying to find me but I didn't answer him. After awhile Miles—that's Tony's cousin— came out and found me. He was disgusted with Mrs. Bannister and offered to take me home. I was so sick at heart that I didn't care what the others thought. I just wanted to get home. So he went in and got my coat and told Tony we were going, and we left in his car.

"That was an awful ride. I never had liked Miles, and I

knew Tony distrusted him. At any other time I would not have gone with him, but that night I did not think of anything but getting away. We hadn't gone far until I realized that Miles didn't intend to go home at once. We drove and drove until I was worried sick. If Tony and his mother got home before we did, they would be justly angry. Yet Miles *wouldn't* go home. I hadn't any idea where we were. We stopped to get something to eat and he had a drink. After we went on he kept taking drinks from a flask in his pocket, and he just laughed when I begged to be taken home. It was an open car, and at last when he wouldn't listen to me, I stood up intending to scream when another car passed us. I don't know what happened then. I guess Miles tried to get me to sit down and lost control of the car. Anyway, I was thrown out against a tree and onto a pile of rocks. When I became conscious, Miles had poured water from the ditch all over me. My hand was hurt and he wrapped it in his handkerchief. He was frightened at the accident and sobered down. The car wasn't damaged so badly that it wouldn't run, so we went on home as fast as we could. It must have been hours after Tony got home, before we did. I've tried and tried to reconstruct all the details of what happened, but it's still pretty foggy. I can remember falling as I got out of the car, and Miles trying to give me a drink and spilling it all over me. I wouldn't let him go in the house with me. When I got there, I could hardly walk. Tony came toward me and I am sure that he smelled the whiskey and thought I had been drinking, for what he said to me was so terrible that I felt like I'd been knocked down again. You know the rest. When I started to Aunt Lucy's house that night, I expected to go back home the next day after I'd talked things over with her. And that's been two years ago, and I haven't seen Tony or the babies since. Marion, *how* can I stand it?"

Marion put her arm around the drooping shoulders and

managed to convey the sympathy she could not express. At last when her voice could be depended on, she spoke.

"But things are going to be all right. God has answered our prayers for you this far, and He will continue to hear us."

"I know that. But my heart keeps crying out for my family. I want God's will in this, but I want it to be my will, too. I've fought the same battle every day for all these weeks since that day on the train when the cloud lifted. Only today have I felt that I've definitely won the victory, or rather the Lord won it. As long as I kept fighting, I didn't get any place. But today I realized I *couldn't* win, and I let loose and told God He could take over. He did, and in spite of my heart crying out that I can't stand it, in spite of the never ceasing ache that fills my whole body, I am going to leave it all with Him. He knows how weak I am, and He will just have to give the strength for each day. And when I cry out, as I did just now, He will forgive because He understands. The thing that stood between Him and me has gone, too. You know what that was, don't you?"

"Yes. You had to forgive your mother-in-law, didn't you? I feel sure that was it, because I've had quite a time forgiving her myself."

"Bless your heart, you're a honey. Yes, that was it. At first I could not even pray because I would get to thinking of her and my prayers would just dry up. When I tried to argue myself out of it, I couldn't find an argument, for I knew she had wronged me and there was no excuse for her. At last, however, it came to me that forgiveness could only be exercised when there was wrong, and that Christ knew when He told us to forgive that it would be hard. It seemed to make a difference when I realized that He knew all about it. He knew all the sharp things she had said that I hadn't even told Tony. He knew the tricks she used to win the children's preference. He knew what underlay the unkind remarks about my family.

Yet He said 'forgive.' And if I couldn't forgive, there would always be the barrier between Him and me. I couldn't stand that, and I told Him so. I don't know what happened then, Marion, but all at once the load was gone. I can go back now and face whatever is to be faced."

"What are you going to do? All of us want to help you all we can. If there's anything that Scott can do before we get there I'll call him tonight."

"I haven't much of a plan. First I want to find out where they are. Then I'll have to know if Tony has remarried or is planning to. I seem to have no doubts about the divorce, although he thought divorce was a terrible thing. He knew how I had been hurt by it. But perhaps it's different when it's yourself that has been wronged. If he has remarried, there isn't a thing I can do except try to make a deal with him about the children. I am asking God to let me be able to give them the Christian teaching I never had. And some way I'm going to manage to witness to Tony. I've *got* to do that. If I've lost him for this life, I want to meet him in the next."

She was silent for many minutes, looking out over the bay at the tumbling water and the clouds and the beating rain. Marion waited with a prayer in her heart. At last, drawing a long breath as if to steady herself for the further explanation, Linda spoke again.

"If I find that Tony isn't married again, I intend to put on the most intensive courtship that any woman ever waged. I don't know how I will do it. It will all depend on Tony's attitude. If he will just let me tell him what happened, I think it will be all right. He is naturally good-natured and reasonable. If he once hears the whole story, he will be kind and understanding. But Miles told me once that if he ever got really angry at anyone, he never got over it. I am afraid that he will be so angry that he won't be willing to listen to any explanation."

"In that case maybe Scott or Bill, or both of them, could make him listen to reason."

"I'd rather not try that until I'm desperate. I want to win him back by myself if possible, and I'll use every wile I possess to do it. That is, if he doesn't freeze me so completely that I can't talk to him at all. If I find he is really unforgiving and angry, I'll seek the privilege of being his laundress or scrubwoman. Anything to attract his attention and show him how I've changed. That may sound unwomanly, but I mean it. When I think that I brought into the world two souls who will live for all eternity and who may never hear of the love of God, I feel as if I would go crazy. I *have* to be able to win them for the Lord. I've prayed and prayed about it. If Tony won't forgive me for my sake, he *must* take me back for the babies' sake.

"But you see the difficulty will lie in the fact that Tony doesn't believe in Christianity at all. He and I decided that there was nothing to it. So before I can speak convincingly I must demonstrate the value of the change in me. And it has to be so convincing that he will know it is a real character change, and not just the result of my accident. I must demonstrate that I am a different person from the spoiled 'brat' he married. I do hope he will love this person as much as he did the other. For, having been born into God's family, I can't be unborn out of it, even for Tony's sake."

Marion was running her hand absently over the head that was leaning against her knee, much in the way she would have soothed Janie in some poignant childhood trial. Now she spoke huskily.

"I am going to call Scott anyway and tell him we are starting home. And I'll tell him we are ready for action and we must all pray harder than ever. We can be at home by the end of the week and Scott should have learned something by then."

"I'll be glad to get back to Sunnyknoll, Marion. It's my ancestral home now. At least it's my birthplace, for there I was born a child of God. And tonight, having told you my whole story, I feel much better. I wish you would tell the others. I want them to know it, but I think it would be hard to tell it again. I don't know what the Lord is going to work out of this, but I'm going to let Him decide what it shall be. There is one thing I am sure of. If we find Tony and he takes me back, I can't be entirely happy until I've won him to the Lord.

"I've done a lot of thinking lately about marriages, and what are the necessary elements of a successful one. At first I thought that a common background was an essential. You and Scott are so happy in each other's love and companionship, that I took you for my example. You've known each other since you learned to walk. You come from the same kind of people, old pioneer stock. You went to school together, and your friends were mutual ones. You understand each other's viewpoint. Tony and I had nothing in common except our love. So I decided that it was the lack of similar training and heredity that was the primary cause of our trouble.

"But then I thought of Dr. Bill and Rosanne. They don't have even the same racial background. When I first knew that his wife had been an emigrant from central Europe, I almost cried. I felt so sorry for him because I was sure he could not be happy with her. Then I saw them together. Even you and Scott live no more harmoniously than they do. I could see that something had done away with all the barriers. I couldn't understand it then, but I do now. I've lived with you all and watched you when you didn't think I was noticing. At last I know what the necessary element is. Didn't we used to be told in chemistry that it is called a catalyst, that element that combines and works on other elements without losing its own identity? My ignorance of chemistry is such that I never did understand how I managed a passing grade. But in this case it helped me to decide what, or rather *who* is necessary for a successful marriage. It is Jesus Christ in the lives of Christians. He, and He alone, can make them truly one.

"I don't mean that non-Christians cannot be happily married. I know they can, for I've seen such cases. But they can't have the deep-down peace and joy together that you and Scott, and Dr. Bill and Rosanne have. Having seen what two lives made one in Christ can be, I'll never feel completely one with Tony until we are one in Him. I can pray for that with greater faith than I can for our reconciliation. I can see, though I pray that it may not be so, that God can have some purpose in keeping us part. But I know without a shadow of a doubt that it is not His will that anyone should perish. And I'm standing on the promise that 'if we ask any thing according to His will, He heareth us.' I am going to work and pray and believe that even though we may never be together as man and wife again, we will spend eternity together because we are one in Christ."

Marion, with tears streaming from her eyes, kissed her wordlessly as she arose to make the telephone call.

Chapter Twenty-two

"Aunt Linda! Aunt Linda! Hey, Aunt Linda, *wake up!*"

"What is it, Dick?"

"Aunt Linda, do peanuts grow on trees?"

"Yes, dear."

"They do *not*. You're still not listening or you're just igernunt."

The little boy looked accusingly at her and stamped his foot. "I don't think you're really igernunt. You just don't listen when I talk. You go right along reading that book that isn't even open."

"I'm truly sorry, Dickie Boy. What is it about peanuts?"

"Janie's teacher told them yesterday that they grow in the ground. It seems *very* queer. Could a teacher be mistaken, Aunt Linda?"

"A teacher could, of course. They are just like the rest of us and don't know quite everything. But in this case, teacher is right. They do grow in the ground. When I was a little girl, a man gave me a plant with the nuts still hanging to the roots."

"Did you eat them?"

"No, they weren't ready to be eaten. After they are dug up, they have to be dried and roasted before they are good."

"That's quite a dissertation on the peanut," said a laughing voice from the doorway. "Is this a botany class?"

"No. Just a quiz conducted by your son, who is bored by three days of cool, rainy weather. I've had to polish up every bit of learning I ever had to cope with these question-boxes of yours. They may make something of me yet."

"It didn't take Dick and Jane to make something of you. You and God, working together have done a pretty good job of that."

"I don't feel that way. I try hard, but it's slow work."

Marion turned to the little boy who was regarding them with gravely puzzled eyes. "Run up to the playroom now, Dickie Boy. Janie wants you to help her fix the sand-table farm. And remember, son, no teasing."

As he scampered away, she put her arm around Linda's shoulders and said, "Come into the den. It's more cheerful there. I've lighted a bit of a fire to dry us out. This is more like November weather than early September. Let's sit down on the davenport. It's time we had a real chat. Since coming home I've been so busy and you've been so undemanding that I've neglected you. I was shocked awhile ago when I realized we have been home three weeks and haven't done a thing for you. I should think you'd be very impatient with us."

"I'm not. I know Scott is spending more time hunting Tony than I could ever pay for. And I would have no idea what to do if I didn't have him to do it for me. I'm more grateful than I can say. But I'm heartsick and tired of not knowing. It's been so little we've been able to find out. The bungalow has been sold, and even the neighbors don't know where Tony went. His old employers don't have any idea. So far as we've been able to discover, he isn't back in his home town. There are no records here of either divorce or remarriage, but that's no sign he didn't move to some other place and get a divorce there. That's all we know, and it leads us exactly nowhere."

"I know how you feel. The hardest thing I ever have to do is to wait when I want to be moving. But that's our task now. And while we wait we are praying. Why don't you do as Bill advised and get a job some place?"

"I know I should," Linda admitted with a quiver in her voice. "I know I'm just sponging off you, and I ought to—"

"You *are not* a sponge, Linda Mitchell, and don't ever say that again. We're all ashamed for having let you work so hard for us. That's what is bothering Bill. He thinks it isn't good for you here where all you do is care for the children and take the heavy work off me. He thinks *you* are spoiling *me*."

"He's crazy. But he should know what I need, and I will try to follow his advice. But what would I do, Marion? I really don't know much in spite of a pretty good education. Until I find Tony I probably couldn't keep my mind on an office job. Maybe I'd better look for a place doing manual labor of some sort."

"I couldn't bear to think of you in a factory. I've been trying to think what to recommend to you. Then a few minutes ago Grandma Willis called. Since she hasn't been able to get about much, she reads every word of the daily paper. At least it seems so to me. She loves the ads and gets a lot of human interest stories out of them. She said she has been watching one especial ad for a week and hoping someone nice would answer it. It appeared again this morning which indicates it hasn't been answered satisfactorily. And suddenly it occurred to her that it might be the place you were needed. That's what I came in here for. I hunted up the paper, found the ad, and —I agree with her. It seems just meant for you."

She handed Linda the paper with the marked item, and watched closely while Linda read it. The color flooded her cheeks, then receded leaving it pale as she looked up and gasped,

"It frightens me. It might be—it could be—. Should I try?"

"Why not?" said Marion casually. "It seems just made for you. Let me read it again and you measure your fitness. 'Strong young woman of good character wanted to care for two motherless children and an aging semi-invalid for the next

180

few months. Must like children and furnish best of references. Reasonable compensation. Call evenings, or write J. C. Ayer, 937 Linden, Reedsville.' Why, that's only twenty-five miles away. We go through it on the way to my folks' house."

Linda had risen and was nervously twisting her hands. "Marion, I couldn't."

"Of course, you could. It just fits you. You are young and strong, and you could do a lot for those children who need mothering. This may be God's way, Linda."

"But—it sounds—like—a mother-in-law!"

"Could be. But you aren't a spoiled youngster any more, dear. Maybe the Lord has sent this to help you prove what you can do. With Him you can tackle even a mother-in-law."

For so long she stood resolutely that Marion feared that she would reject the chance. But at last she looked up with a pathetic attempt at a smile.

"O.K. You win. I'll write at once and let Dick take it to the mailbox for me. I'll ask God to lead. If this isn't His will for me, He can make those folks reject me. I will at least have tried to follow the leading. If I get the job, He will have to supply a lot of courage and strength, for I'm weak at the thought of it. In spite of all my impatience at staying here and doing nothing, I am afraid now to receive any marching orders."

* * * * *

Linda was alone with the baby when the answer to her letter came. The ringing of the telephone had wakened her from an afternoon nap, and she was still drowsy as she replied to a voice asking,

"Miss Mitchell?"

"Yes."

"I am speaking for Mr. Ayer. He will not be home until about eight o'clock. You *are* the Miss Mitchell who wrote about the position, aren't you?"

"Oh, yes." Linda had recovered her poise. The voice was that of an elderly woman but there was nothing but kindliness in it.

"Oh, I'm so glad you answered. I liked your letter. I am Mrs. Davies, Mr. Ayer's aunt. We just haven't had any good answers at all until yours came. The others all wanted too much money. We *can't* pay a great deal, so we will try not to demand too much of you. I do hope you will come over and talk to John about it this evening."

"I will do that if you desire. When would you expect me to begin?"

"Oh, at once. Tonight if you can. You see, John has just been asked to take a trip which will keep him away from home several days. It means a great deal in his work if he can make that trip. But he has to leave tonight and we just couldn't find anyone who would stay. Your references looked very good to me, and if you could stay until he comes back, maybe we could find someone else before he has to go again. Or maybe you'd be willing to stay on with us."

"Your nephew may not want to keep me."

"I think he will. I liked your letter and I like your voice, and I'm sure John will find you acceptable."

As she turned from the telephone, Linda was shaking as with a chill. She wanted to call back and tell Mrs. Davies that she could not go through with it. She did not want to go for that interview. All she wanted was to stay in this safe haven where her friends could take care of her. Surely she could do enough work for them to pay for her board. She would rather stay here and let Scott and Dr. Bill make all her decisions. Maybe if she called Dr. Bill now he would tell her not to go. Or maybe Scott had learned something today that would make this plan useless. Maybe she was not really needed in that home. Mr. J. C. Ayer might be a man whom she could not work for. Just because his aunt sounded like a lady was no assurance that he was a gentleman. She *couldn't* go there tonight and face him.

But all the time she was arguing with herself she was packing. One suitcase would be enough. She might not stay even one night. There was a bus back about eleven o'clock. And if by chance she did decide to stay longer, she could come back for more luggage. When Marion reached home, dinner was ready and the suitcase stood in the hall. Linda's face was pale, but there was no word of her struggle. The battle had been decided on her knees.

After dinner Marion took her to the bus station. As they waited she sensed Linda's tension and fear, and spoke words of reassurance.

"You're going to be all right. God opened this door for you and it is going to lead you back eventually to happiness. We will all be praying. There will be some bad times, of course. We all have them. But you have a Friend who has promised to be with you. Remember this morning's verse? Philippians 4:13, it was."

"I won't forget. I'll—oh, there's the bus. Marion, I'm *afraid*."

"Cheer up, honey. You're not alone, you know. If you decide not to stay tonight call us and we will meet you here. Call in the morning anyway. We'll be waiting to hear. Good-by now. Keep looking up!"

When the taxi which Linda had taken from the Reedsville bus stop drew up in front of the house that the driver declared was 937 Linden Avenue, she had a frantic hope that the place would have been filled. Maybe some kind neighbor would have taken note of the family's need and offered services that would be much more satisfactory than hers could be. Perhaps, after she had talked to the aunt this afternoon, some better prospect had applied. She paid the driver and watched him disappear around the corner as if he were taking her last connection with civilization with him. She looked down the street as if she longed to follow the car, then at the length of walk that lay between her and the front door. Could she ever force herself to knock at that door, and face—what? Even after she pressed the doorbell, she had to fight down an impulse to run. She could still make the late bus, and Marion would welcome and comfort her. She could get a job in a factory and let Scott keep on—

A light was turned on in the hall and an opening door disclosed a tall man silhouetted against it. Linda shrank back into the shadow where she had placed her suitcase. She wondered what would happen when he questioned her and she could not answer. Her throat was so stiff she was sure no sound would come from it. With his back to the light the man peered into the shadows.

"Yes? What is it?"

"I—I—was asked—to come," she said in a breathless tone that could hardly be heard.

"Asked to come? I don't understand. Oh, you mean about the position." His voice changed, betraying a very real, if somewhat belated, interest. "Excuse me. I was not expecting you so soon. Will you step in?"

She stepped over the threshold and stood in the light from the lamp on the table, raising her eyes to his, and waiting for the verdict which would either permit her to stay here or send her back to Sunnyknoll. He stepped back quickly and for a long minute stared at her without speaking. She shook as with a chill, and still he looked as if trying to analyze what lay behind the frightened eyes and trembling, but nevertheless resolute, lips. At length he spoke, and the harshness of his tone cut across her tired nerves.

"Are *you* applying for the position I advertised in the *Herald?*"

"Yes."

184

"I doubt if you understood what I require. I want a strong woman who can do all the work in this big house, as well as care for my aunt who is not well, and my two small children. You do not look strong enough for that."

"I am well and strong. I can do all that is required."

"I must require the very best of references as to character. Can *you* supply those?"

She tried twice before she could force a reply from her dry throat.

"Yes. For a year and a half I have been working in just such a capacity for a family that is well known. I have references from both husband and wife."

He read audibly the letters she handed him:

> To whom it may concern:
>
> This reference is gladly given. Linda Mitchell has been in our home in the capacity of helper and friend for over eighteen months. She is leaving of her own volition and to our deep regret. We will gladly recommend her for any position she desires to assume.
>
> Scott R. Willis
>
> To anybody and everybody:
>
> Linda Mitchell is the best thing that ever came into our home. I am sorry she is leaving, but wherever she goes, God bless her.
>
> Marion Chase Willis.

"H'm. These can be verified later. Just now I would like to ask a few questions. Is that Scott Willis of Warner, Sheffield, and Willis in the city?"

"Yes."

"And you've been there a year and a half?"

"Yes."

"Why did you leave such a place?"

"Their need for me had passed. I could have stayed but I did not wish to. I have other plans that I must be at work on."

185

"Do your plans include this position?"

"If you hire me, yes. For six months, did you say?"

"Approximately. It would depend on how you work out and on my aunt's condition. I will reserve my final decision as to your desirability until I have talked to Willis. Tonight I must ask you to stay if you are willing. I should take a plane shortly after midnight, and I can't leave my family alone. Can a discussion of salary wait until my return?"

"Yes."

"Come into the living room and I can explain the situation and give you some instructions."

Linda had noticed a small rocker standing just inside the living room, and had felt as if it were beckoning her. If only she could sit down in it before her shaking limbs betrayed her by dropping her at John Ayer's feet! Now she moved toward it, but before she reached it he stepped ahead of her.

"This chair, please."

He seated her in a huge overstuffed chair that almost overwhelmed her in its soft depths. Such courage as she had built up during the short interview seemed to seep out at her feet. The man did not appear to notice her perturbation, nor did he seem in any hurry to proceed with the interview. He sat opposite her with one nervous foot tapping the floor and with his eyes downcast. As she waited, Linda grew more calm and took advantage of the opportunity to study his face. It was a haggard face, one that told of heavy burdens, of deep sorrow and of bitterness. It could have been handsome in a happier day, but the lines of care had cut across it, and the bitterness had hardened it into a forbidding mask. As she watched him she could only think of the man's need for One to help him with his burdens.

"I am John Ayer," he began at last. "I lost my wife several years ago. My aunt has been caring for my children. She has tried to give them the love and care that all children need, and she has done an excellent job. Several months ago her eyesight began to fail. She has cataracts on both eyes and can hardly see to do all that must be done. You can understand how she cannot longer be responsible for the care of two lively youngsters. She will become increasingly helpless until she can have an operation, which will be some months from now. I must have help. I am not able to pay a large salary, yet I must have someone whom I can trust. To further complicate things I will have to be away from home much of the time during the next six months. If I am unable to find a good helper here, I shall have to pass up a wonderful business opportunity, which I need badly. I will be frank with you. If Willis gives you the kind of backing I shall expect after such a letter, will you be able to stay with us?"

"I will be glad to do so, and will do my best to prove satisfactory."

"My aunt can talk to you tomorrow. She went to bed with a headache as soon as I reached home. Have you any luggage with you?"

"I left it on the porch."

He brought it in, then led her upstairs to a room at the end of the hall.

"The children's room is next to yours. My aunt is across the way. Will you leave your door open so that you can hear the children? My little girl is very nervous and apt to cry out in her sleep. The boy will want a drink or two, just for the fun of making you wait on him. Don't pay too much attention to him. My aunt will help you to get into the swing of things. She will be expecting you to be down by about seven in the morning. Have you any questions?"

Linda wondered what he would do if she asked all the questions that were pressing against her tired mind, but she only shook her head, and he turned abruptly away. She stood still in the doorway watching as he went down the stairs. As the slam of the front door told that he had left the house, she went to the window and watched as he went down the street.

"No hat or coat. He's not leaving for the trip yet. Just going to walk off his troubles, probably. Poor fellow! He goes as if the furies were after him. And that's not the way to peace."

How long she stood at the window she did not know. When she finally turned away it was to drop to her knees and cry out to the Lord.

"Dear Father, take me and hold me and give me the strength to go on just as you lead. Help me not to ask or claim anything for myself, only Thy will in all that I do. And dear God, please save Tony and my babies, for Jesus' sake. Amen."

After she had lain down sleep did not come although she knew she should be resting for the day ahead that held as yet unknown problems. She went over and over the events of the months since she went to Aunt Lucy's house, the long trial of not knowing how nor why she had come to that place, the goodness of Scott and Marion in welcoming her to their home, Dr. Bill's kind guidance through all the fog that enveloped her, the sudden lifting of that fog and the heartbreak of the weeks since, when she did not know where Tony and the children were nor how they might be faring; when she did not have even a picture of the dear faces to make her feel a bit closer to them. Most of all she thought of the peace that came over her like a flood when she yielded to the insistent call of the Spirit and accepted what Christ had done for her on Calvary. Then she thought of the chance (or was it chance?) that had led Grandma to observe this advertisement. She had not thought she could venture out of the safe shelter of the Willis' home, but here she was, and God, who had led during these other tests would be faithful in this.

She had longed to tiptoe into the children's room and look at them in their sleep, but did not dare go unless she felt a need. Now she heard a sound from that room. She listened for a moment. Perhaps the father had returned and would answer the call. Or perhaps the aunt had wakened. But the other doors remained closed, and the fretful little voice continued. She tiptoed into the room where the light from the hall showed two cribs. From the nearest one came the plea,

"Dwink, please. Dwink, *please*."

She brought water and held the little fellow up while he drank greedily. As she laid him back on the pillow she smoothed the tumbled hair and stooped to kiss the soft little cheek. He was already asleep and had not noticed that it was a stranger who had ministered to him. She moved to the other crib and looked down at the sleeping girl. Dark curls were spread out over the pillow. In the half-light the face looked pale and thin. The tiny outstretched hands twitched as if the sleeper were disturbed and restless. With a choking sob Linda kissed this tot also, then dropped to her knees between the cribs. She was aroused by the sound of the front door closing again, and sprang to her feet. Quick steps bounded up the stairs, and John Ayer met her in the hall.

"What were you doing in there?" he demanded harshly.

"I was giving the little boy a drink. You told me to."

"Yes—yes, I guess so. Look here! I don't like leaving you here. I don't like it at all. Everything I have in the world is in these two rooms. I don't want to go. But I have to or lose an opportunity I've worked for, for two years. I can't find anyone else. But I don't like it. And I'm saying now that if anything happens to my babies, I'll make you answer for it. I mean that!"

Her voice shook, but she answered forthrightly, "I know you have no reason to trust me, but you may do so. I will give you my word of honor," and here she looked at him as if expecting him to scoff at those words, "that I will do my utmost every day to be and do all that you desire. Later, after you have talked to Scott Willis, I will stay if you so desire. You may trust me."

"I *have* to trust you for a few days. I have no one else. This I want you to remember. My aunt is mistress of my home. As such she will receive your utmost courtesy and co-operation."

"Surely."

He looked coldly at her as if weighing again the question of whether to go or stay. His eyes were so steely and icily blue as he gazed at her that she felt again the nervous chill.

"I must go. I will be back on Saturday. In the meantime you are responsible."

Again she watched until the taxi that was to bear him to the station was out of sight. Then she returned to her bed where she lay sleepless through a long night.

Chapter Twenty-three

SHE WAS DRESSED early in the morning. Judging from the quietness of the house, the children and aunt were still asleep, so she tiptoed downstairs and out onto the lawn. The grass was damp from the heavy dew, and the air was sweet with the odors of flower and shrub. Widespreading maples bordered the street. Along the driveway low shrubs formed a bank of bronze and green. The house itself, which she had not seen clearly the night before, was a rambling frame, rather badly in need of paint but having a hospitable air that warmed the heart of this one who was in need of a friendly gesture. She followed the path around to the back of the house, and drew in her breath with delight at what she saw. Here was the old-fashioned back yard of her dreams—asters, zinnias, marigolds, cosmos, dahlias and even some goldenrod and wild asters back by the fence. She had learned to love these flowers and to know them at Sunnyknoll, but there had not been such a wealth of them as she now saw. All around the sides of the lawn, against the garage, bordering the walk they grew, flaunting a blaze of color to greet the sun which was just now coming up over the hill. Under an apple tree that still held on to a few maiden blushes, a sandbox and a swing showed where the children were wont to play. Nearby two lawn chairs and a bench told of the hours of watchfulness by aunt or father.

"This is a lovely place, a homey, comfortable, good place where flowers and folks grow together. It isn't a bit like my garden at the bungalow."

The memory of that little house set in its landscaped lawn with the prim, geometrically designed garden behind it, cast a shadow over the brightness of the hour. With a shiver she turned back to the house. In the hall she met a plump little white-haired woman who was holding a paper in her hand and looking anxiously about.

"Oh, there you are! I've been ten minutes deciphering this note of John's. He tried so hard to make it large enough and black enough for me to see, that he entirely forgot to make it legible. But I'm good at puzzles. I find I've been put into the care of 'I hope, a capable young woman,' he says. Are you she?"

Linda smiled. "I'm Linda Mitchell. I've promised to stay until Mr. Ayer gets back on Saturday. If I haven't done anything *too* wrong, I may get a permanent position."

"Bless your heart, you don't look as if you'd do anything wrong. I'm sure we will get along fine. I'm Aunt Nan to John and the children, and I'd like to be to you. I hear the children now. I'll take you up and tell them who you are."

The children were having a hilarious time bouncing on their beds. Aunt Nan trotted in between the cribs and, seizing each child by an arm, spoke reprovingly.

"Children! Peter! Suzanne! Your daddy told you not to jump on your beds. Don't you remember?"

Peter squirmed guiltily and slid off onto the floor. But Suzanne spoke defensively.

"What I remember is Daddy told me not to jump on *my* bed, and he told Peter not to jump on *his* bed. So we didn't be naughty cause we jumped on each other's bed."

"Well, don't jump on *any* bed. Do you understand that? Now I want you to meet Miss Linda who is going to live with us for awhile. Come, speak to her."

Two little pajama-clad figures approached hesitantly. Linda

gravely shook the little hands offered to her, longing instead to crush them in her arms. Little lovable, motherless tots!

Peter gave her a roguish smile and darted to the bathroom calling out, "I'll be dwessed first! I'll be dwessed first!"

Suzanne did not smile, but raised questioning eyes to meet Linda's own.

"Why are you going to be with us? Are you a visitor?"

"No, I am going to take care of you for several days while your daddy is away."

Suzanne threw herself at Aunt Nan in a panic. "Why is my daddy gone? Is he coming back? Did he go with my mother?"

Aunt Nan stooped and held the little girl close as she said with a quaver in her voice, "No, darling, no. He isn't with your mother. He will be back soon."

"How soon?"

"Five days."

Linda gave a reassuring pat to the brown curls. "Can you count to five, Suzanne?" she asked.

"Y—yes. One—two—three—four—five."

"Then let's play a game. All day today we will fix up fives. Let's put five flowers in some vases. And I have some candy upstairs. We can put five pieces of that in each of two dishes, one for you and one for Peter. We will think of some other fives after while. Then tomorrow when it's only four days until Daddy comes, we will take a flower out of each vase. And you and Peter can each eat a piece of candy. We'll do that every day until there are no more candies or flowers. Then Daddy will be home. Want to try it?"

Suzanne looked up at Aunt Nan who smiled and nodded in approval.

"I guess so," she said soberly. "Maybe it will work."

In mid-morning, after a conference with Aunt Nan, Linda volunteered to go to market. Peter was playing happily in the back yard with the little boy from next door, so Linda offered to take lonesome little Suzanne with her. But the child drew back in panic.

"No, I can't. You're a strange woman."

"I'm *what?*"

"A strange woman. Daddy said I must never go away with a strange woman."

Aunt Nan showed her embarrassment by a nervous apology. "Don't be offended, Miss Mitchell. My nephew is overly anxious about the children. He seems to fear that someone will try to kidnap them. I'm sure he would think it all right for Suzanne to go with you."

"No, she mustn't," said Linda, biting her lip to conceal her own nervousness. "I wouldn't think of taking her until Mr. Ayer says I may. She is an obedient youngster, and I love her for it." Her hand rested lightly on the curly head, and she smiled down into the sober face.

When she reached the corner, she turned to look back. Suzanne still stood at the window looking wistfully down the street. Linda waved, then hurried on.

"I mustn't cry. I don't dare. I'll have to learn not to show my feelings or I will spoil any chance I have of holding this job."

When she reached the house again, she found Suzanne busy with her dolls. She had decided to include them in the game of fives, and was sorting doll clothes with an eye to finding five dresses for each one. The task of finding enough dresses and squeezing the dolls into them consumed most of the day, and at night she went to bed docilely, eager to have morning come, for then she could take a dress off each baby, as well as a flower from each vase, and a piece of candy from her dish. Best of all, Daddy's homecoming was tangibly nearer.

For Linda, the rest of the week resolved itself into an effort to win the confidence of the little girl. Peter presented no personality problem. He was a gay little fellow, full of tricks, with a genius for getting into dirt and trouble. Many times a day he had to be punished for disobedience. And just as many times he came to Aunt Nan or Linda saying,

"I'm saw-wy. I did forget. I'm a good boy now."

Then Linda would gather him into her arms hungrily and kiss the roguish little face. Often when he made them all laugh with a clownish trick, she would find her eyes filling with tears as she remembered that other lovable clown who had been her dad.

It was not easy to win acceptance from Suzanne. Such a sober little girl she was that Linda's heart ached for her. Surely it was not natural for such a young child to be so serious. Many times each day she stopped in her play to lean against Aunt Nan's knee for a few minutes of demonstrated love. At such times Linda longed to hold her as she did Peter against her own hungry heart. But Suzanne would permit no such display of affection. Obviously, she was waiting until her daddy could give his stamp of approval to this newcomer.

She jealously guarded her father's possessions lest this alien hand touch them. She inquired anxiously if she herself might dust his bedroom, and was delighted when consent was given. When through with the rite each day, she carefully closed the door and requested that no one open it. The small rocker in the living room was also sacrosanct. Even Aunt Nan was not allowed to use it.

"That is my Mommy's chair. And Daddy is all that can sit in it. He sits there when he tells us about Mommy. Nobody else can."

One rainy afternoon held them all in the house. As the early dusk came on, Linda began to tell Peter a story. It was a wonderful tale of a dog named Scotty and a yellow cat called Butterfly, who lived together on the farm at Sunnyknoll. Peter was fascinated and sat on a stool at her feet with his chin in his hands and his shining blue eyes fixed on her face. Suzanne stood at the table working with a puzzle. As the antics of the animals became more and more thrilling, she was unconsciously drawn closer to the center of interest. Linda dared not notice her, although she yearned to reach out and bring her close. When the story was ended, the child started as if just becoming conscious of what she had done, and turned quickly to her puzzle again. But her hands moved listlessly among the pieces and soon she began to gather them into the box. As she closed the lid she spoke as if to herself,

"If I had a mommy she would tell me a story."

Linda wondered at that moment if her heart could hold its surge of ache and longing without breaking. Aunt Nan reached for the little figure and drew it onto her lap. Suzanne nestled there and watched Peter and Linda contentedly. After awhile she roused herself to say stoutly, as if challenging anyone to deny her,

"But I don't *need* a mommy. My daddy can tell stories, too."

Aunt Nan kissed her and said shakily, "Bless you, darling. You have the best daddy in the world."

And Linda, feeling her way through tear-blinded eyes, went to her room for an hour alone with the only One who could comfort her.

Chapter Twenty-four

Jᴏʜɴ Aʏᴇʀ ᴄᴀᴍᴇ ʜᴏᴍᴇ on Saturday. The children were riding their trikes on the sidewalk when their shouts and squeals of delight aroused the two women in the house.

"John has come, I am sure," cried Aunt Nan. "I can't see from this distance, but I can tell by the children's noise."

"Yes, it's he," said Linda, looking from the window. "They're bringing him in."

She stood back by the door to the dining room as Aunt Nan hurried to greet the newcomer. She wished she might run upstairs and into her own room, or, better still, she wished she might run back to the friendly shelter of the Willis' home where she would not have to meet this cold, steely-eyed man. But her "verse for the day" came to her and its promise gave her strength.

> The Lord is nigh unto them that are of a broken heart;
> and saveth such as be of a contrite spirit.
> Many are the afflictions of the righteous:
> But the Lord delivereth him out of them all.

Aunt Nan was greeted affectionately by the man who held a child by each hand. In the joyous excitement Linda stood unnoticed until Peter, pulling boisterously, dragged his father into the room.

"Here's Linda, Daddy! She's my Linda. I like her an' like her!"

Linda looked up in confusion as the voice, which had been tender in a greeting to Aunt Nan, now became harsh as he said,

197

"Yes, I see her. How do you do, Miss Mitchell?"

She answered his greeting quietly and turned to the kitchen while the others went into the living room. As she prepared lunch, she heard the happy chatter of Peter, and Suzanne's gay little laugh which told of her joy at her father's return. Aunt Nan's quiet voice and the deep tones of John Ayer joining in, served to emphasize the silence and loneliness of the kitchen where she worked alone.

During lunch the family of four seemed sufficient unto themselves, and talked of things and people unknown to her. Linda sat quietly, studying the face of the man across from her—such a young man to be so broken and embittered. His face looked even more haggard than it had on that other evening, and when he was not speaking his mouth had an unhappy twist that betrayed rebellion of soul.

"Oh God, help me to help them all," she prayed silently.

For several hours after lunch John Ayer and Aunt Nan were together in the little room off the hall that they called Aunt Nan's den. The children were napping, and after Linda had washed the dishes and prepared a dessert for dinner, she went to her room. She was beginning to think of this room as a battleground, for already it had seen some fierce struggles with the adversary. Discouragement, heartache, loneliness, bitterness had all attacked her here this week. But all had been met with the help of One who had promised to overcome, and victory had been won. So again today she knelt by her bed and prayed. Even battles that result in victory are not easy, and this one was fierce. She prayed for this whole household; she thanked God for the privilege of serving here; she pleaded for patience, submission and grace for the trials that beset her. And over and over she begged, "Oh God, give Tony and my babies back to me." At first the prayer was insistent as if she could no longer be denied. But as the time passed, she grew quieter, and at last she prayed brokenly through lips that were steady, "Dear God, let it be Thy will in my life, whether for service and happiness with my dear ones, or for a lonely path of suffering and heartbreak."

A knock at the door aroused her; Aunt Nan stood outside. Linda was thankful that the dim eyes could not note her swollen eyes and flushed cheeks.

"John would like to see you in the den, dear. I am going to lie down awhile. I hope he is going to ask you to stay on with us, but you and he will have to decide that. I want you to know, though, that whatever he decides, *I* want you to stay and will be *very* sorry if you must leave. Will you call me at five-thirty?"

Linda bathed her eyes and burning cheeks, then went back to her room for a few more minutes of prayer. As she went down the stairs, she knew that never before in her life had she been so frightened. And she must not be. She could not forever hide from the realities of life. It must be faced, and this was the course her Captain had directed.

When she stood at the door of the den, John Ayer sat at the desk with his head on his arms. She opened her mouth to say a word which was never uttered. For he raised his head and, at sight of her, his face changed instantly into the mask of harsh dislike that had greeted her before. He arose, however, and asked her to be seated in Aunt Nan's "darning chair." After he had seated himself, he only looked at her gravely for so long that she began to feel that she must get up and go away from that cold scrutiny. When he spoke, however, it was with grave courtesy.

"I find myself in a trying situation, Miss Mitchell. I had returned here with a determination to let you go as soon as I could find someone—anyone—to take your place. I have had a most wretched week. I doubted your fitness to care for my family. You are definitely not the type of person I expected to answer my advertisement. Why did you do it anyway? Can't you find work that is easier and with better pay?"

"I prefer this. I care for only enough money to satisfy my very simple needs. I—I wanted this because I want to—to—work with children."

"I see. Well—I called Willis and he verified your references. But I still am doubtful. However, I see no other course than to keep you if you care to stay under such circumstances. I have to take such help as I can get. Also, my aunt wants very much to have you stay. I owe her too much to refuse her anything that will help to make her lot easier in the trying months ahead. She is facing a serious operation and needs reassurance while she waits. If you are the one she desires to have with her, I must make the best of the situation. But I must also, for my own peace of mind, ask some questions. Do you mind?"

Her hands were cold as they lay in her lap, and her cheeks were hot and flushed. But she answered calmly.

"You may ask what you wish."

"In my office whenever we employ new personnel we like to have a history of their employment during recent years. Could you give me such a history for, say, five or six years?"

For a moment she wondered if the lump in her throat would completely choke off her voice. Then again came the remembrance of the promise of God's presence, and with remembrance came peace. She answered quietly.

"I shall be glad to do so. I was graduated from college five years ago last spring. I was married immediately. For the following three years I was employed only in my home in being a wife and mother."

As she realized that she had uttered the same words that Tony had flung so angrily at her on the night that had ended that home, she stopped in dismay. But John Ayer was staring out the window and apparently did not notice her perturbation. Gripping the arms of the little chair more tightly, she went on.

"Then my home was broken up. I went to live with an aunt. I had a long and severe illness, and it was many months before I was able to work. I held a position for four months as a file clerk with the Dennison Electrical Company. When my aunt had to be sent to a rest home, I took the position as mother's helper in the Willis' home. I was there until last week."

"You said your home was broken up. Is that—er—permanent?"

"It appears to be. There is nothing about it that would interfere with my work here."

He studied the letter opener in his hand as if seeking guidance from it. The twitching of his cheek betrayed nervous strain. His coat, hanging loosely on his thin shoulders, spoke of a time when he must have been many pounds heavier than now. The drooping shoulders told of discouragement. But when he spoke, his harsh voice had in it no bid for sympathy.

"You can understand that I have some problems. I lost my wife several years ago. I had no one to turn to except this aunt who came up from Florida and opened her old home to me and my motherless babies. The adjustment has been hard for all of us. Aunt Nan isn't well, Suzanne is sensitive and difficult, and I am struggling with a new job. Pete, bless his heart, adjusts automatically. His disposition is one hundred per cent sunshine. But the rest of us are problems to each other.

"Then, too, the work is pretty heavy. I have always had a woman come in to do the cleaning and laundry. I expected a woman to answer my ad who could do that also. I can't afford both. I am in a quandary about what to do."

"I can clean and do the laundry."

"You?"

"Surely. I always did it in my own home."

"That was different. It *was* your own home. Under those

201

circumstances a woman would do many things she would not care to do for a not-to-large weekly wage."

"I would like to do it. I am stronger than I look. Or you could keep the woman and deduct the amount of her pay from mine."

"But that wouldn't do. At best, I can't pay enough, and with that taken out you'd not be getting enough to clothe yourself."

"I have enough savings from my work at the Willis home to dress me for a long time. Anyway, I don't need any new clothes. Could you understand if I tell you that it means a great deal for me to make good on this job? It would prove to me and my friends that my illness is really a thing of the past."

"But if you have been ill, you shouldn't work too hard. You are very thin."

"Yes, but I will be all right when I get settled. I will not do too much. I will pay the cleaning woman out of my own salary. The rest of the work isn't too hard. Let me try it on those terms for a few weeks longer. Perhaps some other thing will open up by then."

He leaned his head on his hand as if in utter weariness and despondency. She wished she might speak some word of comfort or sympathy to him, but did not dare try to bridge the gap between them.

"I am reluctant to accept such an offer," he said at last. "I do not wish to be under such obligation to you. But I am forced to accept those terms. I will be in the home office for several days, then I will have a trip of about three weeks' duration. Until I return from that we will let things stand as they are. I will find some other solution. I must. It is my problem, and I do not intend to put it onto anyone else. For the present I can only say, thank you."

He had risen to close the interview, and she hurried upstairs to answer Peter's call of "Linda! Linda!" As she went she whispered, "Thank You, Lord, for these few weeks. Help me to go on just as You lead, one step at a time."

* * * * *

That evening after supper was over Linda sat with Aunt Nan in the den, holding a skein of yarn on her hands while Aunt Nan wound it into a big ball. Crocheting was one thing Aunt Nan could still do, and she found great comfort in it. She had launched a project to make a varicolored afghan, and had a great pile of skeins to wind.

"Let's do them all at once," she said, "while John is here to keep Peter from getting tangled up in them. That is, unless it tires you."

"I can take it if you can," laughed Linda. "And the advantage of being without Peter's assistance is worth considering."

From the living room came the sound of laughter and happy voices as John Ayer romped with the children.

"Bless their hearts," said Aunt Nan softly. "I just love to hear that. It's times like this that save his sanity. When he has had a romp with them, he can sometimes go to sleep without walking himself to death."

"Walking?"

"Yes, that's what he does when things get on his nerves— walks it off. Sometime when you and I are alone I want to tell you about his wife. Then you will be better able to understand his moods."

The noise from the other room had risen to deafening volume, and at last there came a good-natured order to halt.

"Listen, you two! We can't shake the house down. Aunt Nan will be putting us out."

"Then tell us a story."

"O.K. Settle down and we'll see. Here, Pete, you sit on this side and—"

"No!" broke in Suzanne's voice. "That's not how. Daddy,

please," here she caught her breath sharply, "won't you sit in Mommy's chair and talk about her?"

"Yes! Yes! Yes!" from Peter.

Aunt Nan shook her head sadly as if wishing he would refuse. But his answer came with gentle kindness.

"Sure, I will. Come here, sweetheart, and sit on this knee where you can lean your head right against my heart. Now Pete, old fellow, up on the other side for you. That's it! Now what shall we say?"

"What did she look like?"

"Well, what *did* she look like?"

"Brown hair—"

"An' bwown eyes."

"An' a sweet smile."

"An'—an'—an' what did she do?"

"What *did* she do?"

"She made me a sweater—a yellow one!"

"An' a gween one for me!"

"She cooked our dinners."

"An' ouwa bweckfus."

"An' we went on pinkninks."

"An' I wide on hewa lap."

"An' she was good—gooder than anybody, an' she'd sit in this chair an' rock and rock."

"An' she loved us an' loved us!"

"An' she loved Daddy too."

"An' Daddy loved hewa."

Linda got up hastily as Aunt Nan reached for another skein. "Do you mind if we do the rest some other time? I—I have a headache."

"Why, you run right along to bed. You must be very tired. I just take advantage of you and work you too hard. You go right to bed. John will take care of the children. He likes to do it when he is home."

She did go to bed, but not to sleep. She was awake when John Ayer brought the children up to bed, and she heard Peter say shrilly,

"I can't go to bed till I've pwayed. I always pway with Linda. Twice I did, an' I want to now!"

Later she heard heavy steps go down the stairs and out the front door. Evidently they were going for one of the long walks Aunt Nan had described. Hours later she heard them coming back up the stairs. Only then did she sleep.

Chapter Twenty-five

THE NEXT DAY WAS SUNDAY. As she was dressing, Linda thought longingly of the family at Sunnyknoll and of the happy preparations there would soon be for church. Her own church-going days had been so few and recent that she still felt a thrill at the thought of it. How she wished she might introduce Suzanne and Peter to the joys of Sunday school! She had spoken to Aunt Nan about it but had been told that John Ayer would not permit it.

"When he is at home, I go to church by myself," said Aunt Nan. "That is, I did as long as I was able. Now I find it more of a blessing to stay at home and listen to the radio. There are several good services. I do wish John were not so bitter against religion. It isn't right to raise children without the Lord."

"Perhaps you and I can introduce them to Him," Linda had answered. "If we pray and trust the way will open, won't it?"

But today she thought mostly of her own deep need for the spiritual refreshing that a sermon and a visit with Marion Willis would bring. She could not go and get back in time to prepare dinner even though John Ayer has assumed the care of the children. Perhaps she could be free after dinner, however. Maybe she could attend the evening service.

At the breakfast table, in a moment of lull in the excited babblings of the children, she asked hesitantly,

"If I prepare for your supper, may I be away this afternoon and evening? If I am to stay here, I must bring more of my things from the Willises."

John Ayer looked up quickly and answered with a promptness that seemed to betray eagerness.

"You may go anytime you wish. I shall be at home all day, and Aunt Nan and I can run the ship. We have weathered a good many storms together, and we are a complete crew."

There was no doubt that he would be glad to be relieved of her presence while he enjoyed the day with his aunt and the children. Definitely he did not want to count her as a crew member.

"He need not have been *quite* so glad to get rid of me," she thought later as she waited for a bus. "After all, if I'm good enough to care for his children, I ought to be worthy of some ordinary courtesy. Oh, but I'm not! I'm not really worthy of anything. I'm 'fit to be neither a wife nor mother.' Why should I expect to be treated worthily any place?"

For some miles as the bus rolled along she brooded sadly on the wreck of her home and her own fault in that circumstance.

"I was so stubborn and silly," she thought. "I knew what divorce was like, and yet I hadn't sense enough to keep out of it. Tony's mother *was* irritating. No one would deny that. But she wasn't as bad as it has been to lose Tony and the babies. Riding in the back seat that night couldn't possibly have hurt me as much as that wild ride with Miles did."

The bus rolled on through the fields and woods where the first frost had turned some of the leaves into a pattern of gorgeous colors—yellow, red, and green. The drive began to soothe her spirits, and she determined to put the regrets aside and get the rest and peace that the day could bring her.

"In spite of my foolishness, Christ loves me. All the things that have happened are worth while—the pain, the suffering, and the loss. For through them I've found Him. And surely if He loved me enough to take so much trouble to reach me when I didn't even want Him to, He loves Tony and the babies. And some day they will love Him."

She did not go out to Sunnyknoll before church. As the bus drew into the village she realized that it was almost time for the service to begin. Already the children were coming out of Sunday school. So she slipped into the pew where the Willis family usually sat, and was rewarded by their spontaneous smiles of welcome when they saw her. Although no words were spoken, Marion's eyes asked the question, "How goes the battle?" and Linda's eyes reassured her. The battle had been stiff, but there had been no retreat.

All day she rested and relaxed in the friendly atmosphere of the Willis' home. In the afternoon Dr. Bill and Rosanne and their flock of lively youngsters came to add to the fun and fellowship and to display the new baby boy that Linda had not yet seen. What a loving and lovable group they were, thought Linda as she watched them! Scott and Dr. Bill and the two older boys were struggling with a model airplane that wouldn't perform as it should. Marion, with her own youngest on her lap, was talking to Rosanne and admiring the new baby. Three little girls had paper dolls spread all over the floor, table, and chairs in the dining room. As they worked, Scott and Dr. Bill sang softly some song which Linda did not recognize but which she felt instinctively was an old hymn.

"This is just what a family ought to be. And even if I never have a family of my own again, I'm glad I have had an opportunity to see how a Christian home is run. If Tony and I had known how to pray and sing hymns together, we couldn't have grown so far apart. Oh, dear God, give me the chance to help Tony and show him how he needs Thee."

In the late afternoon when the new baby had been put back in his basket and Rosanne was browsing through the books in the library, Linda and Marion went out with baskets to gather the eggs.

"Let's go to the orchard and get a basket of apples also," said Marion. "We finished picking this week, and tomorrow the men will begin to sort them. I love to eat them just out of the orchard, and I want to send a big bag back with Bill. Store apples haven't the same taste at all."

As they turned back toward the house a gorgeous sunset scene was spread out before their eyes.

"Let's climb up on this fence and watch the sun go down and the dusk come. Did you ever sit on a fence and watch twilight settle over the land, Linda?"

"No, I never did. But I want to now. It's awe-inspiring, isn't it? We've been here only a few minutes and already the sky has changed from flaming red and yellow to gray and purple."

"Yes, and look over toward the northwest. See the mist rising off the little pond? And the shadows of the pine trees beyond are already growing dark. Night is a beautiful time, isn't it?"

"Yes, if you're not afraid of the dark."

"My mother taught me not to be afraid of it. She called it the 'velvet dark.' It's such a restful, blessed time after the hurry and work of the day."

"It's a lonesome time, too, Marion. During the day the hands and feet can be so busy with tasks and errands that heartaches can be pushed back into the background. But at night they all come out, and they aren't rosy like the sunset or silvery like the moon. They are just big and black heartaches that can hardly be borne."

"Bless your heart, dear! Don't think we've been forgetting you. Even Dick and Jane pray for you. I know the heartaches are heavy, but I know, too, that you have a Burdenbearer ready to help. Can't you lay it all on Him?"

"Oh, I do. And then I stoop down and pick it up again. I wish I knew my Bible better. There are such wonderful promises in it, but I never can find them when I need them."

"Keep on reading and studying. No one ever became a good Bible student in a few days or weeks. It's a job for a

209

lifetime. Some day you will discover that Christ's words are really abiding in you and are yours to use when needed."

"I hope it will be soon, for I surely need all the help for the present and promise for the future that I can find."

"Is it so hard? Do you want to tell me more about it?"

Until the shadows were dark under the pines and the moon was beginning to come up over the orchard, they sat and talked. Then Scott's voice calling through the dusk brought them back to the light and laughter of the big house.

"If you're going to church tonight, you will have to hurry," he said. "Rosanne says she will stay with the children so we can both go. Mr. Lambert called awhile ago, and when he found out that Bill was here, he asked us to sing a duet. We've been practicing, and I think we're pretty good!"

"Oh, you do?" laughed Marion. "Well, we'll be ready with supper in a jiffy. Then we'll be real kind to Rosanne and let her do the dishes."

That evening service in the small church brought a peace and benediction that Linda knew would last through many days to come. Scott's and Dr. Bill's duet was to her as a message sent especially for her benefit from a loving Father who knew her need.

> Lead me gently home, Father, lead me gently home.
> Lest I fall upon the wayside, lead me gently home.

After it was over and Dr. Bill and his family had started back to the city, Scott and Marion insisted on taking Linda and her suitcases back to Reedsville, while the wife of the tenant farmer watched the children.

"Do you have a key? And are you allowed to be out after midnight?" asked Scott. "Yes? Then we will go around by the valley road. It's less traveled and much more suited to a Sunday evening mood."

So they drove slowly, drinking in the beauties of the cool

210

night and breathing deeply of the frosty air. They loitered on the way for there was a charm about the valley road that encouraged a leisurely pace. When they drew up before the house on Linden Avenue, Scott looked at his watch by the light of the street lamp on the corner.

"Just midnight. And a lamp has been left burning for the wandering child."

"That would be Aunt Nan's thoughtfulness. She loves to mother us all."

But when she had told them good-by and watched from the porch as they drove away, then turned to enter the house, it was not Aunt Nan who awaited her. John Ayer sprang up hastily from his seat in the little rocker.

"You're late enough," he said. "I wondered if I should have to go out after you."

"You need not be concerned. I have a Friend who will care for me."

"Did he come home with you?"

She felt a quickening of her pulse at his concern for her and his unconscious use of the word "home." But she only said, gravely,

"Yes, He did."

"Well, I *was* concerned," he said harshly. "I have to leave early tomorrow morning and I must know you are here to take charge."

"You need not fear, Mr. Ayer. I have told you I will be responsible for things here, and I will. I will not even go to see my aunt or friends while you are away."

"You don't have to be *that* strict. You may leave the children with Aunt Nan for a few hours any time you wish. She is not able to carry the full load any more, but she would enjoy an occasional afternoon with them alone. Please don't stay out or go out alone after dark. She would worry, and I want to save her from that."

211

"I shan't do anything to worry her. My one task while you are gone will be to care for her and the children as you yourself would do."

In the silence that followed she turned to the stairs. Halfway up she looked down to see him still standing motionless.

"Mr. Ayer," she said softly. "Scott and Marion Willis brought me home. The Friend who came with me, who is with me now and always, is my Saviour, the Lord Jesus Christ."

He stared at her in amazement as if doubting either her statement or her sanity. But she continued up the stairs. As she closed her door she thought,

"That's the first time in my life that I ever spoke to anyone except the folks at Sunnyknoll about the Lord. I guess that's what Marion would call witnessing. Dear Lord, make me an effective witness here."

Chapter Twenty-six

IT WAS A BLUSTERY NIGHT. The wind whirled the snow around the corners of the house and piled it in ridges which, by morning, would become great drifts. In spite of storm windows it had been hard to keep the house comfortably warm. Now, at eight o'clock the children had been tucked under heavy blankets, and Linda and Aunt Nan were alone for another of the long evenings they had learned to love. Through the fall and winter they had lived and worked together and had grown very close during the many weeks when John Ayer had been away. Aunt Nan's eyes had grown so dim that she needed more and more help about the few activities left to her; while Linda, hungry for the motherly care that had never been hers, responded with all her heart. They were on the couch in Aunt Nan's den working industriously on the afghan. Linda liked to sit where she could help with the colors that blurred before the dim old eyes. So, side by side, their fingers busy with the wool and their tongues busy with the many common interests they had found, they sat as the wind howled and the hard-driven snow beat at the windowpanes.

"I'm glad I don't have to be out in this," said Linda. "I like snow and I love to play in it when it's nice and soft and feathery, but this stuff has a viciousness that chills me. I wish no one had to be out in it."

"Do you know whom you remind me of? Did you ever read *Snowbound?*"

"I don't think so. I don't seem to remember it."

"I just loved it as a child. My father used to read it to us. And I heard it so often that even now I can repeat almost all of it. I tried it the other night when I couldn't sleep."

"How do I remind you of that?"

"You're like the mother. It's a beautiful story of a family snowbound in one of New England's severe winters. You *must* read it, dear. I have it in an old reader. It tells of a long evening when each member of the family, and even the guests who were with them, contributed something interesting to the fellowship around the fire. Then when it was time to go to bed, the mother expressed her gratitude for the warm, comfortable home her family had at such a time. Then she prayed 'that none might lack, that winter night, for food and clothing, warmth and light.' "

"That's just how I feel. It's snug and comfy here, and I'd hate to think of anyone being out in that wind."

"Yes, I'm glad John won't be home this weekend. He is in Tennessee, and it probably is much warmer there. He wasn't a bit well the last time he was at home. He gets thinner and thinner all the time. And he catches cold *so* easily. He doesn't take care of himself as he should."

Aunt Nan finished one block, and Linda sorted out the colors for another.

"This is going to be a beautiful thing, Aunt Nan. What are you going to do with it? I hope you keep it for yourself. It would be just the thing to throw over you when you nap on this couch."

"I don't know what I'll do with it. When I started it last summer, I knew it would take me a long time to finish it. I had a faint hope then that by the time it was done, John would marry again, and I could give it to his wife."

She felt gropingly among the yarns, and Linda guided her fingers to the right color. Aunt Nan sighed.

"When he was at home the last time, I said that, and he got very cross with me. I guess I'm spoiled, because it made me feel very bad. In all his life he had never been cross with me. He said he did not want another wife, ever. He told me never to mention it to him again. I wish he would marry. It isn't natural for a man as young as he is to stay single, even though he did adore his first wife."

Linda was busy untangling a knot in the yarn, and Aunt Nan chattered on without interruption.

"He probably thought I was tired of the care of the babies. But I am not. I was thinking only of him in his sadness and loneliness. I know what it's like to lose a mate. I lost mine after almost forty years together. One just never gets entirely over it. I don't expect him to forget his wife. But he's a young man and he has two children who need a mother."

"You have done so well with them, Aunt Nan, that he doesn't feel the need."

"I've done my best, for he's all that's left to me since my husband and daughter died. I had decided that my days of usefulness were over, and I might as well go to some old ladies' home and sit on the porch and twiddle my thumbs until I died. Then John's letter came, and in spite of my sympathy for him in his loss, it made me too happy for words to know that someone needed me. John has always been very dear to me. My only son died in infancy, and John seems to take his place."

"Is—is his mother dead also?"

A flush came to Aunt Nan's face. She seemed to wince as if in pain, and when she spoke, her voice showed such unhappiness that Linda regretted the question.

"No-o. No, she isn't. But she and John are alienated. I don't know why. It has something to do with his wife's death, I think, for it all occurred at the same time. Whatever it was, it has completely **separated them. John will** not talk of her, and I know he never gets any letters from her. It makes me quite ill."

Linda murmured a word of sympathy, and Aunt Nan went on.

"Do you ever think that when you get to Heaven you **are** going to have to ask some questions and find out some things that have troubled you on earth?"

"No, I never did. But there are a lot of things I could ask about."

"One of the things I intend to find out about is just what is wrong with my sister. It wasn't just this trouble with John. It showed itself a long time ago in her hatred of me."

"Whatever could make anyone hate you?"

"She does, I know. You see, she is my only sister. She was ten years older than I, and in between were the three boys. When I was six, our mother died, and sister had to take her place. She was fond of the boys and did well by them, but I was her pet. She dominated me completely, for she was a strong type, and I was a timid little girl. I loved her so passionately that I never felt the lack of a mother. As I look back now, it seems to me that my whole life was wrapped up in her. I never had a childhood friend I really loved. I worked at school to earn my sister's praise. I stood at the head of my class because I wanted her to be proud of me. Everything I did was for her."

"What changed her?"

"I have asked myself that question a hundred or more times and I still have no answer. I know *when* it happened, but not *why*. When I was sixteen, sister had a friend who wanted to marry her. He was a fine fellow, but was quite poor and not at all the dashing type that would sweep a girl off her feet. I thought he was wonderful, but sister made fun of him and sent him away. I cried myself to sleep that night. Five years later I met him again, and in spite of sister's opposition, we were married. From that day she has acted as if she hated me. Why? I can't tell. I've asked myself that question until I get dizzy thinking of it. Was she jealous because I married before she did? Did she think I'd thrown myself away on an unworthy man?" Here Aunt Nan's voice broke. "He was the kindest and gentlest person I ever knew. And I was loved and cared for, for almost forty years. And I didn't take him away from sister. She had sent him away long before. If she didn't want him, why was she angry when I married him? Or did she think I should have entered into her plans for a career for me and paid no attention to any man? Did she envy me my family, or did she pity me because of them? I don't know. I have never understood her. It seemed to me that she was always waiting to pounce on everything I said to find some fault with it or me. She wanted to do things for me and the children, but everything carried a sting. To the boys she was still the kind, big sister, but to me she was sharp and cynical. She always got her way with the boys, and I guess she resented not having her way with me."

"She surely can't be very happy to be alienated from both you and her son."

"No, I'm sure she isn't. I think she never has been. She married years after I did. Her husband had a great deal of money, and when John was a little boy, the father died, and sister was left very wealthy. She was fanatically devoted to her boy and kept him away from even her relatives. He had a most unnatural childhood. I longed to be close to him for he looked very much like my boy. But after one summer he spent with us when he was about fifteen, she would never let him come again. I didn't write to him, for I felt it would only anger her more. Only through my brother Charles did I get any word of them. He would often send on to me the letters she wrote him. I knew John had married and had two children. I sent a Christmas card or two, but that was all I knew about them until I got the letter saying he needed me. He knew I'd help him when he needed me."

"That's a sad story, Aunt Nan. I can't help but feel sorry for her. She must be *very* lonely. Think of having two grandchildren like Suzanne and Peter and not being able to cuddle them."

"She is lonely, I am sure. I think often of what she is missing. And it isn't good for John to hold so much bitterness. If he'd only talk of it, he would feel better. Maybe I could make him see things differently. But he won't let me mention her. It's not right though. It just doesn't pay to hold on to the hurts as you go through life."

"I'm sure you're right, but sometimes the hurts hold onto you."

"I guess that's true, but that's where prayer helps. I've had some hurts myself, but I just can't stand to stay unhappy. So I take hold of the Lord in prayer and hang on until He has given me peace. I wish John could do that."

"So do I. But one has to be a Christian to do that."

"Yes. And John won't let me talk to him about it. It's one place where we are worlds apart and can't get together. He is an utter unbeliever. I do not know if his wife was a Christian. I hope she was."

"Did none of them ever talk about her?"

"I hadn't seen any of my family for years. After our daughter died, we closed this house and lived on a little place we had in Tennessee. Then when my husband became ill, we went to Florida, and I stayed on there after he died. My brother Charles wrote to me, but he never was very talkative about family affairs, and I didn't know much until I got John's letter. It was just as if my own son had called for me to help him. I can remember every word of that letter. 'Dear Aunt Nan: Can you come and help me out? I have lost my wife and am

218

alone with two babies to care for. You used to be my answer to every problem, and I need you now. Johnnie.' I used always to call him Johnnie. His mother disliked it, but he was always pleased with it. And I was so glad to be able to help him. I hurried up here, and as soon as we could get the tenants out of the house, we moved in. I think John is as happy here with me as he will ever be any place."

"I'm sure he is, but he can never be really happy with his heart full of bitterness."

"I know that, but I don't know how to change it. It must have been a terrible thing sister did, for John was never an ill-natured boy. We used to say that he didn't know how to get really angry."

"Often a person who is slow to anger will hold the anger longer than one who is quick-tempered."

"Yes, I guess you're right. John is certainly a different person from the mild, easy-going boy that used to visit me. There are times when I think his wife must have been somewhat responsible for the change in him. Then I hear him talking to the children, and I know she was sweet and good or he could not have loved her so much. I wish he would not talk so much about her to them. Suzanne, especially, is so easily disturbed. But he says he wants them to believe that they remember her. Of course, they can't, but he tells them so much about her that they think they do. I asked him once if he had a picture of her, and he said none that he wanted the children to see. Said he didn't want them to think of her as a picture."

The wind continued to howl. Aunt Nan rambled on, crocheting as she talked. Linda, listening as she aided in the work on the afghan, thought she must do something to change the subject, for the pictures of the characters in this unhappy family chronicle were unpleasantly clear before her and gave her a feeling of depression. She could see it all—the tangled personal relations through the years, the growing alienations, the jealousies and hurt feelings, the caustic remarks and bitter answers. And now, a young man sullen and embittered, and an aged woman, unrelenting even in heartbreak. And a young wife—lost?

"Hatred and anger are dreadful things," she said when Aunt Nan paused because of the tremble in her voice. "They are dreadful in themselves, but more dreadful in the things they can lead to."

"Yes, they can, and often do, lead to death."

"They can lead to worse than death," Linda answered with a break in her own voice. "They can, and often do, lead to divorce. And that is living death."

Aunt Nan stared in astonishment at the girl who had dropped her head on her arms while her shoulders shook with sobs. Then she pushed the yarn off her lap and reached out to enfold Linda in arms that had ached with emptiness since a beloved daughter had left her. She waited until the sobs had somewhat subside, and then asked softly,

"Do you want to tell me?"

"There isn't much to tell. My parents were divorced, and because I loved them both so much, I thought I couldn't stand it. I said I'd *never* be divorced, no matter what my husband did. And then—oh, Aunt Nan, I do want to tell you about it some day. I know you can help me. But tonight I can't talk about it. I will have to pray some more before I can talk about it. It's such a mess, and it gets worse all the time."

The telephone in the hall shrilled its summons, and Aunt Nan went to answer it while Linda dried her eyes. Her excited voice carried clearly into the little room.

"Hello! Yes—yes. Oh! Oh, dear! As soon as you can get here? Yes, we will.—No, I won't worry. Tell him that.—Yes, thank you, Doctor."

Linda was standing by her side by the time she turned from the phone.

220

"What—what is it? Is John hurt?"

"No, but he is ill. That was Dr. Moore. John came in on the train about half an hour ago and went to Dr. Moore's office. He is quite ill, and the doctor is bringing him home."

"Ill? What is it?"

"I don't know. The doctor said he would rather take him to the hospital but the road is blocked between here and Seebury, and John must be put to bed as soon as possible. Oh, I'm shaking all over."

"You sit right down in that chair and relax while I fix the bed. If the telephone or doorbell rings you can answer. I'll be back down in a few minutes."

She prepared the room, closed the children's door so that they would not be disturbed by the commotion, then ran down the stairs again.

"I'm going to fix us some tea while we wait," she said. "Aunt Lucy always prescribed tea for every situation, and a hot cup now will help you to relax."

While Aunt Nan gratefully sipped the tea, Linda began to gather up the wools. The telephone rang again, and she answered it with a sick fear clutching at her heart. Perhaps he was worse, and they could not get home with him! But this time it was Marion Willis' voice that spoke to her.

"Linda! I wanted to be sure and get a word with you tonight. All the lines will probably be down by morning. The wind is *awful* here. But I just *had* to talk to you."

"It's bad here, too. But what's the matter, Marion? Is someone ill?"

"No, but I've some news I couldn't wait to give you. Scott will send you the details in a letter later, but he said I could tell you tonight."

"What is it?"

"Well, Scott finally found the lawyer that handled your dad's affairs, and he knew who—the other party's lawyer was.

And Scott talked with him today. Can you take some good news, Linda?"

"Yes, oh, yes. Quick!"

"Then here it is in a nutshell. You're still married to your Tony, Linda. He hasn't even tried to get a divorce. Said he wouldn't do that under any circumstance. We're all praying our hardest. Scott called Bill and he said to tell you that John 14: 13,14 is still true. And we all say, God bless you!"

Aunt Nan, alarmed by the long silence after the receiver had been hung up, came to the door and looked in anxiously. Linda's head was bowed on the telephone table, but this time Aunt Nan knew she was not crying, for over and over she heard the words,

"Oh, Father, thank you, thank you!"

Chapter Twenty-seven

As far as the waiting women could see, the drifts were piled high in the street. Few motorists were out, and the unlucky ones that had ventured forth were having to shovel themselves out of drifts once or twice in each block. It seemed to the anxious watchers that an hour had passed since the call, before they saw a taxi bucking through the drifts at the corner. When it finally stopped before the house, the driver got out and shoveled a path to the porch before they opened the door of the cab. Then with the doctor on one side of John Ayer, and the driver on the other, they came up the walk. Linda had the door open, and they were soon inside. John slumped and would have fallen had not the doctor caught him and lowered him onto a chair. The driver looked at the stairway and said,

"You go on up, Doc, to get things ready. I'll bring him up like I used to bring 'em in when I was in the army."

So, across the broad shoulders of the driver, John Ayer was carried to his room. Apparently the taxi man had joined up with a medical unit again, for as Linda and Aunt Nan came up the stairs he called out,

"I'll put him to bed while you give his women their orders, Doc. Then we'll be ready to start back through them Alps."

"O.K., Dick. Now," the doctor turned to Aunt Nan, "he's going to need some close watching tonight. Can one of you be with him all of the time?"

He looked inquiringly at Linda, and Aunt Nan hastened to introduce her.

"My companion, Miss Mitchell."

"Have you had any nursing experience, Miss Mitchell?"

"None except in the home of friends in cases of slight illness."

"I think you can manage here, all right. Mrs. Davies should not stay up. She needs her rest. But she will be here to help you in case of a real emergency. I don't think you will have any trouble. He is very susceptible to this drug. It may make him very dopey, or he may become delirious. I used it on him last year in a similar attack. But don't worry. He will just talk irrationally awhile, then drop off to sleep. All you will have to do will be to watch the time and give the medicine. If you need me, I can be reached by phone. I'll be over as soon as I can get out in the morning. If the fever breaks, discontinue the medicine."

After the men had gone and the sound of their laboring car had died away, Aunt Nan insisted that she could take the first part of the night watch.

"I'm wide awake now, and I might as well. I think I'd feel better if he woke up and saw me."

"I'm sure he would. But he won't wake up. The doctor said so."

"Well, I don't believe he is too dopey now to see me. I'm going in."

Before Linda could answer, the little lady had tiptoed in and seated herself at the bedside. John was turning his head restlessly from side to side, and breathing hoarsely. Aunt Nan took one of his hands and held it gently between her own until he became quieter. In a few minutes he seemed to drop off to sleep. Linda did not interfere. Aunt Nan could be a very determined lady when she desired. But as the end of the hour drew near, she went in.

"We will have to rouse him to take this tablet. The doctor said we must."

John opened his eyes and stared stupidly at the women.

Shaking his head impatiently he reached for Aunt Nan's hand.

"Aunty, will you go and see if the babies are O.K.? It's so cold."

"Of course, I will. Now don't you worry. I'll be right back."

As she padded away with her quick little steps, John's eyes opened wider and he motioned Linda to come closer.

"Lean down," he said hoarsely, "I don't want her to hear. I'm not too groggy now, but another pill or two will make me silly. I babble like an idiot when that stuff gets to working. I don't want her to hear me. Will *you* stay tonight?"

"Of course," she answered matter of factly in spite of the uncontrollable leap of her pulse. She went out and met Aunt Nan in the hall.

"Listen, dear," she said, "I've given him another tablet and he will go back to sleep, I am sure. Won't you lie down and try to rest? Both he and the children will need you tomorrow, but there isn't a thing you can do now. I promised the doctor you would go to bed."

So Aunt Nan went off to bed to prepare for tomorrow, and Linda returned to the sickroom. The tablet had taken effect, and the patient lay in a stupor. She went to her room and got the comfortable armchair that Aunt Nan had insisted be put there, wishing, as she dragged its clumsy weight across the hall, that she dared use the little rocker from the living room. She placed it so that she could watch the sleeping man but not be too obvious when he wakened.

The light on the desk was turned away so that John Ayer's face was in the shadow. Even so, she could make out every feature—the high forehead, the all-too-thin cheeks, the mouth which was relaxed as he lay in sleep. With his eyes closed and the line of mouth and chin softened by relaxation, he bore little resemblance to the bitter man whose eyes looked on her so coldly. Minute after minute she studied him. It was not pleasant to realize what life had done to the boy who did not know

225

how to get angry, as Aunt Nan had said, to turn him into the cynical man who seemed to delight in hurting her. As she watched, she prayed.

He began to grow restless, and Linda looked at her watch. She must not give more medicine for another ten mniutes. He turned and opened his eyes.

"What are *you* doing here?"

"The doctor said for me to stay so I could give you your medicine."

"You can't do it. You're just trying to get my babies."

"No, I'll never do that. I just want to help you take care of them and Aunt Nan."

"Aunt Nan is O.K., but if *she* comes here don't let her in."

"I won't. No one shall come in."

He closed his eyes, but opened them again and sat up, looking about as if frightened.

"She was here. I saw her. She said she would take the babies. She said a grandmother could do that."

"No one has been here. Aunt Nan is taking care of the children. She will never let anyone have them. Here, take this tablet and you can rest again."

He looked at her glassily, but obediently swallowed the tablet. As his eyes began to droop again, he murmured drowsily,

"Aunty Nan, I hurt. Will you rock me?"

For another forty minutes he was quiet. Linda brought the basket of yarns and busied herself with the afghan. But as she crocheted her thoughts were not on the bright blocks. She was praying over and over the prayer that filled her heart to the exclusion of all other needs.

"Save him, Father, for Thy glory alone. Show him how he needs Thee."

As the medicine lost its effect the restlessness came back.

"It doesn't matter who your grandfather was," the patient

declared challengingly. **"He's dead. You've got to let him stay dead."**

"I agree with you," she said quietly. "We'll forget him."

"Good!" with a sigh of relief. Then he sat up quickly and looked at her sharply. "You're all right. Do I know you?"

"I'm Miss Mitchell, Aunt Nan's companion."

"Oh! Say, look here. Would you run away from home just because—just because—why *would* you run away?"

"I wouldn't."

"Wouldn't you ever? Even if you found that the guy was no good?"

"No, I wouldn't."

"Well, she did. And then *I* ran away. And she said, the other one did, that I was a thankless son. But I'm not. I thanked her for a lot of things."

Then he laughed, a high-pitched silly laugh that made Linda shudder.

"I thanked her for a miserable childhood, and I thanked her for a ruined career, and I thanked her over and over for a wrecked home. Oh, I *thanked* her."

Linda hastened to give him the medicine, anxious to secure for him the interval of quiet that followed. But this time it was shorter than before, and soon he began again his incoherent ramblings.

"Did you know a guy could live without a heart? I knew one once that did. Then he had one made out of—no, it was a spine he had made. It was made of jello!"

"Can't you rest awhile?"

"I'm afraid to. She can't rest. She has to keep running from me. I almost got her once, but she went away in a car and left the fruit on the step. She runs and runs and I can't catch up. She's afraid of me."

"Won't you lie down and be quiet for awhile? For just a few minutes?"

"No. When I do, I get to thinking. You should never think. I've quit thinking. It makes me sick. Why don't you sing to me?"

"Because I don't sing well. It might make you worse. Do you want me to read to you?"

"Yes."

She looked about for something to read, but all she could see was a treatise on Wholesale Credits. She wished she had her Bible but did not want to leave the room long enough to get it. Then she thought of the passages she had been memorizing during her devotional periods. Speaking softly to lull him into quietness if it were possible, she began. The list was not long—the Twenty-third Psalm, the thirteenth chapter of First Corinthians, the fifty-third of Isaiah, and shorter bits that had borne especially on her own problems. When she could think of no more, she went over them once again. She did not know whether he heard or not. But he lay more quietly.

After the three o'clock medicine, he did not quiet at all, and had not the doctor warned her she would have been much alarmed. He became so excited in his delirium that she closed the door lest Aunt Nan be wakened.

The next three hours would live forever in her memory. She sat helplessly by, trying to soothe, answering when it seemed advisable, and praying always as she saw a human soul and its deep hurt and agony bared before her. Sometimes in shocked amazement, sometimes in hot anger, sometimes in heartbroken sorrow, John Ayer relived the years of his troubled life, and she could do nothing to quiet or comfort him. He had known he would react this way when the fever was high, and he had not wanted Aunt Nan to know all the darkness of his soul.

"Do you think there is a God?" he asked after one outburst. "Would a God let *that* happen?"

"Yes, I *know* there's a God. Do you want to know about Him?"

"What about Him?"

"Just this. He loves you."

"He—*what!*"

"He loves you—with an everlasting love."

"Hm."

He seemed to ponder a minute, then broke forth again in bitterness.

"Do you know why it all happened? Well, I do. A fellow with a backbone made of jello can't be anything but a coward. He's a sniveling, yellow coward, and nobody can help him. But it hurts—oh, it hurts!"

Wearily turning his head from side to side as if the ache could hardly be borne, he said,

"If I had it here, I could take better care of it."

"What is it you want?"

"It. You know what. Don't tell, though. Won't you get it?"

"Where is it?"

"In the bottom drawer. Let me hold it."

"Is it the dresser drawer?"

"The bottom drawer, the bottom drawer."

He was becoming impatient, so she went over to the dresser and opened the lowest drawer. There was nothing there that could possibly be meant. Surely, he wasn't interested in any of the neatly piled clothing. He must mean the desk. There she found several small books, none of which interested him. He was becoming so excited that she feared she could not control him, when she lifted out a box that had been behind the books. He struggled to get up, and cried angrily,

"That's mine! Don't you open it."

"I won't. Here it is. Now lie down and try to be quiet."

He took it, handling it as if it were something fragile and

229

precious. As he held it closely, fearing that someone might take it away, he glared at her in animosity.

"Don't you dare touch it. You're supposed to be dead!"

With his treasure protected by an encircling arm, he fell asleep. At six she gave him medicine without fully waking him. At seven, as the dawn struggled through the snow that still swirled, she rose from her cramped position in the chair and stood by the bed looking down at the sleeper. His breathing was easy and regular, and when she placed her hand lightly on his forehead, the moist coolness told that the fever had broken. She withdrew her hand and the motion caused him to stir. He tossed one arm outside the blankets, and as he did so the little box fell open and its contents lay before her—two little figurines. Wonderingly, she picked them up and saw, through tear-filled eyes, that each one had been broken into many pieces and painstakingly mended again. How many hours of patient labor it must have taken! She put them tenderly back into the box and replaced it at his side, then she stood erect and raised one hand to her forehead.

"A salute to a real man, John Chetwolde Ayer," she whispered. Stooping over him she kissed him lightly. She held her breath as a smile passed fleetingly across his lips, but his eyes did not open, and she tiptoed from the room. Tapping lightly at Aunt Nan's door, she said,

"The fever has broken, Aunt Nan. He's sleeping like a log. While you dress the children, I'll get breakfast. Then I'll go to bed for awhile and turn him over to you. He won't want me around when he is awake."

But before she slept, she knelt by her bed, thanking God for His mercy and grace in the past and His promise for the future.

Chapter Twenty-eight

IF JOHN AYER REALIZED who had watched with him during that night, he did not give any sign of appreciation. For several days he was kept in bed, but Aunt Nan was his nurse and companion. He rested, and slept, or read while she crocheted at his side. The children were not allowed in the sickroom, but hailed their father joyously from the hall. When he was allowed to come downstairs, they took immediate and complete possession of him. It was a treat to have Daddy at home all day, and they took full advantage of the rare opportunity to enjoy him. Aunt Nan sat and beamed as she listened or joined in some of the games John invented.

Linda alone was outside the circle. She was not invited into it, and it was made evident that she did not belong. She went quietly about the work, her heart heavy as she remembered Miles' statement long ago, that when his cousin ever really became angry at anyone, he never got over it; but she was cheered and strengthened by the knowledge of God's care and leading thus far and the thought of her praying friends. One more thing gave her hope. It was the picture of two little figurines which she had left in the attic of the bungalow, and which she had seen mended and treasured in a desk drawer. Surely, John Ayer had not kept and mended them for a disinterested love of the ridiculous china figures themselves.

Aunt Nan timidly tried to include her in the family fun, but sensed the coldness in John's attitude and desisted. Peter could not forget her, however. After a hilarious romp one afternoon, the little boy trudged up the stairs and stood in her doorway.

"Why don't you come down and play with us?" he asked.

"I'm busy, dear."

He sighed, then after a moment of hesitation spoke wistfully, "Are you too busy to wock me. I'm *so* tiwed."

"Indeed I'm not," she said reaching out her arms to the weary little fellow.

Later, when John Ayer was whistling about some task in his room, Suzanne came to the doorway. She looked with a troubled frown at Linda holding the sleeping Peter in her arms. Then she turned away to that other room. Linda could hear her say, first with a wistful tone then changing to challenging independence,

"If I had a mother she'd rock me." Then after a silence, "But I don't *need* a mother. Do I, Daddy?"

Then she heard the father move across the floor to meet the child, and knew that Suzanne, too, had found refuge in loving arms.

As day after day passed, and there was no softening of the harsh attitude, she found it difficult to face it. She kept away from the house as much as possible. One day was spent with Aunt Lucy. Another with the Willis' family. And on another she went in for a complete checkup by Dr. Bill.

"You're O.K.," he said after he had finished his examination. "You're my prize patient. From tip to toe you're good as new. A heavy schedule of cooking, cleaning, and baby sitting seems to be all you needed."

"It's been grand to have such a chance," she said. "But it's not all I want."

"Patience," he said kindly. "It will all come in time. I know, for we're all praying. Mrs. Bill said yesterday that it was all coming right soon. And she usually knows. She prays until she has found the answer, then waits for it. And if there's anything else we can do, you'll remember we're standing by, won't you?"

"I surely will, and I won't be discouraged. With such good friends back of me, how can I doubt?"

* * * * *

John Ayer was getting impatient to be back at work, and when the doctor pronounced him fit, he prepared for another trip.

"This delay has been bad," he said to Aunt Nan as she was protesting his departure. "This trip should have been made two weeks ago. Now I will have to combine it with another and be away just that much longer. But if all goes well, I'll be done with the traveling and can settle down to life again."

Linda heard with sinking heart. Did that mean that she would not be needed further after his return?

The days dragged by. The weather was too unsettled for the children to play outdoors. They were weary of the house, and all of Linda's games and stories had ceased to interest them. Aunt Nan seemed to have tired of the afghan and wandered about from room to room as if seeking something she could not find. Peter teased and Suzanne cried crossly. Linda tried to amuse her but was petulantly rejected. The furnace broke, and two entire days had to be spent in the kitchen where an electric heater and the oven of the range managed together to keep the temperature in the sixties. Both children caught cold and Peter had the croup. Linda wondered drearily if any further complications could come to add to the confusion.

She soon found out that this was possible. Suzanne developed an earache. She would not permit Linda to hold her and poor Aunt Nan was worn out. The ear grew steadily worse in spite of Dr. Moore's care. The specialist who was called in advised an immediate operation.

"Can't we wait until her father comes?"

"No—not if we can manage it before. We dare not let the abscess break and tear the membrane. But we must have better co-operation from her. Can't someone control her?" he asked briskly as Suzanne's hysterical screams rose higher. "Can't the young woman do better than the elderly one?"

"I'm sorry," answered Linda. "But she has an aversion for me, and I can't touch her."

"Well, we will have to do the best we can. Is there any way to reach the father?"

"We have his address. I will put a call through at once."

John Ayer's voice was sharp with anxiety as he answered. "I was to start home tomorrow anyway. I'll try to get a plane tonight. But you'd better not wait if the doctor says to operate."

"But she's so wild we can't manage her. Aunt Nan is almost exhausted, and Suzanne won't let me touch her."

There was a pause, then he spoke quickly. "Is she there? Is she able to talk to me? If she is, I think I can quiet her."

"I'll see."

"Wait. I want to say something to you first."

"Yes?"

"I'm—I just want to say—I can't tell you how I feel—but I'm very thankful you are with her."

"Oh—thank you!"

"Now can you put her on?"

Linda turned to where Aunt Nan held the child. "Suzanne, do you want to talk to your daddy?"

"To my daddy? Oh, yes!"

"Then let's try this. Put this to your good ear and listen."

The sobs quieted, and the little girl listened intently. The others could hear the murmur of John's voice, but only Suzanne knew what he said. Her eyes lighted at the sound, and occasionally she gave a happy answer.

"Yes. Yes, I can hear."

"Yes, I do. A secret? A really, truly one?"

"Oh, I will. Just like you said. I truly will."

"Good-by, Daddy."

She handed the telephone to the doctor and reached up to Linda. "I'll go with you," she said.

Aunt Nan stayed with Peter, and Linda went to the hospital with Suzanne. It was over quickly, and when John Ayer called back at midnight, Aunt Nan reported that all was well. Linda would stay at the hospital until Suzanne could come home, perhaps the next afternoon. John had not been able to catch a plane that night, but had a reservation for the next afternoon.

"And when I get home this time, Auntie, everything is going to be rosy. We're all going to live happily ever after."

Chapter Twenty-nine

W HEN THE TAXI DROVE UP in front of the house on the second morning, John gave a bill to the driver and ran up the walk without waiting for the change. He was standing in the kitchen door before Aunt Nan and the children, at a late breakfast, realized he had come.

"How's my sick girl?" he asked, picking Suzanne up and looking at the gauze dressing. "Should you be up?"

"Yes, the doctor said I could this morning. I stayed in bed lots of hours at the hospital, and I stayed in bed here last night. But I'm all well now, and he gave me a penny, and said I was a good girl and could eat brekfus with Peter this morning."

She looked for confirmation of this to Aunt Nan who nodded agreement.

"She has been a *very* good girl. Everyone said so."

John patted her head tenderly. "She's a sweetheart. And how's my pal, Pete?"

He kissed Peter in spite of the sticky condition of his face, and then turned to Aunt Nan.

"I can't say what it meant to me to know you were here when my babies needed you, Auntie. But you know how I feel without my having to say so, don't you?"

He started toward the stairs with his bags, but Peter called reprovingly, "Don't make so much noise. Linda's asleep and needs her west."

"Yes, the poor child has been up the last two nights and is worn out. This sore ear has to be irrigated very frequently, and Linda won't let me stay up. So I sent her to bed awhile ago and she promised to sleep all day."

"An' don't you 'sturb her," commanded Peter. "You go quiet like a mouse."

"O.K., O.K., Mr. Bossy," said John, tweaking his ear. "I'll put my bags in the hall and when I go upstairs I'll take off my shoes. Does that satisfy you?"

"Yes, an' I'll be quiet, too. As quiet as a wat."

"As a—what?"

"As a wat. A big mouse."

"He means a *rat*," giggled Suzanne.

"Well, I *will* be quiet—as quiet as two mouses."

He busied himself with his cereal, and John went to the cupboard to get a plate for himself.

"Sit still, Auntie. It's my turn to wait on me. You babied me enough last month to last us both a lifetime. I'm a well man now and am back in the driver's seat. So you get in and just ride along."

"You're acting mighty frisky," she said, looking curiously at him. "What has happened, John? One would think you'd inherited a fortune. Did the trip turn out so well?"

"The trip was wonderful. I got the contracts signed—bigger ones in several instances than the boss had dared hope for. And there's going to be a nice promotion for the lad who got them."

"I'm so glad! No wonder you're sitting on top of the world."

"I'm on top of the world all right, way up in the clouds. But it's not over contracts. It's a purely personal, extra special, earth-shaking little happening that I will tell you about later. Someone else has to know it first. Now if I will be good, may I have some of that raspberry jam you are hoarding over there?"

She laughed and passed the jam, then lifted Peter down and prepared to wash him.

"Since I don't see so well, I never feel that I've got the food

237

all off him," she said despairingly. "I can't understand how he spreads it so far. Why, even his hair is sticky."

"It's a fine art he learned from his sister. When she was smaller she used her food as paint, and did a thorough job of redecorating the breakfast set at every meal."

Then, catching Suzanne's look of indignation, he added, "But she has grown up to be a real little lady. She hasn't spilled one drop today. Maybe when Pete gets to be a big fellow, he'll reform also. In the meantime we can turn the hose on him."

Aunt Nan went into the hall to help Peter with his galoshes, and John leaned over to whisper to Suzanne.

"When I go upstairs, you come up after me. Be very quiet or Pete will catch you. Come to my room, and I'll tell you the secret."

In her excitement she almost choked on her toast, but she did not answer. Only her sparkling eyes told that she had heard. That conference upstairs kept John and Suzanne busy while Aunt Nan went gropingly about the task of cleaning the kitchen and washing the dishes. Her eyes had grown so dim that she found it hard to perform even the simplest of tasks.

"I've become so used to Linda that I'm almost helpless without her," she thought as she dried the dishes, feeling carefully lest she bump and chip them. "I wonder what makes John so happy this morning. He acts like a fellow who has just been accepted by his sweetheart. I wonder if he's thinking—h'm."

She put away the silverware, passing her hands fondly over the pattern.

"I can feel every leaf of this wild rose design," she gloated. "I'll be growing eyes in my fingertips soon. Linda will wonder how I did all of this. Oh, I hope John isn't planning anything that will send Linda away from me. I do want her here when I have my operation. No one else would fit in as she does. Whatever can John be up to anyway? He has Suzanne all in a twitter. I was hoping he and Linda—oh, pshaw, I forgot.

Linda said she was divorced, and she still loves her husband, I know. And she's not the kind that would remarry anyway. And I wouldn't want John to marry a divorced woman. But I wish she could stay with us always. No, that isn't right. I wish, for her sake that she could fix things up with her husband. She hasn't mentioned him again since that night John came home so sick. She said she would tell me about it some day. But I guess she forgot. I *am* disappointed though. I did hope—" she shook her head impatiently. "Quit thinking of such things," she commanded herself sternly. "It's just exactly *none* of your business."

It was mid-afternoon when Linda came down. The children were taking a nap, and Aunt Nan was in her den listening to the radio.

"Come in, dear," she called. "I've got some very good music. I've had some of the *best* programs today. Radio is really a godsend to us folks whose eyes have gone back on them."

Linda sank down on the davenport with a sigh. "I'm wilted. I didn't feel tired at all when you sent me to bed, but I'm fagged out now."

"You were running on nerve, and when you let down, your body demanded payment."

"I've paid up about eight hours' worth, and I still feel in debt," she said laughingly. "I guess I need a cup of tea. How is Suzanne's ear?"

"Fine. It's still draining, but doesn't hurt."

"I must go look at it."

"She's asleep. Anyway, John irrigated it just before she went to bed."

"John? When did he get here?"

"Just after you went upstairs. He's down—"

A noise at the door made them turn. John Ayer stood looking straight at Linda. As her eyes met his, a rush of color flooded his face, then receded, leaving it as white as chalk. He opened and closed his mouth several times as if seeking for words that would not come. Then, with a rush, he was across the floor and on his knees beside her, his head buried in his hands. Linda's arms went around his shoulders as she slid down beside him.

"Any room for another penitent at this mourner's bench, Tony?" she asked shakily.

They clung together and Aunt Nan waited in bewilderment. All she could hear was John Ayer's heartbroken cry, "Oh, dear God, forgive!" She didn't know what it all meant, but somehow she knew it was all right. Tiptoeing softly, she left them alone. When she reached her own room she sat down weakly.

"Oh, if I could just *see!* I'd like to read over that letter of John's again. I was sure his wife had *died*. No—let me think. H'm. He said he'd *lost* her. Now it looks like he had found her. At least he's found someone who is mighty glad to be found. And Linda said she was divorced. But sister always called John's wife Patricia. Oh, I'm all jumbled up and I'm weak as a kitten. I'd better lie down until I hear the children stir. Those two downstairs don't need me. But what I'd like to know is this: how ever did they live under the same roof all these weeks and keep so cool toward each other? It's just too much for me!"

Chapter Thirty

Back in the den John Ayer rose to his feet and drew Linda into his arms. When he could control his voice, all he could say, over and over, was,

"Oh, Pat! It's been so long—so *long!*"

"And so *lonely*, Tony!"

He sat down on the davenport, still keeping her in the circle of his arms. Taking out his handkerchief he carefully wiped the tears from her face, then from his own.

"I was going to do it all so nicely," he said shamefacedly. "I had a proposal all planned. I've been practicing it for three weeks, all the time I've been gone. Then when I saw you sitting here in that blue sweater like the one I got you that last Christmas, I just couldn't wait any longer. Can you ever forgive me, Pat? I'll spend my whole life making it up to you."

"All I can think of, Tony, is how much I need to be forgiven."

"But when I think that you were sick and needed me, and your doctor was looking for me, and one little ad in the papers would have found you—"

"How ever did you know all that?"

"He told me he looked through all the papers every day."

"Dr. Bill told you that? When did you see *him?*"

"The day I went out on my last trip. I had taken this situation as long as I could. It was driving me *nuts*. That night when you came here first, I was sure you had come to steal the babies. And I was *furious*. If it hadn't been for Scott Willis' name on that reference, I would have called the police. But when you looked me in the eye and told me I could trust you, I knew I could. You never lied to me, Pat, no matter how angry you got. And I knew you meant what you said. But I couldn't understand your game. After two and one-half years why should you come back? The weeks went by and all you seemed to want to do was to work like a slave here. I couldn't understand it. You were sweeter than ever, and I almost went crazy. How could you keep so cool, Pat, when I was all torn to pieces with longing for you?"

"And how could you be so cold and stern when all I wanted was to be held like this?"

"Wasn't it awful?" he groaned. "But I didn't dare let loose of myself or I'd have had you in my arms whether I approved of you or not. But how could I have doubted you so? I should have known that you wouldn't leave us purposely. When I think of these wasted two years which could have been saved if I had just tried to find you, I get sick with regret."

"Don't feel that way, dear. I'm sure the pain and sorrow and suffering will bear some fruit in our lives. And Dr. Bill himself did not try to find you because he feared the effect on me. He thought my memory should be allowed to come back without a shock. And, except for that last day on the train, that is just what happened. Bit by bit it was returning, and I'm sure it was best so. Let's believe it was, and go on from here without looking back."

"But I was so harsh with you even when you came here and helped us. I wouldn't give you a chance to make any explanations. And then I got sick and you stayed with me—say, was I bad that night, Pat? Did I say anything awful?"

"You said enough to convince me that I wasn't the only one that had suffered beyond measure."

"There's something else about that night that I want to know. Did you kiss me or was it a dream?"

Her face flushed, but she answered bravely.

"Yes, I did. But I thought you were asleep. The lid fell off your box, and when I saw my poor little man and woman mended so carefully, I *had* to kiss you."

"I thought it wasn't a dream. You took your foot off the bag then, Pat, and I could have caught you out."

"You slipped a little yourself," she laughed, though the tears were still close. "No hard, unforgiving man spent the countless hours it took to put all those pieces back together. The man who did that still had a soft place in his heart for the woman who loved the little figures. That thought has been my comfort ever since that night."

"Oh, Pat, even when I wanted to hate you I couldn't. And I got an idea about those figurines, and it became almost an obsession with me. I decided that if I could mend them it would be a good omen, and that I would find you again. Believe it or not, I finished it the night before I saw you in Cantrall that time. I know now that you didn't recognize me, but I thought you had and were running because you hated me."

"Oh, Tony, I *never* felt that way. Even the night I left I wasn't angry. I was frightened and my head hurt terribly, and I couldn't think clearly. I had been thinking about Aunt Lucy and longing to see her, and suddenly I decided I just *had* to talk to someone and she was all I had. I never meant to leave you, Tony. You believe that, don't you?"

"I *know* it now, but I didn't then. And after I was sick, I wanted you so badly even though I was still angry, that I didn't dare speak to you for fear I'd take you in my arms. I wasn't yet willing to do that. I had to get things straightened out or go crazy. So that last morning before I left on this trip, I went to see Scott Willis to ask him what he knew of where you had been for over two years. He sent me to your doctor, and did I get it there! But when I found out what had happened and realized I could have found you so easily, I wished the doctor would give me a physical trouncing instead of the verbal one he handed out. I'll never get over it. I get sick all over when I think of you hurt and alone, not even remembering your babies, and I not there to help you."

"Please, darling, don't think of it. It is past and we are here now. At first when I came back to a knowledge of what had happened, I thought I could not stand it. I imagined all sorts of things happening to you and the children when you found I had left. But I reminded myself that your mother could care for the children and that—"

"Mother didn't care for them at all. She left the next morning, and I haven't seen her since. I took the kids over to Ruth Hayes, and she had them until Aunt Nan came. I hope we can go to see Ruth soon and tell her all about it. She has never lost faith in you, Pat. They live in Cantrall now—moved from the old neighborhood last year. I had been helping them the day you saw me. They are grand, both of them, and I don't know what I'd have done without them."

"Oh, what a load you've had to carry!"

"And what a chump I was not to try to find you. Instead, I just 'jumped ship' myself. I quit my job and got another so that no one could ask any questions. I dropped the Chetwolde part of my name and picked up the John that Aunt Nan always used. I decided there was nothing left for me but to care for the children, so with Auntie's help I've been trying to do a good job there. But it has been hard and lonely, Pat. I can hardly believe yet that it is all past."

They sat in silence for awhile trying to comprehend the one big fact that overshadowed everything else—they were together again. Tony picked up her left hand and winced at the sight of the scars across the palm. He kissed each one, then drew from his pocket a white velvet box.

"Before we put these rings back where they belong, I want to tell you something else," he said huskily. "When your Dr. Bill was convinced that I was in earnest, and that all I wanted in the world was you, he gave me another jolt. He told me that even yet there was something lacking. You know what it was, don't you?"

"I think so," she whispered.

"He said you told Mrs. Willis once that you could never again feel completely one with even me unless we were one in Christ. Did you think that?"

"Yes."

"I asked him what you meant, for it was all Greek to me. And that busy doctor took time out that morning to tell me what I'd never heard in all my life before—the simple fact that I was a lost soul, and that God had a plan by which I could not only be saved but could share a new life in Christ with you. He had to make it simple as kindergarten stuff, but I finally got it. It was so wonderful when I did believe it, that I wanted to rush right back and tell you. But I think the doctor was afraid I was just doing it to get you back. He kept telling me it was more important than even my relations with you. He gave me a Bible and suggested that I study the New Testament while on my trip and find for myself what the whole plan was. So for three weeks I've been spending every spare minute on that job and getting smaller and smaller all the while. Do you remember how cockily we once disposed of all faith? And in one short hour God upset all my pompous thinking and put me down where I belong, at the feet of the crucified Christ."

She had been listening in amazed delight. Now she could hardly speak for the joy that filled her.

"You mean—we really are one in Christ, Tony?"

"Yes, and I want to put these rings back on your finger. Then I want the two of us to pray that God will keep us always so close to Him that we can't get away from each other. I can't pray very well yet, but I think He will hear us."

"I know He will."

"Do you remember Jesus' prayer on the night He was betrayed, Pat? I found it the first week in my reading. I am sure I have read it a dozen times since. When I realized *I'd* been included in that prayer, I wanted to jump up and shout 'hallelujah!' like the folks used to do in that camp meeting I told you about once. Remember? I learned that verse and the one following it, and I've been saying them all day long ever since.

"Neither pray I for these alone, but for them also which shall believe on me through their word; that they all may be one; as thou, Father, art in me and I in thee, that they also may be one in us: that the world may believe that thou hast sent me.

"That's what I want to ask of Him, Pat—that you and I may be one in Him. I can think of nothing more wonderful—you and I together in Him."

"I have a verse, too, Tony. It shows how that other can be. I found it one night when I thought you were never going to forgive me. And it brought a promise that some day we would be reconciled. It is Ephesians 4:12.

" 'For he is our peace who hath made both one and hath broken down the middle wall of partition between us.' When we were living in the bungalow and things weren't right, it seemed to me that there was a high wall separating us, and I couldn't do anything to break it down. When I came here, it seemed even higher. Then I found that verse, and I knew that in Christ it could be broken down. Now it has been and it seems the most wonderful thing in the world!"

"I hadn't found that verse yet. But the wall is gone and, please God, it will never be between us again. Here darling, give me your hand."

The rings were back where they belonged, the wedding ring guarded by the diamond. Then Linda and John, for the first time in their lives, came together before the throne for a blessing.

Chapter Thirty-one

Aunt Nan paused at the door and peeped cautiously inside. Then she advanced hesitantly.

"I just *couldn't* stay away any longer. I don't know what's going on here, but it seems so—so attractive that I want to get in on it."

Linda and John sprang to their feet and John gave the little lady an embrace that lifted her off the floor.

"Two foolish people have come to their senses, and to the Lord, Aunt Nan, and we're so happy that we want to tell the world. So come and sit down here and we'll start with you."

They placed her between them and told her the whole story, neither sparing themselves nor blaming anyone else. She listened, often saddened as she realized the cost of the mistakes that had been made, and beaming with joy as they reached the happy conclusion. When they were finished, she spoke briskly.

"I feel as if *I* deserve *some* credit for this. If it had not been for these old eyes of mine, we would never have needed a companion."

"But we would always have needed our mother-girl back," said John quickly. "And even before we knew Him at all, God was working for us."

"Oh, He was!" whispered Linda.

"But there's something more in the tale than you have told me," continued Aunt Nan. "I know my sister, and I am sure she had more than a little to do with this near shipwreck."

John's voice was hard as he answered. "You're right, she did. And she did it purposely."

"Oh, no!" said Linda. "She didn't really mean to break up our home."

"Yes, she did. Well, maybe she didn't expect to wreck our marriage, but she definitely wanted to throw enough monkey wrenches into the machinery to mess it all up. And I let her. Oh, if only—"

"Don't let's keep on saying 'if only,' Tony. No matter what anyone else did or said, it was our fault. The only 'if only' worth thinking about is 'if only we had known Christ and been one in Him it couldn't have happened.' But we *do* know Him now. Let's be so glad about that, that we can't think of anything else. O.K., Tony?"

"O.K., Pat."

But the smile he gave her faded as he turned to Aunt Nan. "My mother said she never wanted to see me again. And I have been glad to keep away from her."

"Where is she now?" asked Linda.

"I don't know."

"I do," said Aunt Nan. "Brother Charles tells me about her when he writes. She is living in that small house your father left her, John. The one where you used to go for weekends away from town. She has one servant with her. She doesn't go out, and will see no one except Charles and his wife. She will hardly talk to them. She is a sick—and heartsick—old woman, John."

They sat in silence, thinking back over the bitter waste of the months of their separation, and of the selfish woman who had been in some measure responsible for it.

Linda reached across Aunt Nan's lap and clasped John's hand in her own.

"You know what we have to do, don't you, Tony?"

"No! We don't have to do anything."

248

"Yes, we do. We've been forgiven so much that we can't refuse forgiveness to anyone else. For *His* sake, Tony. He died to win forgiveness for us."

"She shan't come between us again."

"She can't. No one can—ever."

"She'd try to get us away from Aunt Nan."

"She can't do that, either. Aunt Nan is *ours*. Not even your mother can hurt us now in any way. But there *is* something we can do for her. We can go to her in love and show her we are not angry. She is part of the world that we want to point to our Lord. For *His* sake, Tony, please."

He sat with his head in his hands. The women waited, each praying silently that he would win this first real test of his Christian life. At last he drew a long breath and spoke slowly.

"It will take a lot of praying, and more grace than I ever hope to have in my own strength. But if Aunt Nan will go along, and if both of you will back me up with all you've got, we will tackle it tomorrow. We will make it the first stop on the honeymoon."

"On the WHAT?"

"The honeymoon. All five of us are starting out on one early in the morning. I don't have to report at the office until Monday. I arranged it because I had a hunch I'd be needing a honeymoon about now."

"Well, you don't want an old woman like me along. I'm not going."

"How do you know what I want? I got a message from Linda's eyes just now and we both want you. We won't go without you."

"Where is this honeymoon to be?" asked Linda laughingly.

"Oh, just 'round and 'round. We will go and see Mother first. If we start early, we should have a couple of hours with her and be back by five o'clock. Next day we will hunt up that Aunt Lucy that I never saw. I owe her a big vote of thanks.

From there we will go to Cantrall where we are invited to the Hayes' home for dinner."

"Well—well—how in the world?" Linda looked dumbfounded.

"I went out to the drugstore and called Ruth after lunch. She made me promise I'd let her know when I got home. She's been fattening a figurative calf for three weeks in anticipation. You see, after I had talked to Dr. Bill and the whole riddle had been solved, I just *had* to talk to someone about it. Dr. Bill didn't think I should write to you. He sure put me on probation. So I thought of Ruth. She had always stood up for you and said we'd find out some day that you had done nothing wrong. I had a feeling too, that they'd be glad to hear that we were Christians. They tried to talk to me once about the Lord, and I wouldn't listen. Now when I needed someone to pray for me, I thought of them. So I wrote the whole thing to them and promised to call when I reached home. So she's been praying this afternoon. Maybe you'd like to call her tonight. She's been a loyal friend, Pat."

"I know it. I've wanted so much to see her, but I didn't dare until I'd made things right with you."

"They're right now," he said, picking up the hand with the rings and kissing it. "Now, for the rest of the honeymoon. Friday we are all going to the Zoo. Do you remember how we used to plan to take the kids when they got big enough, Pat? We will see it all from the baby monkeys to the hippo. And then we will be so tired that an evening at home will be most welcome.

"Saturday we are all invited to a real bang-up celebration at the Willis' home. I called Dr. Bill as soon as I got in this morning—called him from the station. They've all been bursting with the news ever since I talked to him that day. He said they hadn't dared contact you in any way for fear of messing things up. The doctor and his family will all be at Willises and he says it's going to be something special in feasts of thanksgiving.

They're a great gang. God was taking care of you all the time, honey, when He led you to them."

"I know it, and I've thanked Him for it many times."

"On Sunday I have planned something that will seem like a big chunk of Heaven here on earth. In Los Angeles I went to church, and I saw whole families sitting together, mother, dad, and a bunch of youngsters. That's what I want to do—all five of us go to church together. O.K., Mommy?"

"O.K., Daddy."

When the sound of a closing door told them that the children had wakened, John said, "They're coming, Pat. Suzanne will be all in a whirl. She knew what I was planning. Won't you come over here to make the setting right?"

He led her to the low rocker, the one that had been denied her all the weary weeks. Peter, coming first, saw her sitting there and smiled happily as John said simply,

"Mommy has come home, Pete."

"She been here a long time," answered Peter calmly as he climbed up on her lap. She held him closely, the happy-hearted little son who looked like her father, and whose loving loyalty had been comfort and balm to her sore heart. As she kissed him she saw the tiny girl lingering in the doorway. Holding out her other arm she spoke softly lest she frighten the child.

"Come to Mommy, Susie-Q."

A smile spread over the usually sober face, and without a question Suzanne took her place on the lap where she had often longed to be. She ran her fingers over Linda's face as if to assure herself that each feature were a part of the beloved whole. She looked long into the loving eyes. Then she settled back comfortably against the shoulder that seemed just made for a little girl's head. Looking across the room to where John and Aunt Nan sat watching, she said happily,

"She's just like you said, Daddy, just ezackly."

Linda raised her eyes and, over the heads of her children, met the love and trust in the eyes of her husband.